MW00931461

NEARLY *Wild*

MAIN STREET MERCHANTS, BOOK 3

LINDA SEED

This is a work of fiction. Any characters, organizations, places, or events portrayed in this novel are either products of the author's imagination or are used fictitiously.

The author is available for book signings, book club discussions, conferences, and other appearances.

Linda Seed may be contacted via e-mail at lindaseed24@gmail.com or on Facebook at www.facebook.com/LindaSeedAuthor.

Cover image by Diana Taliun.

ISBN-13: 978-1533559678
ISBN-10: 1533559678

First Trade Paperback Printing: June 2016

Also by Linda Seed

MOONSTONE BEACH

LIKE THAT ENDLESS CAMBRIA SKY

For Pat and Jennifer

NEARLY

The Nearly Wild rose (floribunda) blooms nearly continuously, thriving in the shade, in the sun, through the heat of summer and the winds of spring. She has stiff, prickly stems that form an almost impenetrable barrier.

—From gardeners' descriptions

Chapter One

Getting dumped sucked under any circumstances. But it really sucked, it turned out, when you had feelings for the guy who was dumping you. Rose should have known better than to have feelings, especially for an asshole like Jeremy.

"You're breaking up with me?" Rose Watkins glared at her date over a basket of fried clams at the Sandpiper, a restaurant overlooking Moonstone Beach. She felt stunned, the sting of tears making her eyes feel raw and hot. "You've got to be shitting me."

"This is what I'm talking about," the date said. "Do you have to be so profane?"

Rose had been dating Jeremy, an English professor at the university in San Luis Obispo, for a couple of months. She'd known he wasn't the one—couldn't possibly be the one, with his self-important smirk and his inane taste in music—but she'd dated him anyway, because he was hot, and she had nothing better to do.

And then she'd gone and cared about him. Stupid, rookie mistake.

"I thought you liked my profanity. You said … Wait, let me try to remember … You said it was 'refreshingly honest.' Or was that just a line of bullshit to get me into bed?" Her voice was rising, and Jeremy looked uncomfortably around the restaurant.

"Rose, I hardly think—"

"That's true." Rose nodded in agreement. "That's absolutely true. You do hardly think."

"Do we really have to make a scene?" Jeremy had that pinched look that always made Rose wonder if there was a pebble in his shoe. Or maybe a stick up his ass.

"Well, yes. I think we do, Jeremy. Because, A, you brought me to a public place to dump me, thinking I wouldn't make a scene, and I hate to be predictable." She picked up a fried clam and threw it at him, and it pinged off the left lens of his glasses. "And B, you're doing it over the goddamned appetizer, so I don't even get a meal out of it." *Ping,* another clam flew into his forehead. "And C, you goddamned well *knew* you were going to dump me before we had *sex* a goddamned hour ago! Which makes you a prick!" She rose from her seat, picked up the entire basket of clams, and dumped it into his lap. "So, yes, Jeremy, we do have to make a scene."

She picked up her purse and stomped out, leaving him there with a lap full of fried seafood. As she left the restaurant, it occurred to her that she should have thrown in some tartar sauce.

Jeremy wasn't worth being upset about. She knew that. She'd known, even as she was developing the dreaded feelings, that the two of them weren't right for each other. But still, right or not, the feelings existed. The hot stab of rejection burned in her chest as she emerged into the parking lot. Then she realized that Jeremy had brought her here, and now she didn't have a ride home.

Shit.

"You're not saying, 'I told you so,' " Rose observed from the passenger seat of Kate Bennet's car.

"Well."

"But you *did* tell me."

Kate had arrived in the parking lot of the Sandpiper shortly after Rose's ill-fated date, and now she was driving Rose home through the sparse evening traffic. As she crossed Highway 1 and headed east into the hills of Cambria, California, she shot a concerned look toward Rose.

"I wanted to be wrong," Kate said. "I hate it that I wasn't wrong."

"Ah, well. I don't care," Rose said stubbornly. She ran a hand through chin-length hair dyed the color of a Tiffany's box. "He was a shithead."

"You do care," Kate said mildly. "If you didn't care, you wouldn't be this mad."

Rose shrugged, her arms crossed over her chest. She realized that while her words said that Jeremy hadn't hurt her, her posture said otherwise. With some effort, she relaxed her shoulders and let her hands fall into her lap.

After a moment, she raised one eyebrow, making her silver barbell piercing jump. "I threw clams in his lap." One side of her mouth quirked up in a smile.

Kate let out a guffaw. "I hope they were hot," she said.

Rose lived east of Highway 1 in a one hundred-year-old cottage surrounded by pine trees. She had neighbors, but the lots on either side of her were vacant, and that, combined with the trees, created the illusion that she was secluded in nature, alone in a world of birds and deer and gentle coastal breezes.

Kate pulled up outside the cottage and let the car idle as Rose gathered her things.

"You want me to come in?"

"No," Rose said. "No. You probably were in the middle of something when I called you for help."

"Nothing that can't wait."

"Still."

"Do you want me to call the girls?" Kate offered. "The girls" were Gen and Lacy, the other half of their quartet of close friends. "We could all get together, drink some wine, and belittle Jeremy's manhood."

Rose gave Kate a half grin. "That does sound fun, but … I think I need to wallow."

"Oh, honey." Kate put a hand on Rose's arm. "I hate to think of you all alone, wallowing. I thought you didn't even like him that much."

"Yeah, well … I maybe wasn't completely honest about that." A fat tear rolled down her cheek, and she swiped it away.

"Oh, no," Kate said. "God, Rose. I … jeez. I'm so sorry."

"And even if I didn't care about him—which I shouldn't have, because it was stupid—I could still enjoy a good wallow, couldn't I?"

"Of course you could." Kate gave Rose's arm a gentle rub. "Just don't wallow too long. And call me if you need anything."

"I will. Thanks, Kate."

Rose got out of the car, waved goodbye to Kate, and let herself into the little house. She flicked on the lights and went into the tiny galley kitchen for a glass of wine. Wallowing was always better with wine.

The house was a one-bedroom, with miniature appliances and a main room with knotty pine paneling, hardwood floors, and a freestanding cast iron fireplace. All of that wood might have been overwhelming—might have made Rose feel as though she were living inside a hollowed-out tree like Winnie the Pooh—were it not for the bursts of color that met the eye no matter where you looked. Rugs in shades of red and gold, the sofa with purple and orange scarves draped across the back, the jewel-toned floral mosaics on the walls that Gen, an art dealer, had found for her.

It was hard to wallow in a place like this, but Rose was determined to try.

In the kitchen, she opened a good Syrah, retrieved a wineglass from the cupboard over the sink, and poured herself a glass. She paced with it a little while, wondering what kind of wallowing would be best, and then settled on the idea of a hot bath.

She went into the bathroom and started the flow of water into the claw-foot bathtub. The tub, with its elegantly curved lines and its chipped enamel, was probably original to the house.

Bathing had become a dicey thing in Cambria, where a years-long drought had prompted residents to stop watering outdoors, abandon washing their cars, and master the art of the five-minute shower. Rose generally did her part, but today, she thought, *Screw it.* A girl who had just been dumped by an asshole she'd been stupid enough to care about deserved a little bathtub wallowing.

The hot water made her feel better almost immediately, as though she could wash the grimy film that was the memory of Jeremy off of her body. But it wasn't that easy. Once she was settled into the tub, still and silent, there was nothing to keep her from running through the whole thing in her mind.

She'd met him in Cambria a few months before, when he'd come into De-Vine with a date to do some wine tasting. He had come back the next day—without the date—to ask her out.

She should have known then that this wouldn't go anywhere. While she'd been pouring two-ounce portions of chardonnays and pinot grigios for Jeremy and his girlfriend, he'd been checking out Rose's ass. When he came back the following day to hit on her, he'd claimed that the girl was just someone he'd dated a few times. She hadn't learned until later that they'd been together for months, and he'd broken up with her to go out with Rose.

Red flag, waving in the breeze. She'd seen it, but had chosen to ignore it.

The breakup had come down to her appearance, as things so often did.

When they'd met, Jeremy had told Rose that he loved the way she looked. The colorful hair, the piercings—the one in her eyebrow and another, a delicate hoop, in her nose—the rose tattoo that adorned her left shoulder. He'd said that he loved her edginess, her unique style, that she turned him on in ways that women with a more traditional look never had.

And, yes, he'd even said that he liked her profanity. He'd said she was "untamed."

She should have known that he would take it as a challenge to tame her.

It seemed Jeremy had a double standard for his women. He wanted Rose untamed in bed, all right, but when it came to the big faculty dinner that was coming up at Cal Poly, turquoise hair turned out to be more of an embarrassment than a turn-on.

First, he'd suggested that she might remove the piercings for the dinner. She'd agreed to that, because, hell. Why not? She could always put them back in later. Then he'd suggested that she dye her hair a more natural color, perhaps the medium brown she'd been born with. Then he'd wanted to choose her clothes.

And then, finally, Rose had realized that he didn't just want to change her appearance; he wanted to change *her*. She'd taken a stand, telling him that he could bring her to the dinner—Tiffany hair, facial piercings, and all—or she could stay home, and he could go alone. But parading her around in front of his colleagues while she pretended to be someone else—someone she wouldn't even recognize—was not an option.

She'd been feeling proud of herself, because it had seemed like he'd heard her, like he'd understood. Then, less than a week after that conversation, he'd taken her out to break it off over fried clams—but not until after he'd had one last naked romp with her blue-haired, "untamed" self.

Shithead.

She felt dirty, having been used by him. And she knew that was at least partly her fault. She'd let him do it. She'd allowed herself to be used.

But why?

She didn't want to admit it, but it had something to do with Kate—and with Genevieve Porter, another one of her closest friends. Kate had found love, had moved her boyfriend in with her, and to all appearances, was living the dream of true romance like a goddamned Disney princess. That was okay, that was fine. But now Gen was engaged to a rich, sexy cowboy who worshipped her.

It was one thing to be single in her late twenties. It was another to be single and watching her best friends get happily paired up, one by one. And being conspicuously single at Gen's wedding in a few months? Yeah, that was a prospect that hadn't appealed to Rose at all.

She sighed, dunked her head under the hot water, and stayed there long enough to hear the quiet, feel the sensation of the warm water fully surrounding her. Then she emerged, dripping, and slicked her hair back from her face. She settled back and sipped some wine.

Jeremy had been a shithead, and he wasn't even that good in bed. She'd been settling, because it had seemed better than being alone. But, screw that. It wasn't better. Being with someone who chipped away pieces of you, trying to create someone who didn't exist? Hell no, that wasn't better. That nagging feeling in your soul that told you that you were selling yourself, cheapening yourself, for the sake of someone who was embarrassed by you? That wasn't better. And getting dumped over a basket of fried clams wasn't better. Even if it had been somewhat satisfying throwing the goddamned clams in his goddamned, limp-dicked lap.

By the time Rose finished the glass of wine and the bath, she'd decided she was done. Done with men, done with dating. If she felt like having a fling every now and then, she'd damned well do it. But relationships?

Fuck that.

Men and their expectations could just go screw themselves.

Chapter Two

Will Bachman was getting sick of birds. Particularly *Charadrius nivosus,* more commonly known as the snowy plover.

The unassuming little brown and white bird was declining in numbers due to a variety of factors, and Will was trying to determine how the species, as a group, was attempting to adapt to such challenges as drought, climate change, and increased human activity in its habitat areas.

At this point, he wouldn't mind if they went extinct so he'd never have to see the damned things again.

He got up from where he'd been sitting in the sand and gathered his binoculars, his spotting scope, his notebook, and the backpack that held bottled water, a jacket, an apple, and some granola bars.

Enough of the snowy plover for one day.

There were times when Will was certain he would never finish his dissertation and receive his doctorate. This was one of them.

Sometimes he worried that his research would stretch on forever and that his future in academia was in peril. Then, he often caught himself thinking that maybe that was okay. If he finished his research, if he completed his dissertation, and if he finally earned the title of Dr. Bachman, it meant he'd have to figure out what came next.

And that prospect was scary as hell.

What if he never finished? What if he just stayed here in Cambria, living the life of a regular Joe who didn't know ridiculous amounts of information about the snowy plover? What was the worst that could happen?

That kind of thinking would lead him down a rabbit hole from which he might never emerge. It was best not to go there.

He packed his equipment into his car, shook the sand out of his shoes, and began the drive along Highway 1 back toward Cooper House, an absurdly opulent mansion where he'd been working as caretaker for the past two years.

The weather was classic Cambria, with clear blue skies and temperatures in the low seventies, a light breeze rippling the tall grass that carpeted the hills beside the highway. Even in March—the beginning of snowy plover breeding season—he rarely needed more than a light jacket.

If he wore that same light jacket at home in Minnesota this time of year, he'd be looking at hypothermia. This was better.

He arrived at the road leading up into the hills toward Cooper House and made the turn. He followed the winding road up to the security gate, entered the code, and waited as the gate slowly retracted. Then he drove up through an alternate universe of obscene wealth—formal gardens with sculpted hedges and sparkling fountains; tennis courts; the swimming pool with its marble statues keeping watch; and of course, the mansion itself.

Cooper House, which had been built in the 1800s by a local logging tycoon, was now owned by Christopher Mills, who'd been Will's roommate at Stanford. Shortly after graduation Chris had invented PlayDate, a dating app that paired people based on their online gaming profiles. As a result, he was now wallowing in more money than he'd ever spend in his lifetime.

When Will had needed to relocate to the Central Coast to study the snowy plover, Chris had offered him a position as caretaker at Cooper House. The place needed a caretaker, because Chris rarely visited—it usually sat empty while its owner lived in a sleek condo in the Silicon Valley.

Will lived in the guest house on the property and managed the legions of maids, gardeners, security guys, pool guys, and maintenance crews that were needed to keep a place of this size in top condition for the twice-a-year occasions when Chris visited, or for the more frequent occasions when he sent friends, relatives, or business associates to spend the weekend.

It was a sweet setup for Will, no question. But living at Cooper House, seeing the hulking Victorian and its grounds on a daily basis, reminded Will of the contrast. Here was Chris, a stunning success by any measure. And here was Will, with his meager bank account, a car that showed more than two hundred thousand miles on the odometer, and a future in academia that might never come to fruition. And even if it did, they didn't pay professors all that much these days.

The money didn't matter, not really. It was the *achievement*—or the lack thereof—that rankled him.

What had Will done, really, that would make his mark? What had he done to help anyone, or enlighten anyone, to change something that needed changing? Chris had done something that mattered. It was just an app, but that app—a dating site with an innovative method of pairing its lonely members—had resulted in marriages, long-term relationships, babies born, families created. That was something.

And Will?

He looked at birds.

He pulled his car up outside the guest house where he lived. The cottage was a miniature version of the main house, with a gabled roof, a wrap-around porch, and gingerbread details in red and blue. He was pulling his equipment out of the trunk when he heard a text message ping his phone, which he carried in his back pocket.

He shifted his stuff to one arm and checked the phone. It was Chris:

Coming March 20 to 26, bringing one guest—a woman! ;) Can you have things ready?

Will texted back with one thumb:

Sure. Someone special?

The reply came:

Time will tell.

Despite being the matchmaker for thousands of couples, Chris had yet to find his own match. But he was trying.

At least he had a date, which was more than Will could say for himself.

The snowy plovers were reasonably good company, but they didn't do much for his sex life.

Rose poured two-ounce portions of a fruity chardonnay for a disgustingly cute couple at De-Vine, the wine tasting shop where she worked. They were young—probably no older than midtwenties—and they were smiling with the glow of young love.

Part of her found it reassuring that couples like this still existed, and another part of her wanted to smack them over their damned heads with a wine bottle.

The two of them sipped the chardonnay and used snooty wine phrases like "oaky bouquet" and "clean finish." They didn't know what the hell they were talking about, but it wasn't Rose's job to tell them that.

"Special occasion?" Rose asked, leaning against the counter.

The petite, dark-haired woman giggled—she actually giggled. "You could say that." She looked lovingly at the guy, a sandy-haired preppy type in a Lacoste polo shirt. "It's our one month anniversary."

"Wedding?" Rose inquired.

"Dating," the guy said with a proud look on his face.

Oh, that's just perfect.

"Wow. That's cause for celebration, then," Rose said, adding another splash of wine to each of their glasses. She felt the burn of bitterness in her stomach. That wasn't this couple's fault, though. Oh, no. Clueless bastards.

"It is, right?" The woman practically bubbled, all fresh-faced and dewy. She clung to her date's arm.

"You bet." Rose tried to keep her voice neutral. "One month—yeah, that's a great time. Everything's all new, and fresh. You're so full of optimism and hope, and love."

The woman nodded, pink-cheeked and glowing with happiness.

"And the sex." Rose nodded knowingly. "The sex is awesome when the relationship is new. God. You barely want to do anything else, am I right?"

The woman looked a little uncomfortable, and the man blushed slightly. That was cute.

"Ah. Well, I—" the guy started.

"Of course," Rose interrupted, "that's when it's *new*. Before he lets on that, yes, he told you that you were perfect, he told you that he loved everything about you, but that was *before* he realized that he hates your hair color, and he doesn't actually *like* tattoos, and he really wishes you didn't wear such skanky clothes." She raised an eyebrow, and the woman looked down self-consciously at her own plunging neckline.

"So then he hints that hey, maybe it wouldn't be such a big deal for you to change this *one little thing* about yourself, and you'd do it if you really cared about him. And then that one little thing becomes *five* little things, and you do some of them because the sex is okay, and you don't want to go back to binge-watching Netflix on Saturday nights. But you don't do others, because, you know, he should like you the way you are, or what's the point? And just when you think it's going pretty well, you're feeling proud of yourself because you drew the line—'This is who I am,' you told him—he dumps you at the Sandpiper over a basket of fried clams."

The woman scowled at her date, who shifted uncomfortably in his seat.

"I don't even eat clams," the guy said.

"That's why I'm done with men," Rose declared. She grabbed a wineglass from behind the counter, splashed some pinot grigio into it, and then swallowed it down in one gulp. "Totally. Done."

"Rosemary? May I see you for a moment?" Patricia Howard, De-Vine's owner, was standing behind Rose, looking at her with scorn.

"Sure, Patricia. Let me just finish up with this tasting."

"Uh … I think we're … We'll just … " The guy in the polo shirt got up from his barstool and whispered something to his date.

"You've got four selections left!" Rose declared as the guy tugged at his girlfriend's arm. The two had a short, whispered disagreement, and then the woman gathered up her purse and the two headed for the door.

"That's just like a man," Rose called after them as they left. "You promise her things! 'We'll have a good time,' you tell her! And then you run like hell at the first sign of trouble!"

"Rosemary," Patricia said.

"They were … I was just … Oh, God," Rose said.

Getting lectured would have been one thing. That would have been fine. But when Patricia led Rose into the back room of the store and looked at her with kindness, with sympathy, well, that was worse. Rose felt tears burning her eyes as the older woman patted her shoulder and cooed at her. Rose was horrified that she needed to be cooed at.

"Honey, do you need to take the day off?" Patricia asked.

"No, no." Rose swiped at her eyes. "I'm fine."

Rose was sitting in an office chair at the battered oak desk Patricia used for bookkeeping, phone calls, and the random business of running the shop. Patricia, a woman in her midsixties wearing pale pastel separates that had never seen a wrinkle, her hair coaxed into an immovable grey helmet, pursed her lipsticked mouth and made a *tsk*ing noise.

"I knew the first time that man came into the shop that he was wrong for you," she said, continuing the shoulder patting. "Someone like that could never appreciate you." *Pat pat.*

"Someone like what?" Rose sniffled and took a tissue from the box on the desk.

"He bought the *chocolate wine,* for goodness sake," Patricia said, uttering the phrase *chocolate wine* as though it were an obscenity.

"Well, there's that," Rose agreed. "You're right. That was a red flag."

"I have a nephew … " Patricia began.

"Oh, no. No way. I mean … thanks, but I'm done."

Patricia shook her head, her lips pursed. "Rosemary, you're twenty-eight. You're *not* done."

"We'll see about that," Rose said.

"Hmm." Patricia peered at Rose through the little oval glasses that perched on her nose. "I suppose we will, at that."

Chapter Three

Being finished with men was especially problematic when one of your best friends was immersed in wedding plans. Rose tried to be supportive, helpful, and enthusiastic as she, Kate, and Lacy sat around a table at Jitters, the coffee bar where Lacy worked as a barista, listening to Gen go on about cake flavors and centerpieces.

"The good thing about this cake design is it's got four tiers, and then the smaller cakes surrounding the base, so we can get eight flavors in there. Something for everybody," Gen said, showing them a photo on her iPad.

"Isn't it a little busy?" Lacy inquired.

"Maybe." Gen peered at the cake on her screen. "But, eight flavors!"

"And it's buttercream instead of fondant," Kate put in. "Nobody likes fondant. I mean, it's pretty, but have you ever tasted it?" She grimaced.

"Rose? What do you think?" Gen said.

Ah, God. She'd been hoping Gen wouldn't ask. But now that she *had* asked, Rose had to be chipper. She wasn't sure if she could pull off chipper.

"Huh. … Flavors are good," Rose managed. She propped her chin on her hand on tried not to sigh.

"Or we could just break out a bag of Oreos," Gen said.

"Really?" Rose said.

"*No,* not really." Gen snatched up one of the bridal magazines she had stacked on the table and smacked Rose on the top of the head with it. "I need to pick a cake! I need to pick *the perfect* cake! Show some enthusiasm!"

"Sorry," Rose said glumly.

Gen put down the iPad. "I kind of suck, right? Making you think about wedding plans when you've just had a breakup? I'm a crappy friend."

"You're not a crappy friend," Rose assured her. "It's just … the whole 'I'm done with men' thing is hard to sustain while you're talking about tiers and fondant and … and … God. Cake toppers."

"I thought you didn't even like Jeremy that much," Lacy said.

"I … kind of lied about that."

"Oh."

The dread in that one word, that *oh,* told Rose what her friends were thinking. That Jeremy wasn't worth the brooding, the sadness, the moping. The guy was an asshole. But Rose wasn't the first woman to have fallen for an asshole, and she surely would not be the last.

"It's not just Jeremy," Rose said.

"Then what else is it?" Lacy leaned forward, her face full of concern.

"It's the cumulative effect of … what? … some twelve-odd years of dating and breakups and recovery from the breakups, and then having to find someone new to date. And Gen is done! Kate, too. You guys are done, and I … God. I'm pathetic."

"I'm not done," Lacy said. "We can suffer together."

"No." Rose shook her head. "No, because I'm done, too. No more men. I'm finished. Because men suck. I'll have books, and wine, and long walks, and … and … I'll probably have to get a cat, because that's what women do when they're done with men. It'll just be me and the cat. And you guys can visit."

"Oh, honey. Men don't suck," Kate said, her eyes brimming with sympathy.

"*Your* man doesn't suck. And, okay, Ryan. But the rest of them do."

"I think there might be a few others who are okay," Lacy said.

"Well, I'm crap at finding them."

"Me too," Lacy admitted.

"Hey, hey, hey." Gen waved her arms in the air in front of her. "We're picking out my wedding cake! We cannot simultaneously bash men while feeling the level of happy optimism that's required for picking out a really kick-ass wedding cake! So if we could just, you know … stick a pin in the angst. Just for right now."

"You're right." Rose nodded, determined to try for Gen's sake. "I'm sorry. Let me see those magazines."

"Thank you. Really." Gen shoved *Brides* and *Martha Stewart Weddings* in front of Rose. "And, honey, you're not done."

"Oh, I'm done," Rose assured her. She flipped through the top magazine. "Jeez, you gotta love Martha Stewart. How do they get icing to do that?"

Will just about had everything ready for Chris's arrival. He'd arranged for Cooper House to be cleaned; the pool guy had come and the water was a sparkling blue; the landscaping looked perfect, the hedges crisply trimmed and the flowers dewy and fresh; and the kitchen was stocked with groceries, including Chris's favorite craft beer and the brand of bottled water his new girlfriend wanted. Everything was *so* perfect, in fact, that Will couldn't think of any further excuse to avoid the snowy plover.

He was just about to get out there again—he was packing his field notes and his equipment into the back of his car—when his phone pinged with a text message from his ex-girlfriend.

I need to talk to you.

Will looked grimly at the phone and wondered how long he could simply ignore the message without being an ass.

On the other hand, this might be an excellent way to put off his research. He decided to yank off the Band-Aid and answer her.

What about?

Call me, she wrote.

Will was standing in the driveway, his car trunk open. He shoved the phone into his back pocket, then paced on the gravel driveway for a while, his sneakers crunching with each step. He looked at the blindingly blue sky, then took a deep breath, ran both hands through his sandy blond hair, and reached for the phone again.

"Melinda?" he said when she answered.

"Hi, Will."

"What did you need?" He sounded angry, sounded stiff and short with her, and he didn't mean to. But an ex was an ex for a reason.

Melinda let out a puff of air. "I wanted to let you know that I've started seeing someone."

Will propped one hand on his hip while the other held the phone to his ear. He paced some more because it gave him something to do other than thinking about Melinda.

"Well … that's great, Melinda, but why are you telling me? Why is it any of my business?"

"Because the man I'm seeing … It's Christopher. I'm dating Christopher."

"Oh." He massaged his forehead with one hand. "But … he's coming out to Cambria this weekend, and he said he's bringing someone."

"Yes. He's bringing me. I wanted to let you know, instead of just showing up there and surprising you."

Will suddenly felt very heavy, and he sat down hard on the back bumper of his car.

"Ah … I see."

"I hope this won't be too awkward," Melinda said.

"Well, I feel pretty safe saying it will be." It would have been awkward seeing Melinda again under any circumstances. But when you added the fact that she was dating his friend, and added to *that* the fact that she'd be staying on the property where Will lived, you had a triple layer cake of awkwardness. "Chris didn't tell me it was you."

"He doesn't know you and I dated. I didn't tell him. And I don't see any reason to tell him now."

Well, that added a new layer to the cake.

"Ah, God. Melinda—"

"Look." Her voice was firm. "You and I dated, and then we broke up, and then I met Christopher. I didn't tell him that I knew you because, at first, it just didn't seem necessary. Then, by the time it *was* necessary, it was too late to do it without seeming like I was hiding something."

"You *are* hiding something."

"But nothing important."

Ouch.

"I didn't mean it like that," she added. "I just meant—"

"I know what you meant." He rubbed at his eyes, hard, with one hand.

"Can we just not tell him?" Melinda said. "Can we just … *not*?"

Will sighed. The sky was so bright he had to squint against its brilliance. "You're going to have to tell him if you two get serious."

"Let's cross that bridge when we come to it."

By then, it's going to be a pretty shaky bridge.

Will was just about to get out there and face the snowy plover when Chris texted him one last thing that he wanted Will to get ready for him before his arrival. Melinda liked a particular Central Coast sparkling wine, and Chris wanted Will to buy a few bottles and put them in the wine cellar.

On one hand, the amount of crap Chris wanted Will to do for him before a typical visit bordered on the absurd. Why couldn't the guy buy his own wine? On the other hand, Will was asked to do very little during the periods between visits—and those periods could stretch for months. In the mean time, he had free living quarters most people would kill for.

So, he sucked it up and thought about where he could get the wine.

The winery that made it was more than an hour's drive from Cooper House, so Will got on the phone with some of the local wine shops to see who might carry it closer to home. On his third call, he found out that De-Vine had a few bottles. Grateful to put off his bird-watching, he got into his car—a 2002 Volvo that was starting to show a little rust due to the constant exposure to ocean air—and drove into town.

Will knew Rose Watkins a little. She was Kate and Gen's friend, and Kate and Gen were involved with Will's friends, so they showed up at the same get-togethers now and then. Of course, beyond that, he'd seen her around. She was hard to miss, with her brightly colored plumage. But they'd never really talked, other than superficial pleasantries. He was a little scared of her, to be honest.

She was on duty at De-Vine when he walked into the store late on a Thursday morning, the day before Chris and Melinda were scheduled to arrive at Cooper House. Her hair, which changed colors a lot, he'd noticed, was a fascinating blend of hot pink, blue, and purple. She had a little silver barbell piercing her left eyebrow, and a delicate silver hoop, so thin that it was barely noticeable, adorned her right nostril. Her makeup was bold—all dark eyeliner, thick mascara, and dark red lipstick—and her skirt was so short that for a moment after he walked into the shop, he forgot why he'd come.

"Hey, Will." She greeted him from where she was straightening a selection of wineglasses, corkscrews, bottle stoppers, and other random items on sale for the tourists. "The Laetitia Brut Cuvée, right? I set aside some bottles for you."

"Ah … thanks."

"Why don't you have a seat at the bar while I go into the back and get them?" She sounded friendly, but there was something underneath the friendliness, something darker. He wondered what it was.

He perched on a barstool and settled in while she went to get the wine. The store was empty, not surprising at this time of day. Sun streamed in through the big windows that faced onto the street. Every surface was crowded with a dazzling array of wine bottles, wine-related signs (WINE—HOW CLASSY PEOPLE GET WASTED), little jars of gourmet food items, decanters, picnic baskets, De-Vine T-shirts, and other items so numerous and varied Will couldn't even name the purpose of them all.

Rose returned from the back room with three bottles in her hands. She smiled at him, but the smile seemed to end at the curve of her mouth. It didn't reach her eyes—didn't reach her heart, he imagined.

"Can I get you something to drink?" she asked.

"Water would be good," he said. She poured it and put it in front of him in a De-Vine wineglass.

He knew he should just pay for his wine and go, but something made him stay on the barstool.

"So." He took a sip of water and cleared his throat. "How have you been?"

"Why?" She looked at him sharply. "What have you heard?"

"I … uh … nothing. I was just … you know. Making small talk." Apparently he'd stepped in something, and he didn't know what it was.

"Oh." Her shoulders dropped, and he could see that she was relieved.

"What would I have heard, if I'd heard something?" The level at which he was intimidated by her was slightly outweighed by the level of his curiosity, so he decided to stay with it and see where it led.

She grabbed a small white towel and started wiping the bar, even though, to his eye, the surface looked spotless already. She scrubbed vigorously at a spot he couldn't see. That didn't mean it wasn't there, he supposed.

"Oh, nothing," she said, rubbing at the spot. "Nothing. Not a thing. Except … there might have been some yelling at customers. And some seafood throwing. Maybe."

He raised his eyebrows. "You threw seafood at customers?"

"No. I yelled at the customers. I threw seafood at my boyfriend. Try to keep up."

Ah, now they were getting somewhere.

"So, you're having boyfriend problems."

"No," she replied in an airy voice. "No, no. Because I don't have a boyfriend anymore, now that I've thrown seafood at him."

"Well, that would do it," Will replied.

She scowled at him. "We didn't break up because I threw the seafood. I threw the seafood because we broke up."

"Ah."

"What does that mean?" she demanded. "What does 'ah' mean?"

He shifted on his stool. "It means I'm not sure what to say. It means I want to be helpful, but I don't really know what you're talking about."

She stopped wiping the bar and looked at him.

"You really *didn't* hear about it."

"Um … no."

"I just thought … you know, you're Jackson's friend. And Ryan's. And I told Kate and Gen, and so I just assumed …"

"Yes, well. Guys don't gossip the way women do."

"You're missing out."

"I'm beginning to get that impression."

They were quiet for a moment, and Will wondered what he should say. He didn't feel that he could simply walk away, having opened the door to something that was clearly bothering her. Tentatively, he said, "So ... are you okay?" It seemed to him that she wasn't, but he wasn't sure it was any of his business.

"Me?" She shrugged. "Oh, you know. Nothing a good hit man couldn't fix. You wouldn't happen to know anyone, would you?"

He couldn't help grinning at her. She was hurt, that was obvious, but her sense of humor made her seem tough, and he liked that.

"Well, for what it's worth, you're not the only one with relationship troubles. This wine I'm picking up? It's for Christopher Mills and his new girlfriend."

"So?"

"So, his girlfriend also happens to be my ex. And he doesn't know."

"Oh, shit." She looked at him with wide eyes, apparently impressed with the awful potential of that situation. "Are you going to tell him?"

"I don't know. She asked me not to."

"But whether you do or you don't, you're going to have your friend-slash-employer and your ex doing the nasty right under your nose. So to speak. Not literally, I'm assuming."

"That about sums it up."

"God." She leaned forward and propped her elbows on the bar. "You sure you don't want something stronger than water?"

He checked his watch. "It's ten fifteen a.m."

"Your point?" She raised one eyebrow at him.

He laughed. "I guess I don't have one. Set me up."

She turned and grabbed a bottle from a rack behind her. "This one's good. It's a Paso Robles chardonnay. Nice. Oaky, kind of light, with apple flavor notes."

She put the glass in front of him, and he took a sip and regarded her. "So why did you and the ex break up?" he asked. "Since it wasn't the seafood-throwing."

"Ah, shit." She ran a hand through her galaxy-colored hair and looked at the floor, as though she might find answers there. "It doesn't matter."

"I'll bet it does."

"Nah." She shook her head. "Not really. He was a class-A dickhead. He didn't seem like one at first, but then ... it turned out he was a stealth dickhead. I'm better off without him."

"I'm sure that's true," Will offered. "But it probably doesn't feel that way."

"Sometimes it does." She went to the little sink set into the bar and began washing a couple of glasses from the last tasting she'd done. "And then other times it feels … Ah, shit." She turned away, dried her hands on a towel, and wiped at her eyes with her fingertips, and Will was horrified to realize that she was crying.

"Ah … I … Kate's just down the street. Gen and Lacy, too. Do you want me to … "

"No." She dabbed at her eyes in a way that wouldn't smear her eyeliner, then took a deep breath, let it out, and changed the subject. "What about you? Why did you and Christopher Mills's new girlfriend break up?"

He thought about that and decided there was no easy answer. He wanted to give her *some* kind of answer, though. He considered it, then gave her his best shot.

"Have you ever gone out with someone and felt like it should have been right, but it just wasn't? You're doing all these things together, and you think it's pretty much perfect, and it should be fun. But somehow, you realize you're playing a part. You're just acting, and there's really no connection between you. There's just this overall impression that you'd make a really great couple, if only you weren't bored to tears."

"Ouch." She cocked her head at him. The way she was leaning forward on the bar gave him an excellent view of her cleavage, though he tried to be a gentleman and not look. Being gentlemanly was a challenge at times.

"You've got to tell Mills, though," she said. "I mean, if you two are friends. It's going to be a shit show if you don't and he finds out on his own."

He shrugged. "Yeah, but she asked me not to tell him, and I figure it's her story to tell, not mine."

"So what do you do?" She looked at him, her elbow on the bar and her chin propped on the heel of her hand. "Just keep your mouth shut and hope the shit show doesn't happen?"

He took a sip of his wine—a very good wine—and put the glass carefully back on the bar. "I guess that's all I can do," he said.

She tilted her head and looked at him from under bangs colored deep blues and purples, the hues of peacocks and spring pansies. "That's a bold position to take, considering the fact that if it all goes wrong, you might lose your job *and* your home."

He rubbed at his forehead with his fingertips. "Now that you put it that way, I'm beginning to think I'm in trouble."

"Here, you'd better have some more wine," Rose said.

Chapter Four

Talking to Will had cheered Rose up some, though she couldn't say exactly why. Maybe it was the fact that his own love life was just as dysfunctional as hers. If he could survive and still be funny and cute and pretty much intact, she figured she could, as well.

At least, she thought so until she got home after a long work day and got a phone call from her mother.

Rose was just starting to relax—she'd just changed from her work clothes into sweatpants and an old Ramones T-shirt, had started a fire in her funky cast iron fireplace, and was getting ready to read a book she'd been wanting to get to for some time—when her cell phone rang.

She picked it up from the coffee table and saw the name on the display: The She-Dragon. A hard knot of tension immediately formed in her stomach.

Shit.

To pick up or not to pick up? If she did, she'd face judgment, scorn, ridicule, and a whole list of demands. If she didn't, she'd still face all of those things, except that they'd come in the form of a voice mail message. Of course she could delete the damn thing, but then her mom would just keep calling.

If she ignored the call, she could delay the pain, but she still couldn't avoid it. If she picked up, she could get the misery over with and move on.

She picked up.

"Mom," she said.

"Hello, Rosemary." Pamela Watkins's voice sounded pinched and tense, but then, it always did.

"What can I do for you?" Rose tilted her head back and closed her eyes, willing this to be over soon.

"Well, Rosemary, you can tell me why, exactly, I had to read online that Ryan Delaney would be marrying one of your closest friends. I assume you'll be in the wedding?"

"I … uh … yes. I'm a bridesmaid." *This* was what her mother had called about?

"Why in the world didn't you tell me? Good lord, my own daughter, and I have to find out about it from Perez Hilton!"

"Perez Hilton knows about Gen's wedding? Why does Perez Hilton care?" None of this made any sense to Rose, but she supposed that if she waited a minute or two, her mother would explain it as though she were giving fingerpainting instructions to a preschooler.

"Because, Rosemary." Pamela was using her longsuffering, patient tone, the one that said she was using every ounce of her personal strength not to leap through the phone and throttle Rose. "Ryan Delaney is a member of the Delaney family. The Delaney family is one of the wealthiest families on the West Coast. And Ryan Delaney, who I might add is quite handsome, was considered one of California's most eligible bachelors. Until now. And that, Rosemary, is why Perez Hilton cares."

"Okay." Rose plopped down onto her sofa. "Well, he's off the market now. And, yeah, I'm going to be standing at the front of the church in taffeta, probably with a big bow on my ass. I don't see why you're angry with me about it."

"Language, Rosemary."

"*Ass*, Mother. *Ass, ass, ass.*"

The momentary silence on the other end of the line was ample reward for Rose's immaturity. She waited for her mother's inevitable lecture about her profanity.

But it didn't come.

"Rosemary, I'm angry about it because you didn't tell me yourself. I don't see why I had to learn such news from an outside source."

If Pamela wasn't going to rant about the *ass* thing, then this really was important to her.

Rose rubbed at her forehead, trying to stave off the headache that had to be coming.

"Mom, again, I don't see—"

"It's the *Delaneys*, Rosemary, for goodness sake. Didn't you think I'd want to know that you would be involved in one of the biggest society weddings of the year? Didn't you think I'd be interested? Didn't you think I'd want to be *invited*?"

Oh. Oh, Jesus. She wanted to *come*?

"Mom. First of all, it's not going to be a big society wedding. Ryan's a pretty simple guy. It's going to be a fairly basic wedding at the lodge here in Cambria. So I don't know what you're picturing, but it's not going to be that. It's not going to be ... oh, hell, I don't know ... five hundred people, with Bill Gates sitting in the front row."

"I'm well aware that Bill Gates won't be in attendance," Pamela said. "Though, I'd think that wouldn't be out of the question."

Yep, here was the headache. Just a wisp of it now, just a ghost of an ache. But that would change.

"And you weren't invited because Ryan and Gen barely know you."

"Well, that would be easy enough to change," Pamela said. "And I'm the mother of a bridesmaid. I should think that would entitle me to a certain amount of consideration."

"Oh, God, Mom. Do *not* make me ask Gen to invite you to the wedding. I swear, if you—"

"I won't make you do any such thing," Pamela assured her.

"Good. Because I—"

"I'm perfectly capable of calling Genevieve's mother myself."

"What? You can't … I don't—"

"If you'd be so kind as to give me her number, Rosemary."

The knot of tension had turned into a boulder, sitting hot and heavy in her stomach. Rose went into her little kitchen, found a bottle of Maalox in the cabinet over the sink, and swigged some from the bottle.

"No."

"And why not?"

"Gen's mother isn't even planning the wedding."

"Then who is?" Pamela sounded impatient. She'd be yelling soon, and Rose wanted to avoid that eventuality if possible.

"Gen. Along with Ryan's mother. And if you knew Ryan's mother, you'd know that she's not going to plan some outrageous—"

"Thank you," Pamela said, then hung up.

"Mom? Mom?" Rose looked at the screen of her phone and saw that the call had been disconnected.

Oh, shit. Oh, Jesus.

She immediately dialed Gen, who picked up on the first ring.

"Hey, Rose. I'm glad you called. I wanted to ask you about the—"

"Do *not* invite my mother to the wedding," Rose said, cutting her off.

"What?"

"My mother. The wedding. Be Nancy Reagan. Just say no." She was pacing the room now, stomping back and forth in bare feet from one end of the little cottage to the other.

"Okay. But … why would I invite her in the first place? I barely even know your mother."

"You *won't* invite her. Obviously. But if you did, it would be because she's about to call to ask for an invitation."

"She is? But *why*?" Gen sounded mystified. Rose could understand that. Pamela was mystifying to anyone who didn't know her.

"Because it's going to be the West Coast social event of the year!" Rose waved her free arm for emphasis.

"No, it's not."

"I know!"

"Then what—"

"My mother *believes* it's going to be the West Coast social event of the year. And since *I'll* be there, she sees it as her opportunity to stick her size six Prada pump in the door and force her way in!" Rose urged herself to calm down, because she was afraid she was in danger of hyperventilating.

"Oh. Okay. Well, she's not invited. I've met her, what, once?"

"That doesn't matter. It doesn't matter that she's not invited. It doesn't matter that you've met her once. She's determined to come. She told me she plans to call and wheedle her way into an invitation."

"Honey, calm down." Gen's voice was gentle and soothing, though Rose had to think that if Gen knew Pamela, she'd be hyperventilating as well. "If she calls me, I'll just tell her, gently but firmly, that our guest list is full."

"Okay, good. That's good. But she's not going to call you. She's going to call Sandra Delaney."

"All right. I'll call Sandra and tell her to make an excuse."

"Thank you. Gen? Really. Thank you." It would be okay. Sandra would tell her to piss off, and that would be that. There was nothing to worry about. It would be fine.

"You're welcome. And, Rose?"

"Yeah?"

"Do you want to talk about it?" Gen asked tentatively. "I know you have a rough relationship with your mother. If you need someone to listen …"

"Thank you, but right now I need you to get off the phone with me and get on the phone with your future mother-in-law."

"But it might help if you—"

"Go! Go now!" Rose disconnected the call and tossed her phone onto the sofa. She grabbed fistfuls of hair in both hands and stared at the ceiling, taking deep, calming breaths.

Gen would call Sandra, and Sandra—a woman who didn't take shit from anybody—would dispense with the Pamela problem. This wasn't a crisis. Of course it wasn't. This was just a minor incident that would not become a major one.

Fifteen minutes later, Rose's phone rang again. She braced herself for another call from Pamela, but it was Gen.

"Well? Did you tell her?" Rose prompted.

"I—"

"Is Sandra going to tell her no?"

"Oh, Rose, I—"

"Oh, God. Do not tell me."

"I was too late," Gen said.

Rose let herself drop onto the sofa. She didn't even answer. She was too horrified to say anything.

"I tried. I called right after I got off the phone with you, but Sandra's line was busy. I kept calling until I got hold of her, but by then …"

"She'd already invited her," Rose finished for her.

"Apparently. She said your mother called with this story about how it just so happened that she was going to be visiting you in June, and her visit was going to coincide with the wedding, and you really wanted her to come but you were too shy to ask her to change the guest list."

"*I* really wanted her to come?" Rose asked, incredulous. "*I'm* too *shy?*"

"Well … Sandra doesn't know you well enough to know how ridiculous that sounds," Gen said apologetically. "Oh, Rose … don't blame Sandra. She was just trying to help."

"I know. I get that."

"Oh, honey," Gen said. "Is she that bad?"

"Wait and see," Rose said. "She'll be at your wedding, apparently. Just wait, and you'll see."

Once Rose got off the phone with Gen, she went into the kitchen, found a bottle of Tylenol, and took two. Then she poured herself a glass of a Central Coast Malbec. Even good wine couldn't salvage this evening, but it was worth a try.

Chapter Five

Will had hoped—fervently—that he would be able to avoid Chris and Melinda as much as possible during their stay at Cooper House. They could do whatever it was they were going to do up at the house—he didn't want to think about it—and he could stay in the guest house or out at the beach working with the snowy plovers. He could keep out of their way, and before he knew it they'd be gone.

That was the plan, anyway.

It was a good plan—one he was determined to stick to, until Chris texted him the day before their arrival, just as Will was walking through the main house to make sure it was ready.

Have dinner with me and Melinda tomorrow night, the message said. *I want you to meet her.*

This was problematic on more than one level. First, there was the Melinda-as-ex-girlfriend level. Then there was the fact that if Chris wanted Will to meet Melinda, he must be getting serious about her. And if he was getting serious about her, that meant she wouldn't be going away any time soon.

He thought for a second and then answered the text:

Tomorrow's no good. I have a date.

He didn't, but Chris didn't need to know that.

Excellent! Bring her. That way you won't feel like a third wheel.

Terrific. Now, not only was he expected to have dinner with his ex, he also had to find a date. Unless he could still get out of it.

Thanks, but I can't bring her to Cooper House for dinner, I promised I'd take her to Neptune.

He realized the folly of that ploy only when Chris answered:

Perfect. We'll all go.

Will stuffed the phone into his back pocket and stared into the gleaming stainless steel surface of Chris's fifteen-thousand-dollar Sub-Zero refrigerator. He saw his own reflection, pointed at it, and said, "You're an idiot. You know that, don't you?"

Will was out at Ryan and Gen's new place helping to work on the front porch when Rose came by to look at dresses. Why she would come to the ranch to look at dresses, rather than going to one of those upscale boutiques women liked, he didn't know.

He was painting the wood railing a nice eggshell white as Rose came walking up the driveway in a black miniskirt, some kind of clingy top, and shiny black boots with high, skinny heels. Well, to say she walked wasn't quite accurate. She sashayed. Rose seemed to sashay everywhere, a fact Will found endlessly fascinating.

"Hey," she called to him. She seemed friendlier and more upbeat than she had the last time he'd seen her. Maybe she was getting over the guy who'd dumped her. She looked appreciatively at the new two-story house Ryan had built for Gen on the ranch property, so they wouldn't have to live with his family. "This place is looking really good."

"Yeah, it's coming along," Will agreed.

"Where's Ryan? He's not leaving you to work on his house without him, is he?"

"No, no. He's out back working on the deck." The way she was looking at him, the way she tilted her head and gave him just a hint of a smile, made him puff up a little, as though the job he was doing were much more difficult and important than it was.

"Well, good. Make him give you a beer afterward, at least."

"I plan to." Will stood up from where he'd been hunched over the railing with his paintbrush and straightened his glasses, something he tended to do when he was nervous. Though why he'd be nervous right now, he didn't know.

"So, how'd the thing go with your ex-girlfriend?" she asked him, leaning a hip against a part of the railing that hadn't been painted. "Did she come to Cooper House yet?"

"This weekend." Will shook his head in dismay. "And I can't even lay low, because Chris wants me to have dinner with them tomorrow night. And I said I had a date, which I don't. So now, not only do I have to see her while pretending we've never met before, I also have to come up with some excuse for why the date I never had in the first place didn't show up."

She grinned. "Why did you say you had a date when you didn't?"

He felt himself blush just a little. The curse of having fair coloring. "I was trying to get out of the dinner. I said I couldn't come because I had plans with someone."

"And he said, 'Bring her along. The more the merrier.'"

"Pretty much."

She crossed her arms over her chest, and he saw a glimpse of the tattoo on her left shoulder, peeking out of her top. "You know, you're supposed to be a smart guy, working on the PhD and all. But I could have told you that would happen."

He set the paintbrush down on top of the bucket of paint and stuffed his hands in his jeans pockets. "Yeah, well. Now I have to confess that I made it up, or say my date stood me up. Or tonsillitis. I could say she has tonsillitis."

"Or, you could just find a date." She batted her eyelashes at him. Was she offering? The idea had some appeal.

"Rose? Are you volunteering?"

"Oh, hell no." She laughed. "I'm finished with men. I thought I mentioned that."

A car pulled up into the driveway, and Lacy Jordan got out. Apparently, all of them—all of the tight group of friends with Rose at its center—were coming to look at dresses.

"Hi, you two," Lacy greeted them. "What's up?"

"Well," Rose began, "Will's ex-girlfriend, who's dating Christopher Mills, is coming to Cooper House this weekend, and Will's supposed to have dinner with the two of them tomorrow night, which will be awkward, as you can imagine. Making things even more awkward, he said he had a date, which he doesn't."

"Ooh." Lacy's eyebrows rose. "That *is* awkward. I'd go with you, but I actually do have a date."

"Well, thanks anyway," Will said. There was that blush again.

"You should do it," Lacy said to Rose.

"I can't. I'm done with men."

"That's okay. You'd be pretending to be his date. Pretending doesn't count."

Somehow, Will had been cut out of the conversation, even though he was the one who faced possible humiliation at the dinner.

"Huh," Rose said, looking thoughtful. "Would I get to visit Cooper House?"

"Uh … we'd be having dinner at Neptune, but we might get invited to the house afterward."

"Ooh. I've never been to Cooper House," Rose said.

"Gen said it was spectacular, after she had sex with Ryan there."

"After …" Will said. "After she …"

"Be careful, Rose. You're embarrassing poor Will," Lacy said.

"Am I embarrassing you?" Rose asked.

"Well … kind of. Yeah."

"Now you really do owe it to him to do this," Lacy said.

What with Lacy's dazzling blond-haired-blue-eyed beauty, and Rose's dark mystery, and the talk of sex, Will found himself feeling a little bit dizzy. It wasn't unpleasant.

"I guess I could do it," Rose said, propping one fist on her hip. "But I don't even know if Will wants me to. We kind of assumed."

"Of course he wants you to," Lacy said. "He needs a girl, and you're a girl."

"I am," Rose agreed.

"Perfect." Lacy rubbed her hands together in enthusiasm. "Will, should she meet you at Neptune, or do you want to pick her up?"

"Uh … I … I guess I'll pick her up."

"Great."

Lacy gave him a friendly pat on the shoulder, and Rose kissed his cheek like she would a brother or a favorite uncle. Then they both went into the house to pick out dresses or make party favors, or whatever it was they'd come here to do.

Will was still standing there, a little bit stunned, when Ryan came around from the back of the house, his dark eyes alive with amusement.

"I heard the tail end of that," he said. "Seems to me they didn't really need you for that conversation."

"I guess not," Will agreed.

Ryan laughed, walked up to Will, and much more firmly than Lacy had, smacked him companionably on the shoulder. "Looks like you got yourself a fake date."

It was interesting how that had happened, Rose thought. One minute she'd been chatting with friends, and the next, she had a date with Will Bachman. It was a fake date, but still. She was completely done with men—she'd decided that, and there would be no going back on it—but that didn't mean she couldn't enjoy a nice evening helping out a sweet guy.

And Will was a sweet guy. She didn't know him very well, but what she did know of him was all good. She knew he was a good friend of Ryan, Jackson, and Daniel Reed, a friend of Gen's who showed his art in her gallery. She knew he was roommates at Stanford with tech gazillionaire Christopher Mills, and had stayed friends with him over the years. And she knew he was smart as hell, with his near-PhD in bird DNA, or whatever it was he was studying.

Aside from that, he was cute, with the sandy blond hair and the trim physique that combined to create all-American surfer boy good looks.

"Hey. I heard you have a date with Will," Gen said as Rose came into the house moments behind Lacy.

"Wow. That news moved fast," Rose commented. "And it's a fake date."

Kate, who was already there when Rose and Lacy had arrived, said, "Aww. Does it have to be a fake date?"

"Yes. Yes, it does," Rose replied.

Gen and Ryan were in the process of moving into the new house, which he'd had built on the Delaney Ranch property about a hundred yards from the main house where he'd grown up and where his parents, uncle, sister, and nephews still lived. The living room, an inviting space with wood floors, butter-colored walls, crown moldings, and a big fieldstone fireplace, was still cluttered with cardboard boxes full of Gen and Ryan's various belongings. The big, comfortable-looking sofa in the middle of the room was strewn with a selection of bridesmaid dresses Gen's wedding planner had sent over for their perusal. Amid the chaos of the dresses and the mess of unpacking,

Rose's friends were chatting and fingering dresses in the shades of blush and gray Gen had chosen as her wedding colors.

"No, it doesn't have to be fake," Lacy insisted. "That's the beauty of a fake date—it doesn't have to stay that way. You just see how it goes. If you like him, it can be a real date. If you don't, you can just say you were helping him out, and walk away at the end of the night with no hard feelings."

Rose was happiest like this, when she was with her friends: Kate, who ran the bookstore in town; Gen, freshly in love and excited about her upcoming wedding; and Lacy, the best barista in Cambria and possibly the town's most sought-after single woman with her kind manner and her ethereal beauty.

"I *will* walk away at the end of the night," Rose insisted. "Will seems like a good guy, and I'm glad to help him out. But men are too much trouble."

"Aww," Gen said, looking sympathetic, as she put a hand on Rose's arm. "Jeremy really hurt you."

"No, he didn't," Rose insisted. "Well, yes. He did. But it's not about Jeremy." Rose thought about how to explain. "It's just … Look. I get that having a boyfriend would be nice, because of the sex, and because of the cuddling—I like cuddling as much as the next person—and because it's nice to have somebody to go places with, and do things with … and to ask about your day and actually care what the answer is."

"But?" Lacy perched on the arm of the sofa to avoid crushing the dresses. She had the little vertical line between her eyebrows that she got when she was worried.

"But, men … God. They come with so many *demands*. So many expectations. They want you to *change* for them, but with every change, you feel a part of yourself dying and being replaced with … with this *artificial* part that you don't even recognize as you."

"I don't know if that's fair," Gen said. She was sitting in a little side chair next to the sofa, looking as concerned about Rose as Lacy did. "Ryan never asked me to change. Maybe the men who want to change you just aren't a good fit. And maybe it's not fair to generalize about all men everywhere."

"I know. I know," Rose said. She hadn't intended to make a speech, but now that it was out there, she could feel the truth of her feelings thrumming through her veins. "I know there are good guys. And I know that both Ryan and Jackson are good guys. But … they're not the kind of guys *I* seem to find, or who seem to find me."

"That doesn't mean you should give up," Kate said. She had just emerged from the kitchen with glasses of iced tea for everyone. She handed a cold, sweating glass to Rose.

"And I just don't see why it's that important!" Rose insisted. "Why should I open myself up to yet another person who wants to criticize me? I mean, now that my mother's been invited to this wedding, all she'll be able to talk about is how I'll never achieve anything in life if I don't change my hair back to 'a respectable color.' " She made air quotes with her fingers. "And change my makeup. And get rid of the piercings. And she knows a guy who's just a genius with lasers who can take care of that 'thing' on my shoulder."

"Oh, God," Gen said miserably. "I'm so sorry about Sandra inviting her."

"She didn't know," Rose reassured her. "The point is, to my mother, I'm nobody if I don't play the part of the perfect society woman. And I think it should be enough for me to be me."

"Oh, sweetie, it *is* enough," Lacy said, her eyes moist, her face full of compassion and love. "*You're* enough. If the men you meet can't understand how wonderful you are, how unique and loyal and beautiful and … how *special* you are, then they don't deserve you."

Rose felt tears come to her eyes, and she wiped them away with her fingertips.

"I love you," she said to Lacy. "Do *you* want to marry me?"

"I would, but … you know. Penises matter."

"Okay," Gen said brightly. "On that note, let's figure out which one of these dresses will make you guys look least like a dollop of meringue."

Will still wasn't too sure about this date-that-wasn't-a-date as he pulled his car up to Rose's house the following evening. Going out with Rose—that part was fine. Better than fine. The trouble was seeing Melinda again, along with the stress of having to pretend not to know her.

He got out of his car and crunched his way over a bed of pine needles to get to the front door of the cottage. The weather was warm and pleasant with a cool breeze rattling the branches overhead. He smelled earth and pines and the tang of ocean air.

The house, with its dark wood siding and big lot, made him feel like he'd arrived for a stay at summer camp. A sign hanging on the front door said, NO SOLICITING UNLESS YOU'RE DROPPING OFF WINE OR WANT TO DO MY LAUNDRY.

He looked for a doorbell, didn't find one, and knocked instead.

Rose opened the door and Will stood there looking at her, transfixed. She had the same multicolored hair in deep blues, purples, and pinks, and she was wearing some kind of short black dress with a skirt that poofed out like a bubble. Looking closer, he saw that the tiny pattern on the fabric was hundreds of little white cat faces. She wore heavy black boots with shimmery black tights. The top of a tattoo peeked out above the sleeve of the dress, and he found himself wanting to see the rest of it.

"Wow," he said.

She did a little twirl. "Too much for Neptune?"

"No," he said. "I like it. You look ... fun." And she did, but fun was only part of it. She looked sexy and dangerous and ... Well. He was right the first time. Fun.

"Come on in while I grab my stuff." She stepped back to let him come inside, and he looked around, speechless, enveloped by color and warmth.

"Is this place yours?"

"You mean, do I own it?"

He nodded.

"No. I've been renting here for the past couple of years. I love it out here with the trees, and the feeling that there's no one else around—even though my neighbors are just fifty yards up the road. If I ever got a chance to buy it, I'd do it in a second. Not that I make enough at De-Vine to buy a place."

"*I Dream of Jeannie*," he said when he finally thought of a way to describe the place.

"Excuse me?"

"Your place. It's like the inside of Jeannie's bottle, but with camping."

She laughed, clearly delighted with his assessment, and her laugh made him feel things he didn't fully understand.

She put her hand on his shoulder. "Just let me grab my purse and my jacket, and we'll go."

He didn't want to date Rose Watkins, and she didn't want to date him. They were clear on that. But when she took her hand away, he felt the lost warmth like a fond memory.

Chapter Six

They arrived at Neptune at seven twenty-five for a seven thirty reservation. The hostess, an attractive blonde Rose knew from the salon where she got her hair colored, told them that Mr. Mills was already at his table. She led them into the restaurant and toward a table at the window looking out onto Main Street.

Rose had expected Christopher Mills to be tall. Somehow, when you knew someone was a billionaire, you expected height. But in fact, he was no more than five foot eight. With her boots on, Rose was easily as tall as he was. Mills had bland Midwestern good looks, with a ruddy face and clear blue eyes. His date, Will's ex-girlfriend, was a medium-sized brunette who was probably pleasant-looking in her natural state. But she wasn't in her natural state; she'd clearly spent a lot of money polishing herself up to attain the next rung on the attractiveness ladder. Expensive clothes, expensive haircut, expensive makeup, and probably expensive plastic surgery, judging by the immobile monuments that were her breasts. The woman's eyebrows alone probably represented fifty dollars worth of spa visits and waxings.

All of the requisite introductions were made, and when Chris saw Rose, when he allowed himself to fully absorb the sight of her, his eyes widened slightly with the impact. She was used to that reaction. He rebounded admirably, she noticed.

That first moment, when they stared or froze in discomfort, was a given. It was what they did next that would reveal whether they and she would get along.

Rose liked the way her appearance weeded people out. The interested, the polite, and the benignly curious could stay to play another round. The rude, the judgmental, and those who thought she was an ideal target for jokes, psychoanalysis, or,

God forbid, fashion advice were eliminated immediately without the benefit of parting gifts.

Having exchanged pleasantries with Christopher, Rose extended her hand toward Melinda.

It was interesting that Rose had never met her. True, Melinda didn't live in Cambria. But Will had dated her long enough that Rose should have encountered her at least once. What did it mean that Will had never brought her around? Nothing good, surely.

The woman gave her a dead-fish handshake as though she were afraid Rose's fashion choices might be viral, exchanged through skin-to-skin contact.

They all sat down, and Chris made some noises about ordering a bottle of wine.

"We should have Rose choose," Will said. "She's a wine expert."

"Really." Chris looked at her with interest. "A hobbyist, or do you work at one of the wineries?"

"I manage De-Vine, here in town," she told him.

"Ah. So you're not a vintner or an oenologist," Melinda said smugly.

"No. I'm self-taught," Rose said.

"I'm sure you've picked up quite a lot bartending for the tourists."

What was this? Was Melinda getting into a pissing contest with Rose? That meant one of three things: One, Melinda was still interested in Will, and she was jealous that he'd come with a date. Two, Melinda thought Chris might find Rose attractive, and was worried that Rose might steal her billionaire boyfriend. Or three, Melinda simply thought Rose was inferior due to her appearance. In any case, Rose had always enjoyed a good hair-pulling catfight.

"Rose isn't a bartender," Will told Melinda. "She manages one of the most successful shops in town. And aside from that, she recommends wines for many of Cambria's best restaurants. Jackson Graham, the head chef here, relies on her judgment."

Rose looked at Will. She appreciated the way he was defending her, but she was a little surprised by it. She hadn't realized Will had given any thought to what she did for a living.

"I've heard a little about Jackson Graham," Chris put in. "They say he's a stickler for quality—a real perfectionist. If he trusts Rose's expertise, then that's good enough for me."

"Not that he doesn't push back a little on occasion," Rose said, picking up the wine list and opening the tall folder. "He's pretty good with wine. But he doesn't have The Nose."

"The nose?" Chris said.

"It's almost like a sixth sense," Rose said. "I can tell just about everything about a wine from the aroma. Jackson can't do that. But it's not his fault. Most people can't."

"That's fascinating," Chris said. He seemed to mean it. "How did you learn that?"

Melinda rolled her eyes.

"Oh," Rose began, "I grew up in Connecticut with high-society parents. They thought I should be educated about the finer things—they thought I should be cultured. They taught me a few of the basics when I was a teenager, but The Nose—that's just something you have to be born with."

"Your mother must be so proud of you," Melinda said, giving Rose a pointed look up and down her body, her glance encompassing Rose's clothes, her hair—everything a high-society mother would loathe with every molecule of her being.

"No." Rose laughed. "Mothers tend to be more appreciative of daughters who look like they just stepped out of a Barbie Dreamhouse." She flashed Melinda a cutting smile.

"Okay," Will said, clapping his hands once to break up the conversation. "Rose, I'd like to … ah … talk to you about the … ah … Could we talk privately for a moment?"

"Of course, sweetheart." Rose batted her eyelashes at him, ran her hand slowly from his shoulder down his arm, and gave him a seductive smile before shooting one last look toward Melinda, who seemed like she might swallow her tongue. Yep, it was the first option. She was still hung up on Will.

Will led her into the foyer and turned to face her. She expected him to scold her for being rude to Melinda, and hell, she probably deserved it. She didn't expect what he actually said.

"Rose, I'm sorry," he told her, looking miserable. "Melinda had a chip on her shoulder from the minute we walked in the door. You shouldn't have to put up with this. If you want me to make an excuse, I'll do it, and we can get out of here."

It was sweet that he wanted to protect her, but she didn't need protection.

"I can handle her," Rose said.

"Oh, I'm sure you can. But you shouldn't have to. I don't know why she's being this way, with the crack about being a bartender, and the thing about your mother …" He shook his head, looking grim.

"I think I have some idea," she said.

"You do?"

She fluffed up the bubble of her skirt, making it more bubble-like than ever.

"I'm thinking you're the one who broke up with her. Am I right?"

"Well, I … no. It was mutual."

"Are you sure?" Rose asked. "Was it maybe a little less mutual on her side than yours?"

Will looked uncomfortable. He fidgeted with the collar of his dress shirt, as though it was too stiff or scratchy. "I—"

"Look, I'm not trying to make you out to be the bad guy," Rose said. "I'm sure you had your reasons. Good ones, from what I can see. I'm just saying, she's still interested in you."

His eyes widened. "No. That's … No."

"Yes."

"Rose—"

"Trust me on this. It's one of the benefits of being a fake date. I have distance. I can see things you can't."

He nodded. "Okay. So let's say she still has feelings for me. That's awkward and weird, but … let's go with that. She's dating my friend, who's also my boss. What am I supposed to do?"

Rose shrugged. "That part, I don't know."

"Terrific."

Rose took a surreptitious peek into the dining room, where Melinda was sitting with Chris, looking pinched and angry. Rose raised her eyebrows thoughtfully.

"Will, how important is it to you that I get along with your ex?"

"What do you mean?"

"I mean, do I have to kiss up to these two? For the sake of your job?"

"Oh, I don't think so," he said. "I've known Chris for years. He's not going to fire me if my date doesn't like his girlfriend."

She nodded. "Excellent." She linked one arm through his. "I'm ready to go back. Lead the way."

Back at the table, Will wondered if Rose could be right. Was Melinda acting hostile because she was still interested in him? It seemed unlikely.

The way he remembered it, she'd been perpetually dissatisfied with him for one reason or another—everything from his clothing choices to the way he loaded a dishwasher. Mostly, though, she was dissatisfied because he'd wanted to use his Stanford education to study birds rather than to found some high-tech company that would ultimately go public, raining money down on his head in an all-consuming flash flood of wealth. In other words, she hadn't wanted *him*—she'd wanted someone like Chris. And that's what she'd ultimately gotten, so why was she upset now? Was she still hung up on Will? Was that possible?

Had he really hurt her?

Speaking of people hurting each other, Will felt an impending sense of doom as he saw the way the women were looking at each other: Melinda with barely veiled contempt, and Rose with barely veiled glee.

If there was going to be a Thunderdome-style cage fighting match, Will would put his money on Rose.

That turned out to be the right call.

Rose had barely ordered the wine—a 2012 Enfield Chardonnay—when Melinda went to work on her.

"So, Will. How did you meet Rose?" Melinda's mouth curved into a delicate smile of feigned interest.

"Ah … my friends are in relationships with Rose's friends, so we were running into each other here and there," Will said.

"Are Rose's friends as … *unique* as Rose?" Melinda raised her eyebrows in innocence.

"Well, I like to think we're all unique," Will said, rallying.

"It's so nice that you can make the effort to see below the … well, the *surface*," Melinda said, gesturing vaguely toward Rose. "Unless the surface is the point. I mean, I can see that for an *ordinary* guy like you, dating Rose would be quite a walk on the wild side."

In just three sentences, Melinda had managed to insult Rose's appearance, call Will ordinary, and insinuate that his association with Rose was some kind of kinky fetish. Will was both horrified and impressed.

"Melinda …" Chris tried.

"Not that I'm judging," Melinda went on. "I mean, for every kind of person, there's *someone* who finds that sort of thing attractive."

"I imagine just about anyone would find Rose attractive," Chris put in.

That gentle rebuke—Chris indicating that not only did he side with Rose in this particular wrestling match, but that he found Rose attractive—caused the color to rise in Melinda's face.

"Oh," Rose said, "there's certainly a 'walk on the wild side' aspect to our relationship, wouldn't you say, Will? We do like to take things to the limit." She leaned toward Melinda and whispered, "Sexually, I mean."

Melinda opened her mouth, closed it, then opened it again. Will was reminded of a trout on a hook.

"Rose," Will began. "I—"

"You don't need to be embarrassed, Will," she told him. "We're among friends here." Then she leaned over and kissed him so deeply, so sensuously, so thoroughly, that the world around him disappeared into swirling colors of orange and red, and a whooshing sound filled his ears.

"Well," a voice said, interrupting them.

Will broke from the kiss, feeling like his body had been turned inside out and then right again, and looked up to see Jackson standing beside the table in his chef's coat. "I came to see if I could offer you a special appetizer. But I see you've already had one."

❖

"Well, that was … interesting," Will said as he and Rose left the restaurant.

"God," Rose said. "I'm sorry if I embarrassed you. I wanted to rip that bitch's face off and stuff it down the front of her dress."

"Kissing me was better, all things considered."

"What the hell did you see in her?" she demanded as they arrived at his car.

"This is what I'm wondering."

"And Chris," she went on. They got into the car and she buckled herself in. "He seems decent enough. What's he doing wasting time with a puffed-up, lacquered, fake-ass skank like her?"

Will sat in the driver's seat, stunned by the evening's developments. "She wasn't like that. Before, I mean. When I was dating her." He stopped to consider whether that was true. She'd been judgmental even then. And superior. And a little bit catty. But not to this extent, surely, or he would have noticed. Wouldn't he?

"I'm sorry," he said as they pulled out of Neptune's parking lot and headed down Main Street on their way toward Rose's house.

"For what?"

"For putting you through this. I'm sure you could have done something much better with your evening. Like, I don't know. Doing your laundry, or … or cleaning your grout."

She gave him a half grin. "I do like a good session of grout cleaning."

That had sounded dirty to Will's ears, and he wondered if she'd intended it that way. And that made him think about the kiss. Never in his life had he been kissed that way. Never had he even considered that such a kiss was possible. It might have been the added thrill of doing it in public, and especially in front of Melinda—the whole exhibitionist aspect of it. But probably not, he thought. A kiss like that probably would have blown his world apart no matter where it happened.

"Well, I'm sorry I took you away from your … grout."

"I'm not." Rose wiggled a little as she settled herself more comfortably into her seat. "When you're facing a bitchy ex, you should always have someone there who's on your side. Plus, I got to eat some of Jackson's food, which is always a plus."

He drove down Main Street and got on Highway 1 north toward Moonstone Beach. He turned right and followed Cambria Pines Road up into the pine-covered hills toward Rose's place.

He'd been quiet for a while, and finally, he sighed. "I have no idea what I'm doing," he said.

Surprised, Rose looked at Will as he drove into the woodsy expanse east of Highway 1. He looked sad and vulnerable, his sandy-haired good looks making her think of the boy he'd once been.

"What do you mean?" she said.

He shrugged, looking at the road. "Why did I have to pretend to have a date? Why couldn't I have just … I don't know. Shown up to dinner alone? Or said no?"

She felt a prick of offense; had it been so bad escorting her? But really, she knew that wasn't what he'd meant at all.

"It's normal to want your ex to think you've moved on," she told him.

"Nah. It's not about Melinda."

Then she understood. "It's about Chris." She turned a little in her seat to look at him. "Right?"

He nodded slowly. "Yeah."

She didn't press. It was clear that he wanted to talk, and he'd do it in his own time.

Finally, he said, "We were roommates at Stanford during our undergrad years. Did you know that?"

"I did, yeah," she said.

"Okay. Well, look how that's turned out. He's ridiculously rich, and I'm buried under student loans, driving a car that should have been put out of its misery fifty thousand miles ago. He runs his own business, and I work for him. I'm his *employee.* And now ..."

"And now, he's even got your girlfriend."

"Well ... yeah. It's not that I want Melinda back ..."

"Horrors." Rose shuddered. "I can't imagine why you would."

"But it's the symbolism of the whole thing. He's got it all, and I've got to talk somebody into pretending to be my date."

A muscle in his jaw flexed, and she found herself wanting to tuck him to her breast and stroke his hair.

"As I recall, you didn't talk me into anything," she said. "In fact, this fake date thing wasn't even your idea."

"Yeah. Well."

"And if you want Chris's lifestyle, go get it. Do what he did. You're ridiculously smart, I'll bet you could do it."

He ran a hand through his hair, which was long enough to curl slightly over his ears and at his collar. "It's not even that. I don't want his lifestyle. I just want ... I don't know. I want to achieve something."

"Okay. So, what is it you want to achieve? What's the big goal?"

He shook his head. "That's the problem. I don't know. Right now, the goal is to finish my dissertation and get my PhD. But after that . . ."

"You're going to teach? Become a professor?"

"I suppose so."

"But you're not thrilled about the idea," she guessed.

His grim silence gave her his answer.

When they arrived at Rose's house, he got out of the car and walked her to her door.

"Do you want to come in?" she asked. Usually at the end of a date, inviting a man into your home meant that you were interested in sex, or at least some making out and groping. But this was a fake date—and she was done with men—so it didn't mean that. What it meant was that he looked sad, and she thought he might need someone to talk to.

"I'd better not," he said.

She dug her keys out of her purse, unlocked the door, and turned toward him.

"All right. And Will? It was fun being your fake date. Even with the whole Melinda raging bitch thing."

He was looking at her in a funny way. He started to say something, and then stopped. Then he started to walk back to his car, and stopped, and came back. "There's something I . . . Do you mind if I do just one thing?"

"Do what?"

He reached out suddenly, held her face in his hands, and kissed her. Before she could think, before she could breathe, she was pressed up against her front door with his fingers entwined in her hair, and his mouth was the whole world and everything in it: the earth, the moon, the stars, her own beating heart.

He kissed her just about as thoroughly and completely as a girl could be kissed, then he let go and backed away. Without him holding her up, she wasn't sure she could still stand upright.

"I … uh … I'm finished with men," she managed to croak out from amid her haze of arousal.

"Oh, I know. I get that."

"Then … "

"I wanted to see if I could replicate the results from … you know. During dinner."

"Always the scientist," she said.

"I was just … gathering data."

"Uh huh. Well, I …" She pointed to her front door.

"Right. Good night," he said, and walked down the driveway to his car.

When he got into his car and drove away, she was still standing there, watching him go.

Chapter Seven

"So, I kissed him, and then he kissed me, but I don't think either kiss counted, because it wasn't a real date," Rose attempted to explain to her friends at Jitters the next morning. They were sitting around one of the small café tables with lattes and muffins in front of them—all except for Gen, who had a plastic container full of fresh fruit. Gen had always been a healthy eater, but she was particularly careful about it now, with the wedding approaching.

"Wait," Lacy said, putting one hand up traffic-cop style. "If there was kissing, how was it not a real date?"

"I told you," Rose said with exaggerated patience. "I kissed him because his ex-girlfriend is bitchtastic, and I wanted to see if I could make her head burst into flames. Which it almost did."

"Okay," Kate said. "So that explains the first kiss. But what about the second one?"

"He was gathering data."

"Gathering data," Gen repeated, a chunk of watermelon on a fork halfway to her mouth.

"Right."

"Wait," Lacy said, waving her arms. "Wait, wait. What kind of data was he gathering, exactly?"

"He wanted to see if he could replicate the results," Rose said simply.

"The results of the first kiss," Kate said.

"Right."

"And what results were those, exactly?" Gen wanted to know.

Rose shrugged and took a sip of her latte. "Well, you know … not much. Except that it was so hot both of our faces almost melted off."

Rose broke into a grin as her three friends stared at her.

"Will?" Kate said, looking perplexed.

"Scientist Will?" Lacy said.

"Well. He *is* a biologist," Gen pointed out.

"Yes, Will," Rose said. "I mean, he's cute, right? He's got that Southern California surfer look going on, which is … good. It's good. But you'd never think it, would you? With the birds, and the studies and the … the data."

"Wow. Your face melted off?" Lacy said.

"Almost. For a minute there, I thought I was levitating."

"God," Lacy said. "I want someone to collect my data."

"I got my data collected just this morning," Gen said, wiggling her eyebrows. "There was really a lot of data to collect. And Ryan collected it *all*."

"Shut up," Lacy said, throwing a wadded-up paper napkin at Gen.

"Let's not get off topic here." Kate, who had the happy, relaxed look of someone who got her data collected on a regular basis, turned toward Rose. "I want an answer to Lacy's question. If there was kissing, then how was it not a date?"

Rose sighed impatiently. "I told you. I only kissed him to piss off his ex."

"But it melted your face," Kate pointed out.

"Well … yeah. That was unexpected."

"One could argue that, beginning at the moment of the face-melting, it became a real date," Gen offered.

"No." Rose shook her head. "No, no."

"But why not?" Lacy asked.

"Because I'm finished with men," Rose said.

"Oh, honey." Kate reached out and put a hand on Rose's arm. "The thing with Jeremy was just—"

"It's not about Jeremy."

"So you've said," Gen put in.

"Well, it's not," Rose insisted. "It's not about him. It's about … everything. And the kisses were just kisses. I enjoyed them. Okay, a lot. But they don't mean Will and I are dating, and they don't mean I'm not done. Because I am."

"All right." Kate nodded. "Do you want me to go to the animal shelter with you to pick out your twelve cats?"

Rose shot her a look. "Not today."

"Birds," Gen added. "She should get birds." She raised her eyebrows meaningfully. "Maybe a snowy plover."

"Shut up," Rose said.

Some days Will hated his time with the birds, and other days he loved it. This was one of the latter. Sitting out here in the dunes, in the quiet of the morning, with the breeze on his face and the sound of the crashing waves in his ears, gave him time to think. Time to get away from himself and just … be. If he sometimes became so absorbed in his thoughts that he got less work done than he should have, well, he considered it a fair tradeoff.

The morning was foggy and cool, but not so cool that it was uncomfortable. The marine layer made everything feel soft, like the world had been wrapped in gauze. Sitting out here with his spotting scope and his notebook, he thought about his career, his goals, and the situation with Chris and Melinda.

And Rose. He thought about Rose.

He hadn't even planned on going out with her. When he'd been pushed into it due to circumstances that had spun out of his control, he'd thought, *Okay, fine. I like her, it could be fun.* And then she'd kissed him.

He couldn't recall ever having been so profoundly affected by a kiss. His body had reacted to her in powerful and unexpected ways. Of course, there was the expected reaction—he'd been relieved that he hadn't had to stand up for a while—but aside from that, there was the sensation that he'd been taken apart and put back together again as someone better, happier, more at peace. It occurred to him that Rose's kiss had done for him in a few seconds what a lifetime of organized religion never could.

And then, for reasons that escaped him, he'd talked to her about things he'd never told anyone. He'd revealed to her his insecurities, his feelings of inadequacy, his uncertainty about who he was and where he was going with his life. How in the world had *that* happened?

Now, having experienced all of that, he couldn't help thinking about her, when he should have been thinking about the birds.

What was the point, though? She'd told him not once but a few times that she was finished with dating. And who could blame her? Relationships were trouble wrapped in annoyance, bound together with guilt and obligation. Just look at the whole mess with him and Melinda.

He couldn't help wondering what would happen if she weren't done with dating. What then? Would the two of them be relationship material? Could they make a go of it?

Which was a stupid thing to wonder about, since he barely even knew her.

But changing that—getting to know her—would be part, or even most, of the fun.

She was interesting. He found himself wanting to know what ancient hurts had caused her to be who she was. She walked around wearing a suit of armor made of hair dye, make-up, body jewelry, and snark. What had made her construct it? And what was under it?

He suspected that the real Rose—the beating heart and soul of her—was just under the surface. No one could kiss like that unless they had easy access to their living, pulsing emotions. He was curious about that real Rose. He wanted to know.

Will spotted one of the snowy plovers that was part of his study, as evidenced by a tag on its left leg. He approached it slowly, carefully. If he made too much noise or frightened it, it was going to take flight, and then who knew when he'd be able to spot it again? He eased forward, slow and stealthy, his movements as gentle as a mother's touch.

Pamela Watkins started in on Rose within days of being invited to the wedding.

"You're going to dye your hair, of course," Pamela told Rose over the phone. She'd called during a lull at De-Vine, on the store phone rather than Rose's cell phone. The strategy was a good one; Rose would never have picked up her own phone knowing it was Pamela, but she couldn't ignore the business line.

"Of course," Rose agreed. "Gen's colors are pink and gray. Well, they're calling it blush, but it's pink. I know gray hair is in fashion, but I've never been a fan, so I thought I'd go with the pink."

"Very amusing, Rosemary," Pamela said in a tone that indicated the opposite. "Your natural brown is rather drab—let's face it—but I think you'd look lovely with some golden blond highlights."

Rose clamped her eyes shut and pinched the bridge of her nose. "Mother. If you're worried about me having drab hair, then I suggest you embrace the pink."

Pamela made a sputtering noise. "You can't possibly be planning to ... at a *Delaney* wedding! You simply can't—"

"Mother," Rose tried.

"You'll humiliate yourself, and me, and I simply won't—"

"*Mother.*"

"Why, the bride will be *mortified—*"

Rose banged the handset of the phone against the bar a few times to get Pamela's attention. When she put the handset to her ear again, Pamela was silent.

"Gen won't be mortified, Mom, because she's my friend, and she loves me, and she accepts me the way I am. Something you might give a whirl sometime."

"It's *because* I love you that I care about these things," Pamela said, slightly more subdued now.

Rose knew she was telling the truth. She knew her mother did love her. The problem was that Pamela equated one's appearance with the success or failure of one's life. If you looked a certain way, it had to mean that you were happy, fulfilled, thriving. But Rose knew from experience that you could have the right hair, the right clothes, the right makeup, and the right dress size and still be miserable as hell, mostly because you were trying to be someone you weren't. And that was the part her mother had never understood.

"Look, Mom, I know. I know you do," Rose said. "But I'm going to look how I look. And as long as it's okay with Gen, it should be okay with you, too."

"I just thought—" Pamela began.

"Hey, Mom? I have a customer coming into the store. I have to go."

"If you could only—"

"Oops! I've got someone on the other line. Gotta go. Bye, Mom. Love you!"

Rose hung up the phone and gazed around the shop, which remained empty except for her. Sandra and Gen didn't want to take back Pamela's invitation now that it had been issued, and Rose understood that. So, she pondered other things that might keep her mother from attending.

Car trouble.

Major illness.

Injury.

Flash flooding.

Since none of those things seemed likely, she was going to have to gird her loins for the onslaught of maternal disapproval.

Ah, well. A wedding was nothing without family drama. Gen didn't seem to have much of that, so Rose would have to supply it for her. It would be a sort of wedding gift. Like a Crock Pot, but with guilt and recrimination.

Chapter Eight

Having Melinda at the house was uncomfortable at best, but fortunately, Will didn't have to see her much. Will mostly kept to himself, sticking to the guest house or staying away from the property entirely, working with the birds or hanging out with his friends.

The afternoon after the restaurant incident, Chris stopped by the guest house, and Will invited him in for a beer. Will grabbed two bottles from the refrigerator and handed one to Chris, and the two of them lounged around the little living room, drinking the cold craft brew.

The afternoon light filtered in through the windows, giving the place a warm, cozy feel that inspired napping and lazy reading. Will would have rather been doing either of those than talking about women with Chris.

"Rose seemed … interesting," Chris offered.

If that was his opening gambit, then the rest of the conversation was likely to go downhill from there.

"She is," Will said. He took a swallow of the cold beer and wondered where this was going to go, and how many times he'd have to lie about topics including, but not limited to, his relationship with Melinda and his relationship with Rose.

"She and Melinda didn't seem to get along."

"No," Will agreed.

"What do you think was going on there?" Chris had his feet up on the coffee table, and he was slumped back into the sofa, relaxing like he owned the place. Which he did.

"Did you ask Melinda?" The response was evasive, but Will hoped Chris wouldn't notice that.

"Yeah."

"And what did she say?"

Chris shrugged. "She said Rose had a chip on her shoulder and was trying to pick a fight."

"Seemed like the other way around to me," Will said.

"Me too."

"Huh." Will stayed silent. Nothing bad ever came from staying silent.

"Well, whatever was going on there, it looked like you two have something good going on." Chris winked at Will. It was a slightly lecherous wink that clearly referred to the kiss that had almost brought the walls down around them.

"You think so?" Will said.

"Don't you?"

Will thought about that, took a slug of his beer, and shrugged. "It's new. We're still getting to know each other." At least that part was true.

Chris guffawed. "If that was her getting-to-know-you kiss, I can only imagine what's going to happen if she decides she really likes you."

That was a thought laden with imagery that made it difficult for Will to focus on the conversation, and in fact, he didn't realize Chris was still talking until the man was halfway through another thought.

"—at the wedding," Chris said.

"What? I didn't … Sorry. What was that?"

"I said, I hope Melinda can be better behaved at the wedding."

Will blinked at him. "What wedding?"

"Gen Porter and Ryan Delaney."

It wasn't making any sense, so Will thought he must have misheard. "Melinda's coming to Gen and Ryan's wedding?"

Chris chuckled. "Well, I am. And I'm free to bring a date, so . . ."

"But why are *you* coming?" Will asked. "Do you even know them?"

He shrugged and shook his head. "Nah. But apparently, that night when I let them use Cooper House, they had a really good time. It made an impression. So, I guess the invitation was a kind of thank you."

"Ah." It made sense. He could see it. The problem was, what had started as one weekend pretending that he and Melinda didn't know each other was now going to be one weekend and a wedding. *And,* Chris was going to expect Will and Rose to be a couple at the event.

Well, maybe they would be by then.

It could happen, if Will had any say in the matter.

"Let's summarize for those of us joining in the middle of the broadcast," Daniel said just before his turn at the dart board.

He, Will, Ryan, and Jackson were at Ted's, a bar off Main Street, on Saturday night after Jackson's shift at Neptune ended. Daniel and Jackson were competing for the Ted's Cup, an award they'd invented for the occasion. They were vaguely aware of the official rules for darts, but found them too complicated, and instead they had their own scoring system based mostly on illogic and grandiosity.

The bar was dim and noisy, and the carpet looked like people had been driving tractor-trailer rigs over it for years. The place smelled like beer, sweat, and french fries.

Daniel continued his thought, ticking off points on his fingers. "Your ex is coming to Ryan's wedding. And she's going to be your boss's date. And your boss doesn't know that your ex is your ex. Meanwhile, your boss *and* your ex think you and Rose are a couple, which you're not. So you'll have to either continue to pretend you're a couple at the wedding, or make up some kind of bullshit story about how you broke up. And finally." He paused for drama. "Your ex and Rose hate each other so much that they might break out in hair-pulling and eye-gouging at the reception."

Will nodded miserably. "That about sums it up, yeah."

Daniel, looking self-satisfied, as one does when one's own problems pale in comparison, took aim and threw a dart. It went high and to the right for four points.

"I hope there won't be hair-pulling and eye-gouging at the reception," Ryan said mildly. "Because then Gen would want to jump in to defend Rose, and she might rip her dress. We paid a lot for that dress."

"I don't know how Chris got invited in the first place. You don't even know him," Will said to Ryan.

"Gen wanted to invite him because of that date we had at his house," Ryan said.

"Must have been a good date," Jackson observed.

"It was a very good date," Ryan confirmed. "I relive that date often."

Daniel threw his second and third darts. One hit the bull's eye, but because it was on his second throw, it didn't count.

"Your rules don't make any sense," Will observed.

"You're just jealous because you were eliminated in the Ted's Cup semifinals," Jackson said. He pulled Daniel's darts from the board and lined up for his turn.

"So, what's your plan, college boy?" Daniel wanted to know. "Are you going to plead with Rose to act like she's your sweetie?"

"I don't know," Will said. He straightened his glasses and thought about it.

"You could always say it didn't work out," Ryan said. He was sitting on a barstool just outside the range of dart fire, sipping beer from a mug.

"Yeah, but then they'd have to pretend to be hurt and awkward," Jackson pointed out. "People who have broken up recently are usually hurt and awkward."

"And pretending to be hurt and awkward would be harder than pretending to be a couple," Daniel said.

"Or," Will said. He cleared his throat. "Maybe we really will be a couple by then."

"Oh ho!" Jackson said. He threw his first dart, and it hit close to the center, though not in the bull's eye.

"Ah, Jesus," Daniel said. "We've already got two men down. Don't tell me we're about to lose another one."

"Yeah, how's the single life working out for you, Daniel?" Ryan wanted to know.

"It's good." Daniel nodded. "Last night I sorted my socks."

"Maybe Will doesn't want to spend the rest of his life sorting socks," Jackson said. He threw his last two darts. One went wild and barely hit the board, and the other was low and to the left.

"So. You and Rose, huh?" Ryan asked. He was grinning in that way people have when they're about to convert someone to their cult.

"Maybe. I don't know." Will shrugged and looked at his feet. He picked up his beer mug and looked into it, then put it back down on the table. "She says she's done with dating. But I like her. I like her a lot."

"And there was the kiss."

"What kiss?" Daniel demanded.

"Last night during the date that wasn't a date, I came out of the kitchen at Neptune to stop by, say hi, ask how everything's going. And college boy over here was in a serious lip-lock with Rose right there at Table Twelve."

Ryan raised his eyebrows and let out a long, low whistle.

"It wasn't like that," Will said.

"It wasn't like what?" Jackson grinned. "Wasn't like you were about to bend her over the salad bar and go for it? Because that's how it looked to me."

"I … it wasn't …" Will tried to explain, but what was there to explain? He *was* just inches from bending her over the salad bar. And now that Jackson had suggested it, he wouldn't stop thinking about that possibility for quite some time.

"Rose is terrific, man," Ryan said finally. "You could do a whole hell of a lot worse."

"Yeah." Will nodded. "Yeah. I'll have to think about it."

"That's your problem, college boy," Jackson said. "You think too much."

It occurred to Will that Jackson might be right. Thinking was great when you were compiling a research report or planning a big career move.

But sometimes you just had to bend somebody over a salad bar.

The next day at De-Vine, Rose called the local wineries to place orders for the shop, did some accounting work on the computer in the back room, served a customer who'd come in to buy champagne for a silver anniversary party, and then consulted with a local restaurant about their wine list.

With all of that done, she opened her laptop on the bar and pulled up information on the wine and viticulture program at Cal Poly San Luis Obispo.

The college was only about forty minutes from Cambria, so the commute would be doable. What would be less doable would be juggling her job at De-Vine with her studies. Or paying the roughly eleven thousand dollars a year she'd need for tuition and books.

Her salary at De-Vine wasn't terrible, but it wasn't notably generous, either. Rose couldn't blame Patricia. Rose did the books, so she knew what Patricia could and could not afford to pay her. Her paycheck was enough to cover the rent on her cottage as well as her basic expenses, but it would never be enough for her to pay for college.

Rose's mother had enough money to fund her education, and she'd be happy to lend it to Rose, or even give it to her. But Rose knew what the conditions would be. The money had strings attached, and those strings led straight to a hair salon and a dermatology appointment for laser tattoo removal.

And that would be just the beginning.

There were student loans, of course, but then she'd be saddled with more than forty thousand dollars in debt when she graduated, and that didn't seem like a very appealing prospect.

She could do community college for the first two years—get the general education requirements out of the way relatively cheaply—and then transfer to Cal Poly for the last two years. That would bring her student debt down to a mere twenty thousand.

But that was assuming she could keep up with the course work while still managing De-Vine, and that thought worried her. She could study during slow times at the shop, but she'd need time off to attend classes. Patricia was great, and she'd do what she could to accommodate Rose. But Patricia could only do so much. Rose couldn't manage the store from San Luis Obispo. She had to be here.

She was still pondering it when the little bell over the front door jingled, and she looked up to see Will walking in.

Her heart did a little flip when she saw him. And what the hell was that? She was *not* interested in Will Bachman. She wasn't interested in anyone. And she was going to *stay* not interested in anyone, no matter how brilliant a kisser that someone might be.

"Hey," he greeted her, waving his fingers at her in a way that was endearingly shy and tentative. He looked all mussed and wind-blown from being outside, probably on the beach. He was wearing old jeans, a grey T-shirt with Stanford across the front in red lettering, and Teva sport sandals.

Rose did not want to rip off his shirt and run her hands all over him. Not at all.

She straightened from where she'd been slumped over the computer.

"Hi, Will. Did you need something?"

"Yeah. Uh … Chris and Melinda want some of that Enfield chardonnay we had at dinner. Do you have any?"

"Sure." She cocked her head at him. "I thought you were the caretaker. You have to do his shopping for him, too?"

He cleared his throat. "I had some stuff to do in town, so … I volunteered."

The first thought that popped into Rose's mind was that he'd volunteered so he could see her. But that would be stupid since they weren't dating, not even fake dating anymore.

She went to get the wine. "How many bottles?" she called over her shoulder as she went into the back room.

"Six. Two to drink, four for the cellar, he says."

"Six it is."

When she came back with the wine, he gestured toward the laptop. "So, what had you so absorbed when I came in?"

"Oh … nothing. Nothing important, anyway. Just … yearning and broken dreams."

He raised his eyebrows. "That doesn't sound like nothing."

She flipped the laptop around on the bar to face him. He peered at the screen.

"Wine and viticulture," he read. He looked up from the screen. "You want to go to college."

She shrugged. "Yeah. I didn't go right out of high school because … well, because. And now, with the costs and my job here, I wish I'd gone when I had the chance."

"Why didn't you?" He pulled up a stool at the bar and settled in.

"Ah, jeez. It's a long story."

"Every minute I spend listening to you is a minute I don't have to spend at Cooper House with Melinda," he said.

"Good point. Is she leaving soon?"

"Tomorrow. Thank goodness. But don't change the subject. Why didn't you go to college?"

He looked so cute with his messy blond hair and his sunburned cheeks, his glasses and his earnest blue eyes, that she found herself pouring out the whole story.

"I grew up in Connecticut," she began. "Darien. All white, all rich. I went to private school and my parents bought me a Mercedes for my sixteenth birthday. My mother expected me to get straight As, go to cotillion, and date a future lawyer."

"Huh. That wouldn't have been my first guess."

She raised her pierced left eyebrow at him wryly. "You don't say. Anyway, I was supposed to go to Yale. My mother had it all planned out. My extracurricular activities, student government, debate team—it was all designed to look good on my application. I volunteered at a soup kitchen twice a week because my mother said the admissions office would like that. Of course, there are no soup kitchens in Darien because there are no poor people in Darien. We had to drive to Hartford."

Warming to her story, she propped her elbows on the bar and leaned forward, getting into it. "I had a college admission coach. I had an SAT tutor. I had a Yale student mentor."

"Okay," Will prompted. "So what happened?"

Rose stood up straight and let out a sigh. "I got accepted."

"You did."

"Yes."

"And?"

She crossed her arms over her chest and leaned her hip against the countertop that ran behind the bar. "I ran away."

"You … "

"Right after high school graduation, I got in the Mercedes and ran out of there like I was escaping from a hostage situation. Which, now that I think of it, is exactly what it felt like."

"What happened then?"

She gave him a kind of side-eye. "Do you really want to hear this?"

"Are you kidding? This is a great story."

The bell on the front door jingled again, and a middle-aged couple came in the door and started browsing among the IT'S WINE O'CLOCK signs and the jars of tapenade.

Rose greeted them and asked if they were interested in wine tasting. They were. She got them situated at the bar with a sheet listing the wines available for tasting. When they'd selected their first wine, she poured one-ounce portions into their glasses and returned to where Will was seated a few feet down the bar.

"So, anyway. My parents cut off the money. Of course. I sold the Mercedes for ten thousand dollars and took a bus out here to the coast. I got the tattoo at around the halfway point, at a place in Lincoln, Nebraska." She lowered the left shoulder of her top slightly to show him the red rosebud with the thorny stem.

"That was brave," the woman put in as she sipped her ounce of pinot grigio. She was a trim fifty-something with tidy hair who looked like she might work in a bank. "How old were you?" She looked apologetically at Will. "Sorry. I came in in the middle."

"I was eighteen," Rose said.

"Jeez," the man said, shaking his head. If the woman looked like she worked in a bank, the guy looked more like an insurance salesman. "It must have been hard to give up that Mercedes."

"Not really. It wasn't me. I liked the bus better." She turned back to Will. "Anyway. Now here I am, ten years later, and I want to go to college, but I can't afford it. I should have gone to Yale when I had the chance."

"No." Will shook his head. "No. You'd have flamed out at Yale."

"Hey," she said sharply. "Thanks a lot."

"You'd have flamed out because it wasn't what you wanted. Because someone else was trying to shove you into a little box, and you were too big for the box." He spoke with conviction, and she felt a thrill of excitement at the thought that he might understand—he might really get it—in a way other people rarely had. "This time, it's for you," he said. "This time, it's about becoming the person *you* want to be, not the person someone else wishes you were. That's why this time, it's going to work."

His speech had gotten her so fired up she almost forgot she was broke. But then she remembered, and her shoulders fell.

"Yeah, but I can't afford it."

"There's always a way," the guy down the bar said. "Loans, financial aid."

"But loans mean debt," Rose pointed out.

"Yeah, but a college degree means more earning potential," the woman added helpfully.

"What do you think?" Rose asked Will. "You're a Stanford guy. That can't be cheap."

"It's not," he agreed. "And I didn't get much help from my parents. They did what they could, but they just didn't have the money to give."

"So, how'd you manage?" the bank lady asked.

"Scholarships, loans, work study." He turned to Rose. "If I did it, you can. Anybody brave enough to leave home at eighteen with nothing but a suitcase and a Mercedes can figure out how to pay for college."

"Yeah." Rose wanted to believe it, and she felt a little seed of hope begin to sprout within her. "Yeah. Maybe."

"Can we try the Opolo sauvignon blanc next?" the guy wanted to know.

Chapter Nine

Will drove back to the house with the six bottles of wine in his car. He couldn't stop thinking about Rose.

Unfortunately for him, the story she'd told about leaving home at eighteen had left him more enamored than ever. The reason it was unfortunate was that he thought she might really mean what she said about being through with men.

Someone that strong, that determined, that *brave*, probably didn't need anybody. But that didn't mean he couldn't be good for her. That didn't mean he had nothing to offer.

He wondered if she realized that his errand to get the wine had been an excuse to see her. Yes, it was really for Chris, and yes, he did do those kinds of things sometimes as part of his job. But he'd bent the truth a little when he'd told Rose about it. He hadn't just volunteered to get the wine. He'd been the one to suggest buying a few bottles in the first place. And he'd done that to have an excuse to go into the shop and talk to her.

Pathetic.

He thought she might be out of his league, but then he wondered why he should believe such a thing. He was a Stanford-educated PhD candidate. By any measure, he was good relationship material.

On further consideration, he concluded it was the pure force of her personality that made him feel lacking by comparison. If he was a light breeze, Rose was a hurricane.

It probably wouldn't hurt him to pick up his own wind speed a little.

He was still thinking about her, about his chances with her, and about how he might best approach a woman who had sworn off anyone bearing a Y chromosome, when he pulled up in front of Cooper House to deliver the wine. Rose had given him a cardboard box to carry the bottles, and he hefted the box from the trunk of his car and carried it up the front walk and onto the porch.

He was so preoccupied as he waited for someone to answer the doorbell that it never occurred to him that the person answering the door would be Melinda. But there she was, in bare feet and some kind of long, flowy dress that had probably cost more than the current value of his car. Which, he had to admit, wasn't saying much.

She had a certain look when she opened the door, a certain grandiose attitude, that told Will she was practicing to be lady of the manor. When she saw that it was him, her face dropped.

"Oh. Will."

He cleared his throat and shifted from one foot to the other. "Chris asked me to get him some wine from town." He lifted the box slightly in demonstration. "Here it is."

"Of course. Would you bring it in for me?" She stood back to allow him to enter.

Will looked around as he came into the house. "Is Chris here?"

"He and his tennis coach are out on the court."

Will's brow furrowed. "He has a tennis coach in Cambria?"

"No. His coach from the Bay Area came down for the lesson."

"Ah." It was at precisely that moment that Will realized he and Chris were no longer friends, and were now simply employer and employee. What kind of person made his tennis coach drive four hours to give a lesson, especially when Chris would be returning home the next day? Will had known that he and Chris had grown apart over the years, but at this moment the gaping chasm between them seemed unbridgeable.

"Would you mind bringing the bottles down to the cellar?" Melinda asked. She was moving ahead of him into the house, floating about in a peculiarly airy way, as though her association with Chris and his vast wealth meant she were somehow no longer tethered to the earth.

"Sure." Will nudged the front door closed with his foot and followed Melinda.

Of course he knew where everything was in the house—knew it better than Melinda did—but for some reason she felt the need to escort him into the kitchen and through the big oak door that led down into the wine cellar.

When they were down there in the dim light amid the racks of bottles and the smell of oak barrels kept purely for show, Will put the box on a table in the center of the room.

"Okay. There you go," Will said. "I'll just ..." He gestured toward the stairs and headed in that direction.

"Will."

He stopped and turned toward her, waiting.

"This thing between you and that *woman* can't be serious," she said. She'd uttered the word *woman* as though it were an offense to her mouth.

"It can be whatever Rose and I want it to be," Will said, keeping his tone casual. This wasn't the place to get into a fight with Melinda. "What's your problem with her?"

She looked at him incredulously, her arms folded in defiance over her chest. "My *problem*?" She shook her head as though she couldn't believe he could be this obtuse. "You broke up with me, and then ... you end up with her? *Her?*"

"This isn't about Rose," he said. "Whatever's got you upset, it's not about her."

"No." She walked over to the cardboard box, took a bottle out, looked at it, then set it on the table. "You're right. It's not about her."

"Then what?"

She shook her head. "Will. How can you be so dense?"

"Melinda—"

In a second, in a breath, she crossed the room, put her arms around him, and kissed him. This wasn't the old, familiar Melinda kiss, uninspired and dutiful. This was a kiss full of determination, anger, and maybe a little desperation.

He put his hands on her shoulders and pushed her back until she was at arm's length from him.

"Melinda, what—"

"You can't want her more than you want me," she said, her face flushed. "You just can't. It doesn't make any sense."

"You're with Chris," he said. "What do you think you're doing?"

"He doesn't have to know."

"There's not going to be anything to know. Except what we're already keeping from him—that we used to be together. We *used to be* together. But we're not anymore. And that's all there is to tell."

He let go of her, then climbed up the stairs and out of the wine cellar, leaving her down there, alone, to think her unknowable thoughts.

Tomorrow, she'd leave. It wouldn't be a minute too soon.

He wanted to talk it out with someone, but it seemed unlikely that any of his friends would be available. Jackson would be at the restaurant, Ryan would be out herding cows or doing whatever it was he did on the ranch. Daniel would be in his studio blowing glass into amorphous shapes.

And even if he could get hold of them, any of them, he realized they weren't the ones he wanted to talk to. They weren't the ones whose advice he wanted.

He pulled out his cell phone and called De-Vine.

"Can you have lunch with me?" Will asked when Rose answered the phone.

"Oh."

He heard her hesitation and rushed to reassure her. "I know you're done with men. You told me. But this isn't a date. It's just … you know. Lunch as friends. I kind of have stuff going on, and I need someone to talk to, and … You know what? Never mind. It was a bad idea."

"No. Wait. Patricia's here between noon and two. I can slip out for an hour during that window."

He felt his heart lift. "Twelve-thirty?"

They met down the street at Robin's, where they sat on the patio and ordered fish tacos for him, and a pastrami sandwich for her. The early afternoon was mild, with overcast skies and a slight breeze that kissed her skin.

"So, what's this stuff you've got going on?" she asked, when they were settled in with their food. She picked a stray piece of pastrami from her plate and put it in her mouth.

"It's … I don't even know how to handle this," he said.

"Will. Handle what?"

"Melinda made a pass at me. Today. In the wine cellar. She kissed me and said Chris doesn't have to know." He shook his head, avoiding her eyes. "He's my boss, and my friend. At least, he used to be my friend. This is pretty messed up."

Rose felt a surge of hot anger in her core. It was pushing out and threatening to erupt. If she didn't know better, she'd have thought it was jealousy. Which was crazy, because she didn't have feelings for Will.

"So what did you do?" She kept her voice even, the voice of a neutral observer and not of somebody who wanted to commit murder with her bare hands.

He shrugged. "I pushed her away and left. What else could I do? And she's leaving tomorrow, which is great, but then she and Chris are coming to Ryan and Gen's wedding, which is going to be awkward, to put it mildly."

She put down her sandwich. "They're coming to the wedding?"

"Yeah."

"But what the hell for?"

"That's what I wanted to know. Apparently, Gen and Ryan had a good date at Cooper House."

"Ah." Rose nodded knowingly. "Skinny dipping and library sex."

Will closed his eyes and put up his hands, palms out. "That, I didn't need to know."

He picked up a taco, took a bite, chewed carefully, then wiped his mouth with his napkin. "She trash-talked you some more, said I couldn't possibly be serious about you after I'd broken up with her." He shook his head mournfully. "Help me out here, Rose. What does all of this mean? Because I'm a guy, and I don't speak woman."

Rose put aside her feelings about Melinda kissing Will, and about Melinda insulting her. She already thought Melinda was rude, superior, and snotty. What Will was telling her didn't change that. Sure, Rose wanted to walk out of the restaurant, drive to Cooper House, and slap the woman's skanky-ass face. But right now, Will was coming to her, as a friend, for her insight. She tried to focus on that.

"Well, it could mean a few things," Rose offered. "It could mean she still has real feelings for you. Or it could mean she's competitive; seeing you with me made her feel like she had to one-up me, just to prove she's the better woman. Which she's not, by the way. Or it could mean she's got some sort of score to settle with Chris, and kissing you was a way to get back at him. Or, it could mean that she's so pissed at you for dumping her that she wants to get you in trouble with Chris, maybe get you fired."

"Wow." Will raised his eyebrows in wonder. "I didn't even know there were that many scenarios."

"Oh, there are. And probably a few more I haven't thought about." She chewed a bite of sandwich thoughtfully. "What's your gut feeling? You know her a hell of a lot better than I do."

He shrugged. "It's hard to say. I'd be surprised if she still had feelings for me. I mean, the reason we broke up was that she didn't seem to like me that much anyway. She was always criticizing me about one thing or another. Usually my career path. She doesn't think biology professors make enough money, apparently."

"Huh." Rose thought about that. "Well, if money's what she's after, she should be happy now, with Chris."

"Right." Will nodded. "You'd think so. She's got what she wanted. So what's to be unhappy about? And why risk that by messing around with me?"

Now that the initial shock of Will's revelation had worn off, Rose found that she was ravenously hungry. She dove into her sandwich, which was sublime. The flavors of salty pastrami and spicy mustard mingled on her tongue. "God, this is fabulous," she told him. She figured that a messy pastrami sandwich was probably a poor choice of food to eat on a date. But this wasn't a date, so that was okay.

"Anyway. Melinda." He tried to get her to refocus on the problem.

"Right. Sorry. Do you think it's the competition angle? She sees you with another woman after you dumped her, and she's got to prove she could get you back if she wanted to?"

"Maybe." He looked thoughtful. "I could see that. I think I wounded her ego when I broke up with her."

"Of course you did. It's impossible not to get a wounded ego when you get dumped. But that doesn't mean you were wrong to do it, and it doesn't mean she gets to mess with you afterward just to prove a point." She pointed one finger at him, the nail lacquered in deep blue.

"Right, I get that."

"In the end," Rose pointed out, "it doesn't matter why she did it. What matters is what you're going to do about it."

"Do?" He looked surprised. "I'm not going to do anything. I'm not going to sleep with her, if that's what she's after, and I'm certainly not going to tell Chris about the kiss."

"Okay." Rose nodded, the big, messy sandwich held together in her hands. "But be alert. If it's the competition/ego thing, you hurt her ego even more when you pushed her away. And she's going to want payback."

"Payback?"

"If it's the ego scenario, yeah. Because now you've rejected her not once, but twice."

"Ah, God." Will looked miserable. "You women are so complicated."

"Hey, don't blame me," Rose told him. "I'm not the one who kissed you in a wine cellar."

"No. You kissed me at Table Twelve of Neptune." He grinned.

And that thought distracted her from Melinda entirely. All she could think of, now that he'd brought it up, was the kiss, and the second kiss outside her house, and the nagging question of whether there might be another kiss, at another location, sometime soon. But that was a stupid thing to contemplate, since she was not interested in Will Bachman or his kisses.

Much.

"What are you going to do about the wedding?" she asked.

"What about it?"

"Well." She cleared her throat and felt a little tremble of nervous energy under her breastbone. But why should she be nervous? It wasn't as though what she was about to say meant anything. "You know. She thinks we're a couple, and Chris thinks we're a couple. And they're going to be at the wedding, and we're going to be at the wedding. So ..."

"Ah. Right. You think we should keep up the charade?"

"What? Oh." She pretended to be surprised by the question, as though that hadn't been what she was getting at all along. "I guess if you think we should ..."

"It's just easier, don't you think?" he said. "I mean, otherwise, we'll have to pretend we broke up, and then we'll have to act like two people who just broke up."

"Complicated," Rose said.

"Yeah."

She sighed. "Maybe it's best—easiest, I mean—if we have another fake date for the wedding. If you want to. Just, you know, to save yourself any trouble with Chris." She felt a shimmer of excitement up her spine, but she ignored it. This would be a fake date, not a real one. And if it involved another fake kiss, so much the better.

Chapter Ten

After lunch, Will headed out to the snowy plover nesting area to do more field research. The thing was, he didn't really need to do any more field research. He finally had everything he needed to persuasively show that a combination of global warming and the California drought had resulted in a change not only of the snowy plover's markings, but also its bill length. Furthermore, the changes were occurring at a faster rate than anyone would have predicted.

He knew his data was adequate—more than adequate. He needed to get off the beach, get into his cottage, and start writing the data analysis section of his dissertation so he could just get his doctorate already.

But somehow, he was blocked. He couldn't seem to make himself sit down in front of his laptop and do the work. He knew he was being self-defeating. He knew the only thing standing in his way was his own reluctance to finish the project. What he didn't know was why.

Or, maybe he did.

Will's career path had been set for some time now. Get the PhD, then secure a teaching job in the department of evolutionary biology at a reputable university. It was a good career path. It would lead to job security, prestige, good benefits, a pension. What could be wrong with a solid pension?

Deep down, under the surface layer of ambition and practicality, Will was scared. What if he got the doctorate, and no one wanted to hire him? What if they did hire him, and he didn't like teaching? What if wasn't good at it, and didn't get tenure? It all seemed so fraught with potential failure.

It seemed easier somehow to continue collecting data on the snowy plover, because it meant he could hang out on the beach and live on the grounds at Cooper House, which wasn't at all a bad deal, when you thought about it. The longer he delayed, the longer he could stay in Cambria, which increasingly seemed like the place he wanted to be.

He hadn't discussed any of this with anyone. Not with his friends, not with his family, and not with his dissertation adviser, who checked in every now and then wanting to know when Will was planning to finish. How could he talk about the problem, when he'd only just figured it out himself?

The fact that he was out here in the foggy morning amid the dunes and the birds, but didn't need any more data, allowed him to let his mind wander.

He'd liked talking to Rose over lunch. He'd liked sharing his concerns about Melinda, confiding in Rose, just sitting there sharing a meal and being with her. He'd intended to ask her to go to Gen and Ryan's wedding as his date, and he'd been prepared to pretend it wasn't a real date. Pretending that he was pretending; there was a lot a therapist could say about that.

But he hadn't had to ask her, because she'd suggested it herself. That had been a nice bonus. He wished he could just ask her out on a real date—no pretending—but he didn't think she was ready for that. He was pretty sure she'd say no out of a knee-jerk pain avoidance reaction due to the injury she'd suffered at the hands of her ex.

If Will made his move now, Rose would run like a rabbit fleeing a hawk. She seemed tough on the surface, but inside, she was vulnerable. Sort of like the Goliath birdeater, the biggest spider in the world, with a body as long as a dollar bill. The Goliath birdeater had very little venom, defending itself only with its fearsome exterior. Rose was like that. Her appearance was intimidating, but it was a ruse to avoid becoming prey.

If he wanted to approach her, he had to be careful. He had to move slowly.

The wedding was in the middle of June. If he played it right, if he approached her with care and with a gentle spirit, maybe they could go together as a real couple by then.

He thought about her career goals, and his. She wanted to go to college, he wanted to work at one. Rose was so self-confident in most areas (if not in regard to relationships) that she would succeed in whatever she decided to do. He wished he could say as much for himself.

He needed Rose not just as a romantic partner—though the thought of that kept him awake nights, spinning happy, wishful scenarios—but also as an inspiration, as a reminder of what was possible when one was fearless, the way she'd been fearless when she'd left home.

And she needed him, whether she knew it or not, to inspire her to be fearless in matters of love.

They'd be a perfect match, he thought. Now he just had to make her realize it.

With the wedding quickly approaching, Rose found herself occupied with bridesmaid-related activities. The bridal shower had to be organized. Dress fittings had to be done. The invitations had been sent out three months ahead of the big day, because so many people would have to travel to Cambria for the event. Responses were beginning to come in, and someone had to sort through them to determine a likely guest count.

Shoes had to be bought. Consultations had to be made with the caterers, the photographer, and the guys who'd be setting up the dance floor in the old barn near Gen and Ryan's new house, along with enough tables and chairs to seat two hundred. None of this was primarily Rose's responsibility, of course, but she'd agreed to help out however she could.

Of course, with the Delaney wealth, Gen could have hired a wedding planner to deal with all of the details. But the Delaneys were do-it-yourself kinds of people, so such a thing had never seriously been considered.

Which was fine, because helping with the wedding was actually kind of fun.

This evening, the women had gathered after work to sit around Gen's kitchen table in the new house, drinking wine and assembling place markers for the reception. In keeping with the theme of Gen's career as an art dealer, they were splattering pastel paint on little three-inch-square canvases to create abstract paintings that complemented Gen's color scheme. When the tiny paintings were dry, they would be placed on equally tiny easels, and then each would bear a banner-like ribbon with the guest's name.

According to the messy nature of the task, they were dressed in jeans or sweats and T-shirts, all efforts to be fashionable abandoned. Gen's wild red curls were gathered into a messy bun on top of her head, and Kate's short, spiky hair was all askew. Lacy managed to look effortlessly elegant, as usual, as though a stylist had picked out her white cotton tee and had supervised the tearing of her jeans at the knees.

Gen and Rose were dripping and splashing paint on the canvases, Lacy was assembling the easels, and Kate was carefully writing on the ribbons with fabric pens.

The idea of making two hundred of these might have been overwhelming, but the wine and the conversation were making it seem more like a party than a task. It reminded Rose of one of those paint-and-sip places where everybody drank during an art lesson. That combination probably didn't result in very good art, now that she thought about it.

"Hey, Kate," Rose said. "When you get to my mom's name, could you maybe misspell it or something? There's a lot you can do with Pamela. Maybe Hamela. Or, wait. It's a wedding, she might be drunk. Try Pamelush."

"Huh." Kate appeared to be considering it. "Pam rhymes with damn. And SPAM."

Gen laughed. "As interesting an idea as that is, I don't think it's the best way to nurture your relationship with your mother."

"I'm not sure I want to nurture it," Rose said. "I think I've given up. I mean, she's not a bad person, not really. She just wanted a different kind of daughter. Someone I don't know how to be." Suddenly her throat felt thick, and she silently cursed at herself; she hadn't wanted to bring her family drama into what was supposed to be a fun evening. But now that she'd started talking about it, she found it difficult to stop. Plus, she needed their take on something.

"Oh, honey." Kate put a hand over Rose's on the table. "We don't have to talk about your mother if you don't want to."

"No, I do need to talk about her. Because I have to decide whether to ask her to pay for me to go to college."

Gen, Kate, and Lacy all stopped what they were doing to look at Rose.

"College?" Kate said.

"Wow! I didn't know that was something you wanted," Lacy said.

Rose shrugged and went back to dripping blush-pink and pale gray paint on a little white square. "It's something I've been thinking about. There's a viticulture program at Cal Poly. But it's more than ten thousand dollars a year, and the pay at De-Vine isn't exactly lavish. My mom is loaded. She probably spends more than that on her hair stylist."

"I'm not sure that's a good idea." Gen's look of concern was punctuated by the drop of pink paint on the tip of her nose. "From what you've told me about your mom, she's likely to use it as an opportunity to control you."

"I know that," Rose said irritably. "Don't you think I know that? But what are my other options? Student loans? I can do that, sure, but … I've never had debt. As broke as I've been sometimes, I've always managed not to have debt."

"Ryan and I could lend you the money." Gen looked at Rose earnestly.

"No, no. I can't—"

"You could pay us back when you're ready. I know Ryan would say yes."

Rose knew he would, too. Ryan was one of the kindest people she knew. It made her both jealous of Gen and over-the-moon happy for her.

"Thank you. Really," Rose said. "But I can't. Friends and loans don't mix. Or, they do, but they create a chemical reaction that explodes and levels entire cities."

"That's true," Lacy admitted.

Rose dripped some pink paint onto a canvas in a loose S formation. "Borrowing it from my mother … Our relationship is so damaged already that it hardly seems to matter."

"What does Will think about the whole college idea?" Lacy asked.

The mention of his name in this context seemed incongruous, like she'd been putting together a jigsaw puzzle and had found a piece from a different box.

"How did Will get into this conversation?" Rose wanted to know.

Lacy shrugged. "It's just … you've been spending time with him lately. I thought it might have come up."

"It did," Rose admitted grudgingly.

"So how did that go?" Kate prompted her.

Rose shrugged. "Talking about wanting to go to college led me to talking about why I haven't gone yet. And *that* led to me telling him my running-away-from-Yale story. Which is really quite a story, you have to admit."

"It is," Lacy agreed.

"So what did he say?" Kate paused with a tiny ribbon in her hand.

"He said I was brave." Even as she said the words, they seemed to shimmer inside her, and she felt herself getting choked up. "He said … he said anyone brave enough to do what I did then is brave enough—strong enough—to do this now."

"Oh," Gen sighed.

"Wow." Kate looked a little choked up herself. "That's … wow."

"He's right, you know," Lacy said.

Rose wanted to think so. She really did.

Rose had a lot of opportunities to ask her mother for the college money, it turned out, because Pamela called her repeatedly with questions about the wedding.

"It's black tie, I assume," Pamela said one evening over the phone as Rose talked to her during her drive home from work. "It didn't say on the invitation, God knows why. You'd think the *Delaneys* would know how important it is to indicate a dress code."

"No, Mom, it's not black tie. It's … you know. Not casual, but not dressy. Nice, but not *too* nice."

Rose's car wasn't a recent enough model to have Bluetooth, so Rose had her iPhone on the passenger seat, on the speaker setting.

"Well, that doesn't clarify things at all," Pamela pouted. "Nice but not too nice? Dressy but not too dressy? Could you be any less helpful, Rosemary?"

Rose scowled at the phone. "Mom, this isn't like the East Coast. This is California. It's casual here. Just wear a dress. Not formalwear, just … you know. A dress."

Pamela sighed. "I should have known you were not the person to ask about fashion."

"Yes, you should have."

"At least I won't have to worry about what you'll be wearing," Pamela went on. "I assume Genevieve is choosing your dress, since you're in the bridal party."

"You can rest easy on that account," Rose assured her.

"But your *hair*. For a wedding, surely you plan to—"

"Uh-oh, Mom. I've got to hang up. I'm heading into the hills and there's no cell coverage!"

"Rosemary, I—"

Rose reached over to the passenger seat and ended the call while Pamela was in midsentence. Apparently she wouldn't be asking about the money today.

Maybe tomorrow.

Chapter Eleven

It might have been purely by chance that Will was assigned to work with Rose to select the wines for the reception. It might have been, but it wasn't. Will had asked Ryan to put him on the job so he could spend more time with Rose.

Rose thought they were being set up by their well-meaning friends; she said as much when she let Will in the door of De-Vine after closing one night.

"Do you know anything about wine, Will?" she asked him, her arms crossed, leaning her hip against the doorframe after she unlocked the shop for him.

"Uh, no. Not particularly. Why?"

"Because Jackson does. Why wasn't he given this job?"

"Well, I … Maybe because he's coordinating the food?"

"Maybe." She raised one eyebrow at him. "And maybe it's because you and I are being set up."

He cleared his throat. "Set up?"

"Yeah." She backed out of the doorway so he could enter. "Gen thinks we should be dating."

"Ah." He moved into the empty shop carrying two manila folders in his hands. He took a seat at the bar and put the folders on the polished dark wood. "The guys might have said something about that, too. They think we'd be good together."

She locked the door behind him and went behind the bar. "We probably would, *if* I were still dating, which I'm not, and probably never will again."

"That's a shame."

"Why?" She pulled a wineglass from under the bar, poured some chardonnay, and passed it to Will.

He shrugged. "Because you're a really good person. And if you don't want to date now—which, believe me, I get that—you still should be open to it someday. You've got too much to offer not to ... you know. Offer it. To somebody." He rearranged his glasses, which he knew would make him look nervous, but he couldn't help that. He *was* nervous.

She looked at him in a way that made him feel warm all over.

"That's sweet." She nodded toward the folders. "What did you bring?"

He held up one folder for her to see. "Menu for the reception, including appetizers, and including all of the ingredients for each dish."

"Great. And the other one?"

"That's ... ah." He paused and took a sip of the wine she'd given him. It was good—very good. "It's some information I compiled on scholarship opportunities in viticulture. And some others for returning college students." He pushed the folder toward her.

Wordlessly, she picked up the folder and opened it. She leafed through the pages Will had printed from his computer, and then she looked at him with wide eyes.

"You researched scholarships."

"Well ... yeah. I had some time, and I thought—"

She leaned over the bar, put her hands on his shoulders, and kissed him.

The kiss was different than the ones they'd shared before. The first had been intended to display her passion for him in front of Melanie, and, accordingly, it had been lusty and decidedly PG-13. The second one, the one outside her cottage, had been more tentative, but still infused with a heat that had seared him to his very core. This one, though, had something else behind it, something more genuine and pure. This was a kiss of sweetness and affection, a kiss that acknowledged that he saw her, and she knew it, and she was grateful.

Still, regardless of the nature of the kiss, he felt as though his body were alight with heightened sensation, as though the touch of her mouth on his was bringing his every nerve to glorious life.

"Will. Thank you," she said as she pulled away from him.

"Anytime." He straightened up on his bar stool. "And I mean that. Anytime."

She grinned at him, and he knew he had to change her mind about this reckless determination to give up on men. He needed to be with her, and even if that were not in the cards, even if she remained set on her decision to shut him out, this woman needed to be with someone. She was simply too lovely, too interesting, too *everything* not to share her glory with a man.

But he really wanted to be that man.

"Look," he began, trying to regain his composure. "There are some good opportunities in there. Lots of stuff available to older students. Not that you're older, just ... older than eighteen. And there are fewer things available in viticulture specifically, but there are some. I know you'll have to supplement with loans, probably, but this will give you a start."

She nodded. "Okay. This is ... thank you."

"And if you need any help with your applications, I've done about a thousand of them myself over the years. I can help. I'd really like to help."

"I'll keep that in mind," she said. She tucked the folder under the bar and propped her elbows on the bar top, leaning toward him. "Now, what's say we look at that menu?"

She knew she shouldn't have kissed him again. She knew it would give him the wrong idea, because she really wasn't interested in a relationship, and she didn't intend to let one fabulous kiss—or three—derail her from her chosen course. But she'd been so surprised, so touched, when he'd shown her the information on the scholarships. He'd put thought into this—real thought. He'd actually gone home and pondered how he could help her make her dream happen.

And how sweet was that?

Even though she wasn't going to date him, she had to admit that he was increasingly becoming a friend—someone she could talk to, someone whose company she enjoyed. Someone who would support her in the things she wanted to do. And if kissing him made her feel as though her insides had turned hot and liquid, well, that was something she'd just have to live with.

❖

"You two certainly do kiss a lot for people who aren't dating," Kate told Rose over coffee the next day at Jitters.

"How do you know about the kiss? The last one, I mean."

"Will told Jackson, and Jackson told me." Kate peered at Rose innocently over the rim of her cup.

"Well, why is Will talking to Jackson about kissing me?" Rose demanded.

"You talk to me about kissing him," Kate pointed out.

"True."

"Maybe he needed advice."

"Men don't ask other men for relationship advice." Rose scowled. "Do they?"

"I don't know." Kate shrugged. "Probably. But I imagine it goes something like this: 'What the hell was she upset about this time? What did I do?' 'How should I know? Women are crazy.'" She'd made her voice low, first in an uncanny imitation of Jackson, and then Ryan. She'd also put a wide-eyed look on her face that could only be described as "clueless male." Rose laughed.

"Anyway," Kate said, "Will tells Jackson, Jackson tells me, you tell me, I tell Jackson"—she waved a hand around airily—"It's what people do. No harm, no foul. Let's get back to the point."

"Which is?"

"You and Will kissing," Lacy called from behind the counter, where she was steaming milk for a cappuccino. "I'm all the way over here, and even I know. Keep up."

Rose sighed. "It was nothing. It was an appreciation kiss. It was ... " She grasped for a word. "Polite! I was being polite."

"Oh, honey," Kate said. "When my high school counselor gave me a list of available scholarships, I said thank you. I didn't give him tongue." She shuddered slightly. "He was eighty-three."

"Now there's an image," Rose said.

It was midmorning, and both De-Vine and Swept Away, the bookstore Kate owned, were scheduled to open in an hour. The coffee place was half full, with people chatting, working on laptops, and enjoying lattes and baked goods. The shop smelled like fresh ground French roast and mildew from the damp ocean air.

"Wait, wait, wait!" Gen rushed in the front door, looking harried. The slim black dress she wore for a day of work at the gallery was pristine as ever, but her hair was askew and she hadn't applied her lipstick yet. "I'm here! I'm here! Don't talk about the kissing without me!"

Rose turned to Kate. "Gen knows, too?"

Kate shrugged. "Ryan must have told her."

"I can fill you in," Lacy said from behind the counter as Gen scurried in and took a seat at the small café table. "Rose says she was just being polite."

Gen raised her eyebrows. "What, like 'How was your day?' and 'Nice weather we're having'?"

"No," Rose said. "More like, 'Thank you for being a very sweet and thoughtful person.' I thought the moment called for something."

"It called for you to buy him a cup of coffee or maybe send a nice card." Lacy brought Gen's coffee—black—and set it on the table in front of her. "It didn't call for an exchange of body fluids."

"Why are you guys harassing me?" Rose demanded. "I came here for coffee, and, you know ... companionship. And girl talk. I didn't come here to be harassed."

"This *is* girl talk," Kate said, stirring her cappuccino with a long wooden stir stick. She licked the foam off the stick thoughtfully. "Girls, talking about kissing. What could be more companionable than that?"

Gen shifted in her seat to turn toward Rose. "Even thought I missed the first part, I have to jump in here and say that if we're harassing you, it's because you're being stupid. I'm sorry, sweetie. I love you. But you are."

"Stupid? How am I stupid?" Rose demanded.

"Because you're sticking with this whole 'I'm done with men' thing when you should just drop the act and date Will. Then you can kiss him whenever you want to without having to make excuses about it," Lacy said as she bagged up a muffin for a middle-aged man in a Cambria shirt and madras shorts.

"She's right," Kate said.

"Yeah. She is," Gen added.

"It's not an act. And I don't want to date Will."

"Well, he wants to date you," Kate added. "And not these ridiculous fake dates, either. He wants to date you legitimately, with actual feelings and kisses that you both can acknowledge are real kisses."

"He does?" Rose looked at Kate, stunned.

"Of course he does." Kate scoffed at her.

"He ... I ..." Rose shook her head. "He does not. What even makes you think that?"

"What, are you new to this conversation?" Kate demanded irritably. "Will told Jackson, and Jackson told me. Jeez. We've been over this."

"Wait, he ... did he ... are you sure?" Rose found that processing this new information was surprisingly difficult. She knew that he liked her, of course. And she knew that she liked him. But when they'd gone out to Neptune, he'd made it clear that they were pretending for the sake of Chris and Melinda. Hadn't he?

Rose wasn't sure what it all meant. She'd found Will to be safe and uncomplicated, but if he was genuinely interested in her for something more than friendship and the occasional *we're just pals* kiss, then that meant he wasn't safe or uncomplicated at all. Now, he represented potential heartbreak. She tried to tell herself that didn't matter, but it did. There was a reason she'd instituted her no-men policy.

She shook her head to clear it. "Well, I'm going to have to nix that. That's just ... no." She almost felt as if she meant it.

"Oh, don't do that," Kate said. "He's nice. And he's smart. And he's cute as hell. He's way better than Jeremy was."

"I know he is!" Rose said.

"Then what's the issue?" Gen wanted to know.

"He's better than Jeremy!" Rose wailed. "He's so much better than Jeremy! And if Jeremy ripped my heart out and stomped on it—which he did—how much worse do you think it's going to be if Will does that? Because Jeremy was nothing! He was nobody! And Will ..."

"He's somebody," Gen said, a sigh in her voice.

"Yeah. He's somebody."

Chapter Twelve

Will knew he shouldn't have told Jackson about his desire to date Rose—or about kissing her again and how that had made him feel—because guys didn't talk about those things, except in terms of actions. Who did what, and who should do what next. Guys didn't talk about things like crushes and feelings and longing.

Except that Will didn't know what to do next in response to his feelings. So, it had seemed to fit.

He'd told Jackson that he seemed to keep kissing Rose somehow, even though Rose didn't want a relationship and had repeatedly said as much. And he'd asked Jackson for advice on how to change Rose's mind about him.

That was the guy part, right there. *What should I do? What action should I take?* Guys specialized in doing, not feeling.

So they'd talked about actions, and which ones Will should take.

The vague, niggling feeling that it had been a mistake was grandly, vividly confirmed when Will looked up from where he was sitting on the beach to see Rose crunching toward him over the sand, her fists balled up, looking seriously angry.

She was a beautiful, awe-inspiring sight.

"Uh … hi." He scrambled to his feet and brushed sand off the rear of his jeans.

"You told Jackson you wanted to date me." Her hands were on her hips, and she said the words as though she were accusing him of abusing kittens.

"Well, I—"

"We are *not* going there, no matter what you told Jackson," she demanded, her eyes fiery, her colorful hair blowing in the ocean breeze. She was magnificent. He'd never wanted to kiss her more than he did right now. But under the circumstances, he thought it would be ill-advised.

"Okay. How did you know I'd be here?" he asked. The beach was mostly deserted today, with just a few people strolling along the waterline as the gulls wheeled noisily overhead.

"I called Ryan, and he told me this is one of your places."

"My places."

"So I drove past the parking lot, and I saw your car."

"Ah."

"Don't change the subject," she said. She was wearing some kind of perfume, something spicy and delicious, and the combination of that and the smell of the ocean almost made his knees weak.

"I wasn't trying to. I—"

"Is this where you study the birds?"

Now she was the one changing the subject, and he was glad about it, since the original subject had involved her being angry with him.

"Ah, no. The birds are up the coast a ways. I was just out here thinking." It was a good thing he hadn't been here studying birds, or she'd have inadvertently stomped on a nesting area, the way she'd come barging over here. And even if that hadn't happened, she'd have scared them so badly they'd have flown off in a panic.

"What were you thinking about?" she wanted to know.

Interestingly, she didn't seem mad anymore. This was one of the endlessly fascinating things about Rose. She could be spitting fire one moment and cheerfully curious the next.

"You want to hear about it?" he said.

"I wouldn't have asked you if I didn't."

"Then come over and pull up a blanket."

He'd spread out a blue cotton blanket on the sand, and that's where he'd been sitting to do his thinking. Now, he brushed some sand off the blanket and smoothed it out for her.

She looked at him suspiciously. "If I do, it doesn't change anything. Sitting on the beach talking about your thoughts is just … well, it's just what it is. It doesn't mean anything."

"I understand that." He pushed his glasses back up on his nose.

"And there's not going to be any more kissing."

"Okay."

Still side-eyeing him, she gathered up her skirt and sat down on the blanket. He settled in beside her, leaving some room between them so she wouldn't go off on him about his intentions in relation to her no-men vow.

"So," she said once she was comfortable. "Your big thoughts."

"I didn't say they were big," he corrected. "Just that they were … thoughts."

"Hmph."

She took off her shoes—some kind of sandal with thick platforms that put Will in mind of something Herman Munster might wear—stretched out her feet, and wiggled her toes in the sand. Her toenails were painted deep green, the color of pine trees and summer grass. She wore a thin silver ring around the second toe of her right foot, and the sight of it distracted him so much he forgot what they were talking about.

"Don't tell me you were thinking about bird DNA," she prompted him. "Because I've got to tell you, that would be disappointing."

He grinned. "I don't study their DNA. I study how they're physically adapting to environmental challenges like drought and human encroachment on nesting areas. You see, the length of their bills—"

Rose threw her head to the side, closed her eyes, and made a loud and elaborate snoring noise.

Will laughed. "All right. I get it. I'm boring."

Rose smiled and nudged him with her elbow. "No, you're not. I'm just teasing you because it's all very scholarly. I could never do what you do."

He gave her a wry half smile. "I'm not so sure I can do it, either."

She looked at him with interest, squinting her eyes against the bright midmorning sunlight.

"What do you mean?"

He shrugged. "It's taking me forever to finish my dissertation, and the other day I was thinking about that, about why it's taking me so long." He picked up a handful of sand and let it run through his fingers. "And I kept coming back to two things: fear, and how much I'm going to miss all of this when I finish." He looked out to the ocean, to the foamy, crashing waves. Out in the distance, harbor seals bobbed in the blue water.

"What are you afraid of?" She brought her knees up to her chest and wrapped her arms around them, her voluminous skirt hugging her legs.

"When I get my degree, I'll be getting a university teaching job, I guess. But what if that doesn't happen? What if no one hires me? What if I'm no good at it?"

"Those are big questions," she agreed.

"And this arrangement with Chris was only supposed to get me through my dissertation work," he continued. "When that's done …"

"You'll be leaving," she finished for him.

"I guess so."

"And that's why it's taking you so long to finish the work," she concluded. "It's because you don't want to go."

That was it in a nutshell. He had friends here, a community, a home. And hopefully, at some point, he would have Rose.

"That would seem to be the case," he agreed.

"Well. You don't have to leave the area just because you start teaching. Cal Poly's got to have a biology department, right?"

"They do." He nodded.

"And that's only forty minutes away."

"Right." He sounded hesitant even to his own ears.

He rubbed at his nose and adjusted his glasses.

A guy with his dog walked by along the waterline. The guy periodically threw a stick into the waves, and the dog leaped after it, then emerged, wet and dripping, before shaking off the water in a wild spray and doing it all over again.

"You know, one thing I learned when I ran away from Yale is that sometimes you've just got to leap, even if you don't know where you're going to land. You've just got to do it and hope for the best." She gave him a tender smile.

The smile made him want to kiss her again, but that idea was fraught with potential peril. Instead, he reached out and took her hand. She looked surprised for a moment, and then she relaxed and let her fingers intertwine with his.

And it was enough, for now. If it turned out that she didn't want him, fine. He'd hate it, but he'd deal with it. For now, it was enough to simply be with her, listening to the ocean and feeling the warmth of her hand.

Chapter Thirteen

If Pamela had called Rose to warn her she was coming to Cambria more than a month before the wedding, Rose would have prepared. First, she would have pleaded with her mother not to come. If that hadn't worked, she'd have scheduled herself for long hours at De-Vine, hours so long that she would barely emerge for air, let alone family togetherness. Or she would have asked one of her friends to engineer a personal crisis that required Rose's intervention. Or, if all else failed, she'd have left town until the crisis passed.

But Pamela, with her many years of experience in dealing with Rose, had not called to warn her, and instead had opted to show up on Rose's doorstep, unannounced, on a warm morning in May.

"Mom. You're here. Oh, God," Rose blurted when she opened the door to find Pamela standing there in a Chanel suit, clutching a Hermes purse the size of a small suitcase.

"Is that any way to greet me?" Pamela demanded. "Let me in, I'm exhausted. My flight came in to San Luis Obispo last night—I had to fly on the most rattletrap little plane, it didn't even have first class. And I was forced to stay in the most dreadful hotel. The room was designed to look like a cave. Good God, I'll be having nightmares for months about being buried alive." She shuddered and pushed her way into the cottage.

"What … what are you doing here?" Rose stammered. "I … You didn't call. Did you? Did I miss a call?"

"Why, my dear, I'm here for the wedding." Pamela looked at her as though that were obvious.

"But the wedding's next month!"

Pamela waved a hand dismissively. "I thought I'd come early and spend some time with you. Have a little vacation. How have you been, darling? It's been too long." She leaned in and gave Rose an air kiss a full two inches away from actual contact. As she did, Rose caught a whiff of a Baccarat perfume that she knew cost more than six thousand dollars per ounce.

"You're not staying *here*, are you?" There was that blurting thing again.

"Oh, good God, no." Pamela scrunched up her nose at the thought. "While your place has a certain … charm, it's far too small for the two of us."

Thank God, Rose thought. At least, this once, her mother's disapproval of her and all of her choices would pay a dividend.

"Well … where will you be staying, then?"

"I've rented a house at the beach," Pamela declared. "Check-in isn't for"—she glanced at her Cartier watch—"four more hours, so you and I can spend a little girl time together, shall we?"

Four hours of girl time. With her mother. Rose felt the panic a field mouse must feel when it sees a falcon coming at it at two hundred miles per hour. She opened her mouth to make an excuse, and then, stunned by shock, was unable to think of one.

"Good, it's all settled, then. Is there anyplace in this godforsaken town that sells a decent cup of coffee?"

Rose took Pamela to Jitters, not because they had the best coffee—which they did—but because Lacy would be there, and Rose needed an ally. Even if there was nothing Lacy could actually do to help her, Lacy's presence would be a soothing balm that might make the difference between Rose surviving for the next few hours and her running, screaming, into oncoming traffic.

It was just Rose's luck that she didn't have to work today. Of course, Pamela didn't know that. After she parked her car on Main Street in front of Jitters, Rose led Pamela down two doors to De-Vine.

"While we're here, let me just pop in at work. I have to … I'm just going to talk to Patricia." It had been a couple of years since Pamela had been to visit Cambria, and that last time, she'd said loudly, in front of Patricia, that De-Vine had veered dangerously left at "quaint" and had detoured deep into "tacky." Rose hoped Patricia wouldn't remember.

"Rose," Patricia said from behind the counter. "What are you doing in here on your day off?" Then Patricia spotted Pamela, and her face went from warm and welcoming to a stony mask of neutrality. "Oh. Pamela."

She remembered.

"What do you mean, Patricia?" Rose asked desperately. "It's not my day off. Don't you remember that you and I traded shifts? I'm supposed to start work in …" She looked at the clock mounted above the bar. It had wine bottles for hands. "… in about an hour. Don't worry, Patricia, I didn't forget!" Rose laughed the laugh of the desperate.

"No, dear, we didn't trade shifts," Pamela said patiently. "It's Tuesday. You don't work on Tuesdays."

"But …" Rose did this winking, head tilting thing that was meant to covertly indicate Pamela, but that looked instead as though she were shooing away bees without benefit of her hands.

"What my daughter is trying to say," Pamela interjected, "is that she'd like you to invent some sort of work-related emergency to allow her to avoid spending the day with me. Isn't that right, Rosemary?"

"Uh … well … now that you mention it."

"Now, about that coffee," Pamela prompted her.

"Right." Rose's shoulders fell as she headed out the door and down the sidewalk toward Jitters.

Once they were outside, Pamela turned to her. "Would you mind telling me what that was all about?"

Rose shrugged miserably. "I just … This is a surprise, that's all."

Pamela gathered up her purse and put the handle over her pink-Chanel-clad forearm. "It's a surprise, darling, because I knew that if you had warning, you'd find some way to escape. Now, let's see if this coffeehouse of yours can make a decent espresso."

Pamela was halfway through her espresso and her blueberry scone before she made the first remark about Rose's hair. Which was probably the best she could do, Rose had to acknowledge.

"So I see it's blue this time," Pamela remarked. "You look remarkably like a Smurf."

"No, I don't," Rose answered, staring glumly into her latte. "Smurfs have blue skin, not blue hair. If I dyed my *skin* blue, then I'd look like a Smurf."

"I imagine the idea has occurred to you at least once." Pamela held a bit of scone primly between two fingers and gave Rose a tight-lipped smile.

"Is this what we're going to do? Is this what the next month is going to be?" Rose demanded. "You making snide remarks about my hair and my piercings, and … and my tattoo?"

Pamela popped the tiny bite of scone into her mouth. "Oh, I imagine we'll also talk about your choice of career and your love life."

"Fabulous."

Lacy, apparently sensing the tension, came over and stood at their table. "Is everyone doing okay?" Her hands were clasped in front of her apron, and she had a nervous look on her face. "Is there anything else I can get you?"

"Cyanide would be good," Rose said. "If you've got any."

"Is that for you or for me?" her mother inquired, one eyebrow raised.

"I'm still deciding."

"Okay then," Lacy said. "I'll just … um …" She scurried back behind the counter and busied herself washing some demitasse cups.

If that was Lacy's idea of rescuing her, it had been a pathetic attempt. Unless she actually came back with the cyanide.

At three p.m., after an excruciating morning and early afternoon that included shopping (Pamela had complained that there were no designer stores in Cambria) and lunch (she'd bemoaned the dearth of restaurants with Michelin stars), it was time for Pamela to check in at her rental house. Rose silently thanked God that shortly, her mother would be settled into her place and Rose could excuse herself, retreating into the silent lack of judgment of her own little cottage.

They went to the rental office, picked up the key, and followed the map to the house in the Marine Terrace neighborhood, not far from Kate's place. When they arrived, Rose thought, *This can't be right.* That thought was confirmed when Pamela got out of the car, slammed the car door, and boomed, "*What in the world is this?*"

Rose came to stand next to her mother in the driveway. "This is it," she said cheerfully. "Your home away from home."

Pamela rummaged inside her purse for her cell phone, grumbling something that sounded like, "Over my dead body."

Suddenly, Rose was feeling much better.

The house in front of them was not the five-bedroom, modern style, oceanfront showplace that Pamela had been expecting. Instead, it was a tiny, 1950s-era structure with white clapboard siding, a garden gnome grinning up from a bed of yellow flowers, and a sign hanging beside the door that said LIFE IS BETTER IN FLIP-FLOPS.

The look of horror on Pamela's face suggested she would be more amenable to spending the month in prison.

The situation made Rose feel unreasonably happy, though it shouldn't have; it would certainly mean hours of effort in trying to sort the situation out, and then, if that failed, hearing Pamela moan about the unbearable, ruined state of her vacation.

But right now, Rose might have had Disney bluebirds flying around her head, singing and fixing her hair. "Wow, Mom. This place is *adorable*. Look at the gnome! And that outdoor shower is going to come in handy." She took the key that was hanging limply from her mother's hand and unlocked the front door. "Oh, look!" Rose exclaimed. "They've got a Barcalounger!"

Pamela had dialed the rental company and was holding the cell phone to her ear with a look of fury on her face.

"Yes!" she said into the phone. "This is Pamela Watkins. I've just arrived at the so-called *house* you sent me to, and it's simply unacceptable. I arranged to rent a five-bedroom house at the waterfront, and this … this is … Well. This is *not* the house I rented. Yes, certainly, I'll wait."

After a moment, the conversation resumed. "I see," Pamela said. "Well, I hardly see how that's … No. Well, of course I expect a refund, but this is … I see. But you can't possibly … Yes. Well, your supervisor will be hearing about this, I assure you."

Pamela ended the call, put her phone back into her purse, and leaned against the car in a defeated posture that almost made Rose feel sorry for her.

"What did she say?" Rose ventured.

"It seems I was given this house by mistake. The one I reserved was double-booked. Someone else is already in it."

"Oh. But there are other—"

"Everything else is booked, except for a studio over a garage. With a sofa bed."

"Ah. Well, at least come inside and check it out," Rose said. "I hear those Barcaloungers are really comfortable."

After an hour of hearing Pamela on the phone trying, and failing, to find accommodations that were up to her standards, Rose thought that she might beat her mother to death with the garden gnome.

She decided it was best to make her excuses and get the hell out of there, before she found herself having to pay for a broken gnome.

"Look, Mom. I'm just going to go home and let you … you know. Get settled in."

Pamela was so dejected at this point that she didn't even try to argue. "That's fine."

"For what it's worth, I like the place," Rose said. "It's cute and cozy. I even like the gnome."

"Coming from you, darling, that doesn't surprise me." The words were right, but the delivery lacked the usual sting. Rose almost felt sorry for her.

"You could always go home and come back in time for the wedding," Rose said hopefully.

"We'll see."

Rose gathered up her things and scurried out of there before Pamela could change her mind and insist on dissecting the state of Rose's love life. At least that, at the moment, would be a short conversation.

Chapter Fourteen

The discussion of Rose's love life came the next day at De-Vine while Pamela was sitting primly at the bar drinking a glass of port. Gen had popped in during a break at the gallery to get Rose's opinion on a selection of hairstyles for the big day.

"See," Gen said, showing Rose a couple of magazine clippings, "this one has that tumbling-curls thing going on, kind of natural but sumptuous, but this one is more elegant and classic. What do you think?"

"Genevieve," Pamela said dryly. "You're asking Rose's opinion on *hair*?"

"I love Rose's hair," Gen said, always the loyal friend. "And she knows me, knows my taste. So what do you think?" She turned back toward Rose. "I can't decide."

Rose looked over the two pictures and scrunched up her nose in thought. "I think this one." She pointed to the more loose, natural style. "With a more casual, outdoor ceremony, and the reception at the ranch, you don't want to look too formal."

Pamela peered over at the magazine clippings. "You know, I believe she's right," she said, surprise in her voice.

"I am?" Rose said.

Pamela nodded thoughtfully, then pointed one impeccably manicured finger at the picture. "The other one is more appropriate for an evening church wedding. This one looks … more in harmony with nature."

"I'm right?" Rose said again.

"Well, darling, you know what they say about the blind squirrel and the acorn." Pamela sipped some port.

Once Gen had scurried off with her magazine clippings, Pamela turned to Rose and raised one eyebrow. "It must concern you that all of your friends are getting married, and here you are, alone."

Rose faced her mother, one hand in a fist on her hip. "It doesn't concern me, and it's not *all* of my friends. It's *one* of my friends, Mother."

Pamela cocked her head in a gesture of reluctant assent. "Still, it makes one think."

Rose propped her elbows on the bar, leaning in toward her mother. "And what does it make one think?"

"It makes one think that people aren't meant to be alone," Pamela said. "Look at me. It's five years since your father's death, and what's left for me? What do I have?"

"A four-thousand-square-foot house in Connecticut and a Jaguar?" Rose said.

"Be serious."

"I am! You act like Dad left you nothing. You have everything!"

"I don't have companionship," Pamela said. "I don't have someone to spend my life with. And I don't have grandchildren."

Rose rolled her eyes extravagantly. "Ah. Grandchildren. What do you even want with them? I can't exactly see you getting down on the rug and making the Millennium Falcon out of Legos."

"Well, dear, you're a lost cause, and I thought if I had grandchildren, I could bend them to my will."

"Mother!"

"I'm joking, darling." Pamela scowled. "I want someone to carry on the family, of course. And since you show no interest in any of the wealth your father left me, I want someone who can inherit when I'm gone."

A surge of dread swept through Rose's chest. "Mom? Are you … Is anything wrong? You're not sick, are you?"

"I'm fine." Pamela waved a hand dismissively. "But I'm not going to live forever, dear. Meanwhile, it appears that you're not even dating."

Rose thought about telling her mother she was through with men. Because, after all, she *was* through. But if she did that, she'd have to explain why, and that would mean she would have to tell Pamela about Jeremy, and that just seemed like an exhausting prospect.

So instead, she lied. The lie came out so quickly and easily that Rose hadn't even known she was going to say it.

"I am dating someone."

Pamela's eyebrows rose. "You are?"

"I … um … There's a guy I've been seeing for a few weeks now."

Pamela eyed her keenly—it was a look Rose remembered from her childhood, employed whenever Pamela wanted to extract information from her. Seeing it now made Rose wonder if the lie had been a terrible mistake.

"And who's your suitor this time?" Pamela inquired. "Motorcycle gang member? Tattoo artist? Marijuana farmer?"

"He's a graduate student at Stanford!" she blurted out. "He's getting his doctorate in biology!"

Pamela froze for a moment, and it was clear she didn't know what to make of it.

"Does this gentleman have a name?" she asked, rallying.

"His name … is Will Bachman." Since she was going there, she might as well go all the way. "He lives here in Cambria. At Cooper House."

"Hmm," Pamela said. "I'll look forward to meeting him."

Rose felt a pang of guilt, but then she rationalized that she and Will already had an established history of pretending to date one another in order to appease others. This would be no different. She'd done Will a service by pretending to be his date in front of Chris. Now, Will could just return the favor.

She'd expected him to be annoyed when she told him, but he seemed more bemused than anything else.

"So, we've been dating for a few weeks, and it's getting serious. Serious enough that you … well, let me apologize in advance about this, but … you have to meet my mother."

"Huh," Will said. He was at Ryan and Gen's place, helping to finish up the back deck, and she'd come out there to fill him in. She'd just gotten off work, and the early evening sky was beginning to darken. The air, which carried a light breeze, was full of the scent of pine trees and salt water. "Have I gotten to second base yet?"

"Of course you have." Rose waved a hand airily. "We're getting serious enough for you to meet my mother. Do you really think I wouldn't have let you feel me up?"

"Well, that's good to know," he said.

Will had a hammer in his hand and had paused in the act of building stairs leading up to the deck. Ryan was a few feet away, working on the railing.

"Are you guys getting pretend married, too?" Ryan wanted to know. "Because we could just add you in to the ceremony. Make it a double kind of deal."

"No." Rose waved him off. "Or, wait. That could be … No." She shook her head to clear the idea away.

"Well, you did it for me with Chris. And you're going to do it again at the wedding. I guess playing it up for your mom is the least I can do," Will concluded.

"That's what I thought," Rose said. "I have to warn you, though. She's going to examine your every pore with a microscope, and then she's going to judge the crap out of you. It's her hobby. Kind of like knitting, but with the systematic crushing of souls."

"Ah."

"Oh, shit. Now you look scared," Rose put in. "I don't want you to look scared, because then you're going to back out. And you can't back out."

"I, uh … no."

"Make sure he doesn't back out, Ryan," Rose said.

"Well, I guess I've got to keep him in, because there's bound to be entertainment," Ryan said.

"You have no idea," Rose agreed. "Okay, thanks, Will. I'll get in touch. I've got to go before you … I just have to go. Bye." She rushed toward him, pressed a kiss to his cheek, and hurried off to her car, her short leatherette skirt swishing, her sapphire hair tousled in the breeze.

❖

Will watched her go, still feeling the spot on his cheek where her lips had been.

"So, when are you going to tell her that all this fake dating isn't fake on your end?" Ryan wanted to know.

Will shrugged, placed a nail, and hammered it in. "As soon as I win her over."

Ryan grinned. "When do you think that's going to be?"

"Sooner rather than later, I hope." Will set another nail in place, then missed it with the hammer and almost hit his thumb. With the memory of Rose all over him, he was distracted. Hammering was a bad choice when you were distracted. "Might help if I make points with her mother."

"I'm not so sure about that." Ryan put aside what he was doing and leaned against the side of the house, his arms crossed. "I mean, Rose's whole adult life has been about defying her mother, right? If her mother likes you, you might never get to second base." He waggled his eyebrows.

"Well, that's an interesting point." Will put down the hammer and pushed his glasses up on his nose.

"On the other hand," Ryan speculated, "if she's got a hidden, burning need to get her mother's approval, which she's never gotten so far, then I could be wrong."

"Well ... what am I supposed to do, then?"

Ryan went to an ice chest he had sitting on the back deck, opened it, and took out two cold, sweaty bottles of beer. He handed one to Will.

"Well, hell. When all else fails, be yourself."

Will screwed off the top, took a deep drink, and nodded. "Yeah. I can do that."

Chapter Fifteen

Pamela had met most of Rose's friends on her last visit to Cambria a couple of years earlier, so there was no need to introduce her around. Still, it seemed to Rose that there was a kind of insulation in numbers, so she invited everyone for a get-together at Pamela's rental house. That would account for at least one evening when Rose wouldn't be expected to deflect her mother's criticism or respond to an interrogation about the status of her life.

She'd wanted to invite everyone to her own cottage, but Pamela had insisted that the place was too small, too run-down, too dark, too far from town—pretty much too everything, and not enough of everything else. Although Pamela was horrified by her little rental house's size and décor, at least it had an ocean view, and a fairly decent back patio looked over a vacant lot next door that was carpeted in green grass and colorful wildflowers. Pamela admitted, grudgingly, that an afternoon cocktail party outdoors might be acceptable.

Picking a date and time that worked for everyone was tricky, but Rose settled on a Monday at five p.m. Monday was the slowest business day for the shops, so Rose, Kate, and Gen were able to get away. Jackson didn't work on Mondays, and Will, Ryan, and Daniel, who pretty much did their own thing, found the timing was good for them as well.

Pamela had imagined a sedate, dignified gathering with cocktails and canapés, and that's what she had prepared for. So she was both surprised and flustered when Ryan and Gen arrived with cold beer, Kate showed up with chips and salsa, Daniel came in hefting a couple of pizzas, and Jackson rummaged around on the patio, pulled the canvas cover off the gas grill he found there, pronounced it acceptable, and then left in his truck to get some steaks and corn on the cob.

"He's going to *barbecue?*" Pamela hissed to Rose once Jackson had backed out of the driveway. "I planned a cocktail party, not a … a hoedown."

"Relax, Mom," Rose told her. "Jackson's the best chef in Cambria. If he's going to grill steaks, believe me, you're going to want to eat one."

"Well," Pamela replied, skepticism in her voice.

Pamela had prepped for the party not only by purchasing hors d'oeuvres and a selection of high-end liquors and mixers, she'd also systematically removed everything she considered tacky from the little house—except for the Barcalounger, which was too big to hide in a closet. The end result was that the cottage looked stark and plain without the garden gnome greeting visitors and without the various signs that declared BEACH THIS WAY and THIS HOME IS BUILT ON LOVE AND SHENANIGANS. Rose had liked it better the other way, but she thought it best to keep her opinions to herself.

Rose's friends greeted Pamela warmly, and received polite acknowledgments in return. Then they all fell into the easy, comfortable banter of people who had known each other long enough not to have to impress one another, or worry what anybody thought. All except for Will, who hadn't arrived yet.

Rose wondered if maybe he'd backed out, and it occurred to her that she wouldn't blame him if he had. She wished she could get out of it somehow herself, but since she was the cohostess, that seemed unlikely.

"Where's this gentleman of yours?" Pamela asked once everyone else had arrived, Jackson had left for the food, and Lacy was moaning happily while the shiatsu setting of the Barcalounger worked its magic on her.

"That's a good question," Rose said. She was just about to reach for one of the beers Ryan had brought, but she decided she'd better call Will first.

He picked up on the first ring.

"Where the heck are you?" Rose asked without preamble. She ducked into the cottage's single bedroom and closed the door for privacy. "My mother's asking about 'my gentleman,' and I haven't had time to get drunk yet. I can't handle her grilling me about my love life until I've had a chance to get drunk."

"Sorry," he said, sounding flustered. "My car broke down."

"That's a likely story," she said. "If you didn't want to do this, you should have—"

"No, really. I'm stranded on the side of Highway 1." She heard the sound of traffic in the background.

"Oh. Shit. Okay, hang on. I'll come get you." She got the details of his location and went out to get her purse and her keys.

"Wherever are you going, Rosemary?" Pamela wanted to know.

"Will's car broke down. I have to go get him."

"Sit down and relax. I'll do it," Ryan offered.

"No, no." Rose saw her chance to get out of her mother's immediate vicinity, and she wasn't about to let it get past her. "I've got it. You're drinking already." She pointed to his beer, the contents of which hadn't gone down more than half an inch. "I haven't had anything, so it's best if I go."

"Are you sure?" Daniel asked.

She stood on her tiptoes and pressed a kiss to Daniel's cheek. "You're sweet, and very gentlemanly, both of you, but I'll do it. I won't be a minute." Hopefully, there would be a tree down in the middle of the road, and she'd be much, much longer than that. One could dream.

❖

Rose found Will just north of the Cambria limits, parked at a rest stop overlooking the beach. She got out of her car and stood there appraising Will's old Volvo sedan, which would have looked okay had it not been for the black smoke still drifting out from under the hood.

"That's not good," she said.

"That was my expert opinion, too," he admitted. "It started sputtering out on the highway, and I just managed to limp over here. Had to push it the last twenty feet." He ran a hand through his sandy-blond hair and gave the car a stern look as though he could shame it into behaving.

"Huh. What do you want to do? Call a tow truck?"

"Nah. I'll do that tomorrow. For now, it's okay here. Let's just go to the party."

Rose gaped at him. "Really? This is our out. I mean, *your* out."

"I don't want an out. I want to meet your mom."

Her left eyebrow, adorned with a silver barbell, shot up. "What the hell for?"

He grinned at her. "A deal's a deal. One fake date is entitled to another. I've got to pay my end."

"But you don't have to—"

"Let's get going," he said, and went to her car and got in.

"Thanks for coming to get me," he said as they got onto the highway and headed back toward Cambria.

"Think nothing of it. If you hadn't had an emergency, I'd have had to invent one."

"That bad?" He winced in sympathy.

"No. Not really. I mean, yes, but ..." She shrugged. "She acts like everything's beneath her! The rental house, the garden gnome, the damned Barcalounger."

"The ... Wait. I don't—"

"It doesn't matter." She blew a puff of air upward to move the bangs out of her face. "It just gets annoying sometimes."

She'd said it didn't matter, but Will thought that it certainly did. Because Rose's mother's disapproval didn't stop with garden gnomes and Barcaloungers—whatever those particular items had to do with anything. Will suspected that Pamela Watkins disapproved of a great many more things, her daughter among them. He thought of his own parents—steady, reliable, supportive. How much would it hurt if nothing he did was good enough? He felt a rising tide of sympathy for Rose, and something else: an anger, an indignation, that anyone would treat her that way.

"It's her issue, you know," he said after a while, with the blue water passing by on their right as they moved south on Highway 1.

"What?"

"Your mother being critical of you. It's her issue, not yours. Parents—they bring a lot of their own baggage. I don't know what your mother's baggage is, but she's got some. Otherwise, she'd be able to accept you the way you are."

Rose shot him a quick look of surprise, started to stay something, and then stopped. She looked back at the road in front of them.

"I keep hoping, you know?" she said after a while. "Hoping that my relationship with her will somehow magically heal itself. It's stupid. What kind of idiot keeps hoping for something that's never going to happen?"

"It could happen," he said.

She glanced at him. "You think?"

"Yeah. But if it does, it's going to be because she changes, not you. Because she's the one with the baggage."

She let out a bitter laugh. "Yeah, well, I'm not gonna hold my breath for that."

They got off the highway and headed down Ardath Drive toward Marine Terrace. He'd been trying to think of what to say to her, and he finally just settled on the truth.

"Rose?"

"Hm?" She looked at him briefly before settling her gaze back on the road.

"She should be proud. To have a daughter like you, I mean. Your mother should be proud."

They arrived at Pamela's rental house, and Rose found a parking spot on the street and turned off the car. Then she faced him, hesitated, and suddenly leaned forward and kissed him.

She smelled like lavender and vanilla, and she tasted like ripe promise. The sudden release of all of his tensions felt like his body sighing. Everything he knew vanished and became this, this moment, this one kiss. His hands moved up and buried themselves in her hair.

"Rose," he groaned when she separated herself from him.

"This is just ..." she whispered. "Just a thank you. For what you said."

"Is that all it was?" His voice sounded too loud in the confines of the car, in the confines of this moment, and he softened it to a whisper. "Just a thank you? Because, to me, it feels like more."

"No, no." She shook her head as though clearing it. "I'm not ... I'm ..."

"You're done."

"Yes."

"I know. You told me. Except, the thing is? I don't think you're really done. And when *you* realize that you're not really done, I want to be the one you're not done with." He felt nervous, tingly, the rush of the kiss still pulsing through his veins. He hadn't meant to declare himself—not now, not when she wasn't there yet—but he couldn't seem to help himself. And now that it was out there, he was glad. "You're not ready yet, and I get that. And we can just go on and do our pretend dating until you are ready. But you should know that for me, it's real." He leaned forward, gave her a chaste peck on the lips, and got out of the car.

He came around to the driver's side and opened the door for her. She was still sitting in the same position as when he'd kissed her, immobile.

"Rose?" he prompted her. "You coming?"

"I … uh … yeah."

He held out a hand to her and she took it and climbed out of the car.

"All right," he said brightly. "Let's go convince your mother you have a suitable boyfriend."

She simply nodded, the power of coherent speech apparently still eluding her.

Chapter Sixteen

"So, here's the thing," Rose said as she and Kate moved around the tiny kitchen of the rental house, Kate gathering plates and silverware and Rose putting a salad together from ingredients Jackson had brought from the market. "You were right. Will wants to date me—you know, for real."

"You don't say." Kate's delivery was deadpan.

"How did you know about it before I did?" Rose demanded.

Kate shrugged. "I don't know. Maybe because it was ridiculously obvious."

"What? No, it wasn't! I thought we were just … you know. Putting on a show for the various judgy people in our lives. I never thought—"

"You didn't? Even when he was kissing your face off?" Kate smirked at her, a load of plates and napkins in her arms.

"That was all part of the act!" Rose insisted.

"Hmm. How many of those kisses have there been?"

"Three," Rose said. "Well, now four, including the one just now in the car."

"And how many of them actually happened in front of other people?" Kate still had that damned smirk.

"Well … just one."

Kate raised her eyebrows. "You need a little work on the whole 'putting on an act' deal. When you're doing something to fool other people, it helps if you do the thing where those other people can see it."

She walked out of the kitchen to take the plates to the patio.

Rose scowled and went to work cutting tomatoes for the salad.

Kate was wrong. She was just wrong. One of the kisses had been for show, and one or two had been just … friendly. And if a few friendly kisses had led Will on, well, she'd just have to deal with it.

Later. Maybe after a few more friendly kisses, possibly after some friendly sex.

But that would *really* lead him on, and Will was a good guy. If he actually was beginning to have feelings for her—which, according to him, he was—then it would be wrong to get him into bed purely for her own pleasure, knowing that it wasn't going anywhere.

Wouldn't it?

She was still pondering the cost vs. benefit analysis of having friendly sex with Will when Lacy came into the kitchen to get a serving platter for Jackson's steaks.

"Kate says Will wants you," Lacy said in an offhand way. "To which I said, 'Duh.'"

"I'm thinking about friendly sex. With Will." Rose put it out there as she began slicing radishes. "But, you know. Just friendly. Because I'm finished with relationships."

Lacy paused halfway to the door with the platter in her hands. "What, like, 'You're helping me out by putting on a show for my mom, so to say thank you, I'm going to let you put your penis into my vagina'?"

Rose raised her eyebrows in an expression that said she was considering just that. "Would that be so wrong?"

"Yeah, it would." Lacy gave her a hard stare. "Because he likes you. He really likes you. And he's a sweet guy."

"And I'd be messing with his feelings."

"Yes."

Rose put down the knife and propped one fist on her hip. "Well, jeez. Men do that all the time. Why is it okay for men to do that, but not for women?"

"It's *not* okay when men do it," Lacy pointed out. "And it's not just men and women we're talking about, it's you, and it's a real man who we all like."

"Yeah," Rose conceded, her shoulders sagging.

Lacy left, and Rose was alone in the kitchen with her vegetables. She went back to work on the radishes. Lacy was right, and Rose wasn't happy about it. It would be wrong to mess with a nice guy who had real feelings. But, God. Had she ever been kissed the way he kissed her?

And that was a large part of the problem, the reason any sex between them couldn't be anything more than friendly. If she let herself feel things for him—really feel things—then she'd lose herself in the magic of those kisses. And if that happened, she might never be heard from again.

At first, Pamela refused to eat Jackson's steak. A woman of good breeding, she refused in the politest way she could manage, saying that the food looked lovely, but that she tried to avoid red meat. Rose knew from years of experience that what Pamela actually tried to avoid was anything one might produce on an outdoor grill while wearing a "Kiss the Cook" apron. Rose knew Pamela was still quietly brooding over the fact that her elegant little cocktail party had been taken over and turned into a Kiwanis Club cookout.

Pamela, sticking steadfastly to her original plan, was holding a tiny plate of crab puffs and onion tartlets, a glass of white wine on the table beside her, as Jackson eyed her from where he stood by the grill.

"Uh oh," Kate told Rose. "I know that look. He's upset because she won't try his food."

"Well, she's a fool if she won't," Rose replied. "I guarantee he's as good as any of those snooty chefs she gets for her dinner parties in Connecticut."

"Right. And he knows that. But *she* doesn't know that. And it's bugging the hell out of him."

"You really can see that Jackson Graham temper bubbling up under the surface," Rose observed. "I think I detect a little wisp of smoke coming out of one ear."

Kate sighed. "That's just what we need. For Jackson to throw a tempter tantrum in front of your mother."

Rose perked up. "Oh, I don't know. I think it would really liven things up."

Kate looked worried, so Rose decided it was time to take action. "I'll handle it," she said. She went over to Jackson and whispered in his ear. Still scowling, Jackson put a steak on a plate, drizzled sauce over it from a small bowl on the work table of the barbecue, and then garnished it with a sprig of something green. Rose grabbed a fork, a steak knife, and a napkin from the patio table and brought the food to her mother.

As Kate watched, Rose whispered something to Pamela, who grudgingly set aside her plate of hors d'oeuvres and cut a tiny bite of the steak. Pamela gingerly placed the bite into her mouth, and then her eyes widened in surprise and wonder. With no further hesitation, Pamela dug into the steak with gusto.

"There," Rose said with satisfaction as she walked back to where Kate was standing.

"What did you say to her?" Kate wanted to know.

"I told her Jackson used to cook for the Obamas."

"What?" Kate laughed. "He never cooked for the Obamas."

"I know that. But my mother doesn't."

"Genius," Kate said.

A few minutes later, Pamela crossed the patio to Jackson, said something to him, put a hand on his shoulder, then threw her head back and laughed.

"Wow," Kate said. "That Obama line really worked. She's actually fawning."

Rose shrugged. "Piece of cake. You just have to know which lever to pull."

"If you're this good at manipulating her, then why don't the two of you get along better?" Kate wondered.

"Manipulating her into liking Jackson is one thing. But I'm her daughter. I shouldn't have to manipulate her into liking me." Rose felt heat behind her eyes—tears threatening to come—and she blinked a few times to push it away. "Anyway," she said brightly. "I need some of that steak. I'm starving."

Once Will felt the full force of Pamela Watkins's scrutiny, he couldn't help understanding Rose's attitude toward her. What would it have been like to feel that tacit disapproval as a teenager, when Rose was still unformed and insecure?

"William Bachman," Pamela said thoughtfully, her eyes cast upward in thought. "Would I have heard of your family?"

Will and Pamela were inside the cottage, on the Naugahyde sofa that sat adjacent to the Barcalounger. Will had a beer in front of him, but he hadn't drank much of it, because he wanted to be sharp for the inevitable interrogation. Pamela was nursing a glass of white wine.

"I don't think so, ma'am. Unless you lived in Duluth at some point and needed a plumber." He smiled affably, as though he didn't know that coming from a blue collar family would brand him as unacceptable for Pamela's little girl. "My father has owned his own plumbing and heating shop for twenty years. My mother's an English teacher."

"I see." Pamela looked as though she were smelling spoiled meat. "And you're a graduate student at Stanford. Coming from that kind of background, that's impressive."

Will didn't like the way she said *that kind of background,* as though his parents had been crackheads or welfare scammers instead of hard-working, honest people who gave the best of themselves to their kids.

"The background they gave me was one of appreciating hard work," he said mildly. "I imagine that's what got me into Stanford."

"Of course." Pamela smiled tightly, apparently stung by the mild rebuke.

"Is everything okay in here?" Rose peeked her head in the patio door, looking nervous. "Are you two doing all right? Anything I can get you?"

"We're perfectly capable of having a conversation without your supervision," Pamela said, and Will could see how it was with them: Rose tentative and unsure, Pamela harsh and critical.

"We're fine, but it was nice of you to check on us," Will told Rose. "Don't you think so, Pamela?"

"I would have said 'nosy,'" Pamela told him, turning away from Rose, who backed meekly out the door and closed it behind her.

He knew he was supposed to placate her. He knew he was supposed to make a good impression so Pamela would be satisfied and would get off Rose's back. He knew the role he'd been assigned to play, but he just couldn't play it. He stood up, took a fortifying sip from his beer, and looked down at Pamela as she sat primly perched on the edge of the sofa cushion, as though the cheap fabric might at any moment bite her in the rear.

"I think we're finished," he said.

Pamela pursed her lips. "Excuse me?"

He started to say something—the word *shrew* came to mind—then stopped, gathered himself, and started again. "Mrs. Watkins, you seem to think I need your approval in order to be with Rose. I don't. I need Rose's approval, and I think I've got that. Now, you can judge my 'background,' my parents, and whatever else you'd like. But I'm dating Rose. I just am, and that's how it is. I'm a good guy. I'm nice to people. I like my family, and I like my friends, and I drive an old car that broke down on the way here." He shrugged. "And I think it's fine if you don't like me. I really do. Because you don't seem to like Rose much, either, and she's one of the best people I know. So I figure that puts me in pretty good company. Excuse me, ma'am. I'm going to go back to the party."

He walked away and left her there on the sofa, her mouth open in surprise.

Chapter Seventeen

When Will came back out onto the patio, everyone was sitting around with the last of the beer and wine, and the sun was setting over the calm ocean. The breeze was light, and the weather was still warm, though it was cooling down enough that they'd soon be driven inside.

Kate and Jackson had decided to take a walk on the bluffs at Fiscalini Ranch, Lacy and Daniel were starting to clean up, and Ryan and Gen were snuggling in a chaise longue, whispering to one another and occasionally laughing in low, intimate voices that made Rose burn with jealousy.

As much as she was happy for Gen and Ryan, she couldn't help but brood over the fact that she didn't have what they did—and never would, if her man moratorium held out.

When Will came outside into the twilight and sat on a patio chair beside her, Rose wondered whether the man strike had actually been a pretty bad idea. She felt herself being pulled toward him, not just her body, but her soul—and that created a feeling of fear and dread inside her that she didn't know how to handle.

"So, what happened in there?" she asked him. The sky was streaked in pinks and oranges, and the crash of the waves murmured in her ears.

"I told your mother that you and I are going to be together, if you want me, and that she wasn't going to have a say in it. I told her … Well. I said that if she doesn't approve of me, I don't care. But if she doesn't approve of you, then she's a fool." His jaw was set in an expression of determination and what might have been anger.

"You said that?"

"Well, not in so many words. But that was the gist."

"Oh, Will."

"Look," he said. "I know I was supposed to be nice to her, make a good impression. And I know I was supposed to put on this act, but—"

She wrapped her arms around him and kissed him. It was their fifth kiss, and they were getting good at it. She melted into him, into his taste and his scent—salt air and sandalwood soap—and she heard a moan and realized it was coming from the depths of her own throat.

She pulled back slightly, still so close she could feel his breath on her, and murmured so that only he could hear, "I think we should just have sex."

He jumped slightly in surprise. "What?"

"Will … Kate says it's wrong for us to have friendly sex, because you have feelings for me, and I get that. I do. Because I don't *want* to have feelings, and if we have sex, and you feel things and I don't, then …"

"Rose."

"But I think we can have friendly sex, and you can feel whatever you feel, and I can feel … well … like I'm having fun, and we can work out all of the rest of it later." She touched his face, ran a thumb along the line of his lower lip. "Okay? Will?"

"Ah … no."

He pushed her away slightly, and she felt the hard sting of rejection. But why was he rejecting her? What man didn't want to have friendly, no-strings-attached sex?

"What?" She wanted to be sure she'd heard him correctly.

"Rose, I just … Thank you, but no."

"But why?" She could hear the petulant child in her voice, and she didn't like it, but she couldn't seem to help it.

He looked at Gen and Ryan, who were on the other side of the porch, within earshot if he were to raise his voice. "I think I'd better go," he said.

"You don't have a car."

"Ah. Good point."

"I'll drive you home," she said.

"That's … No, thanks. I'll catch a ride with Ryan and Gen."

Not only didn't he want to have sex with her, now he didn't even want to be in a car with her? Indignation and hurt swelled up in her like the rising tide.

"Will, what the hell's wrong with you?"

His lips tight in an expression of frustration, he took her hand and led her around to the front of the house, where they wouldn't be heard.

"Do you think that was a good offer? Friendly sex? Really?" The hurt in his voice took her by surprise and made her step back as the sky darkened around them.

"Well … yes. I thought it was a damned good offer."

He turned away from her, kicked at a pebble in the driveway, and turned back to face her. "So that's all I think you're good for? A one-night stand? Is that it?"

"Wait. I never—"

"Rose." He drew closer to her and spoke in a voice that was low and intense. "When you and I have sex—and I hope we will—you're going to feel something other than that you're having fun. You're going to feel something for me, you're going to want *me*, not just some casual fling. Now, I'm not opposed to casual sex. Some people like that kind of thing. I've liked it on occasion, myself. But not with you. With you, it's going to matter."

Then he walked back around the house to the patio, leaving Rose standing alone, stunned, in the driveway. She heard his voice, now falsely perky, saying, "Hey, Ry? You guys think I can get a ride home with you?"

"He turned down sex? That's interesting."

Rose was getting her morning coffee at Jitters the next day, and Lacy pondered the situation while steaming milk for Rose's latte. "Guys don't usually do that."

"They don't," Rose agreed. "He went on about feelings. He sounded more like a girl than I did."

"Well, God. That's kind of refreshing, don't you think? A guy who wants the sex to mean something?"

"Sure, it's refreshing. But shocking, right? I mean, I didn't even know such a subspecies existed."

Lacy slid the latte across the counter to Rose. Then she moved to the register, where she rang up some cappuccinos and scones for a couple of tourists. That done, she came back to the coffee machines and started working on the couple's drinks, while Rose stood across the counter from her.

"So what are you going to do about it?" Lacy wanted to know.

"Do? What can I do?" Rose threw her hands up in despair. "I'm going to eat too much chocolate, drink too much wine, and watch too much Netflix. What do any of us do when we're not having sex?"

Lacy pulled a shot of espresso and gave Rose a side-eye. "Or you could admit that you really do care about the guy and give a real relationship a chance."

Rose's expression hardened. "I don't know what you're talking about."

"Of course you don't."

At that moment, Daniel came in the front door of the coffee house, throwing a friendly wave to both of them.

"Low-fat mocha?" Lacy asked him.

Daniel pointed a finger-gun at her. "You got it."

Lacy finished the tourists' cappuccinos, delivered them to their table with the scones, and then started on Daniel's mocha.

"Hey, Daniel," Lacy said as she worked. "How obvious would you say it is, on a scale of one to ten, that Rose has a thing for Will?"

"What, with one being not obvious, and ten being obvious as hell?"

"Right."

He rubbed at the stubble on his chin. "Well, last night when I was helping to clean up after the party, I walked outside and saw her practically in his lap, with their lips glued together. So, I'd call it a solid ten."

Lacy gave Rose a pointed look.

Rose waved her hands around. "That was just—"

"I know," Lacy said. "Friendly. Or, you were saying thank you. Or pass the chips, or some damn thing."

It had come to this: Her friends were mocking her transparent attempts to have a relationship while pretending that she was not having a relationship.

"Well … God," she said.

Daniel leaned his forearms on the counter next to Rose. "For what it's worth, Will's a good guy. If you've got a thing for him, I think you should just go with it. He's not some asshole. He's … decent."

Rose focused on her latte so she wouldn't have to answer him. "Could we just change the subject?" she asked finally.

"Sure," Lacy said. She passed Daniel his mocha, then asked Rose, "How are things going with your mother?"

"Ugh." Rose rolled her eyes extravagantly. "She hates the rental house. She belittled Will. And now, with weeks to go before the wedding, she's already starting in on me about the hair and the piercings. Apparently, if I don't go all WASP Barbie for the ceremony, I'll ruin all of Gen and Ryan's hopes for happiness. Thank God I have work today."

"Huh." Daniel sipped his mocha and made appreciative sounds. "I saw her being friendly with Jackson, so there's that."

"Yeah," Rose agreed. "She tried to hate him, but once she tasted his steak she couldn't keep it up anymore."

"That happens a lot with Jackson." Daniel tapped his knuckles on the counter. "Well, ladies, I've got to go. I've been commissioned to make a ceiling fixture for a casino in Vegas. Like the one at the Bellagio, only a lot cheaper."

"You're the cut-rate Chihuly now?" Lacy wanted to know.

"Hey, I'll take it," Daniel said cheerfully. "It pays the mortgage."

He grabbed his coffee cup, gave them a friendly wave, and headed out the door. Lacy leaned precariously over the counter to watch him go.

"Hey. Are you checking out Daniel's ass?" Rose's voice held a hard edge of accusation.

"So what if I am? It's a nice one."

"I suppose. Is there something going on there I should know about?"

"No." Lacy eased herself back to the floor behind the counter. "I've just been celibate for so long that a nice ass makes me dizzy."

"Huh. Maybe there should be something going on there," Rose offered.

"Look who's talking." Lacy looked at her pointedly. "Miss *I'm done with men, but I can't keep my hands off Will.* You need to get your own love life under control before you worry about mine."

Lacy had a point. What was the worst that could happen if Rose were to give up the pretense and start seeing Will for real? How bad could it be?

Rose thought that if she were really going to give up her man moratorium, it would have made more sense to start with some eye candy she didn't give a crap about. Too late for that. Will had gotten under her skin, like a mosquito, or a heat rash. She figured that any way she looked at it, she was pretty much screwed.

Will busied himself fixing the pool filter at Cooper House, because it was easier than working on his dissertation, and it was certainly easier than thinking about Rose. The filter had been wonky for a while now, and he probably should have just brought in a pool guy to take care of it. But Will figured he ought to do something to earn his salary around here, and anyway, the work gave him something to occupy his mind so he wouldn't think about his woman problems.

That was the idea, anyway. The trouble was, filter or no filter, he was still thinking about his woman problems.

There was a small problem, and then there was a big problem.

The small problem—which would have been the big problem under other circumstances—was Melinda. After the kiss in the wine cellar, he'd thought the issue was done with. He'd made it clear he wasn't going there, and that should have been the end of it. But she had texted him several times since then, each message more suggestive and then hostile than the last.

She'd started off simply enough, with a text that said, *I'm thinking about you.* Will had black-holed it, deleting the text and deciding to pretend it had never happened. Just like the kiss. The next text, about a day later, had said, *We both know you want me back. You're just scared.* Part of that was true, anyway: the part about him being scared. He was scared of losing his job and his place of residence if Chris got wind of what Will's crazy ex was trying to do. The part about wanting her back? Not a snowball's chance inside an active volcano.

He'd stuck with the strategy of ignoring her, but that had just seemed to make her mad. The texts after that took on an angry tone.

You're pathetic.

I wonder what other body parts she has pierced.

And finally, alarmingly:

Fuck you fuck you FUCK YOU!!! >:(

He thought the emoticon was a nice touch. Very mature.

He was increasingly puzzled by the why of it. Melinda was with Chris now. He seemed to be everything she wanted. So why the anger toward Will? And why now?

Will thought about it as he worked on the pool filter under a sky that was clear and bright. He'd disassembled the filter, cleaned it, and reassembled it, and there was still water leaking out of the backwash line. His shorts were dotted with pool water, and he smelled like chlorine.

If he'd had a pet rabbit, he reflected, he might worry about coming home one day to find Melinda boiling it in a pot on his stove. But since he didn't have a rabbit—or any pet, for that matter—he stopped worrying about that and started thinking about Rose.

The big problem.

Rose wanting to sleep with him would not have been a problem of any size—it would have been cause for jubilation—if it weren't for the fact that he had fallen for her. He was willing to settle for second best in many areas of his life. His career path wasn't going the way he wanted, and he hadn't expected to still be a student at twenty-nine. So there was that. But he wasn't going to settle when it came to Rose. Either she'd sleep with him because she was falling for him, too, or it wasn't going to happen at all.

He really hated to think that it might not happen at all.

She'd started as a small thing in his life—a small but pleasant thing—but the place she held in his world was gradually getting bigger and bigger until he worried that she would eclipse everything else.

And that would be okay, would be great, even, if she decided she felt about him the way he felt about her. But if she didn't—if she kept on with her insistence that she was finished with men—then the enormous space she took up in his mind and in his heart was going to be filled with pain and unbearable longing, and he didn't know how we was going to get by day to day like that.

He'd just have to work the problem.

He knew a little about why Rose was so down on the idea of a relationship. She'd had a breakup, and it had hurt her. He didn't know much more than that. Maybe if he knew—if he understood the root of the hurt—then he would know how to make her trust him.

In any case, it was better to have information than not to have it.

He disliked the idea of sneaking around behind her back to ask her friends about her, but he thought it was going to come to that. Rose wouldn't tell him herself.

With pieces of the faulty pool filter in his hands, he decided he'd have to do it. He'd have to ask Kate, or maybe Lacy. Or, if they wouldn't talk to him, maybe Kate had told Jackson, and he could go that route.

Little by little, he began putting the filter back together, hoping that if he just applied himself to the issue, he could fix whatever was wrong.

Chapter Eighteen

"Ah, jeez, Will. I don't know."

Will had come into Swept Away, Kate's bookstore on Main Street, during a morning lull. The shop was empty except for Kate and Jane Austen, the Swept Away cat. Jane Austen was curled up on the counter next to the cash register, and Kate was stocking shelves with new books she was unloading from a cardboard carton.

"Look. I know it's a lot to ask. Whatever she told you, she told you in confidence. I get that. But … I just want to understand. She's got this whole 'no men' thing going on, and I know it has nothing to do with me. But it also has *everything* to do with me, because I'm … Okay. I might as well say it. I'm in love with her, and I can't get out of the friend zone."

Kate paused from her work, both hands full of books. "You're in love with her?"

He ran a hand through his hair. "I think I am. No, forget that. Who am I kidding? I know I am."

She put the books in their place on the shelf, then turned to him, hands on her hips, her eyes appraising him. She was looking at him the way his mother used to when he'd done something wrong and she was deciding whether to ground him.

Kate sighed. "You can't tell her I told you this. Or, wait. Yes, you can. I don't want to keep secrets from my friends."

"Okay."

Kate went to the front counter, scooped Jane Austen into her arms, and then sat in one of the leather chairs she provided for customers who wanted to sit and read. Will sat in the chair across from her as Jane Austen settled into Kate's lap.

"Rose was dating this guy named Jeremy," Kate began.

"Do I know him?"

"I don't think so," Kate said. "He's a professor at the university in San Luis Obispo. They were together for a few months."

Will waited. Kate's hesitation before she continued made him think the story was going to be a bad one.

"At first, it was good," Kate said. "Or, it seemed like it was. Rose seemed happy, and Jeremy seemed … Well. I won't say I took an immediate liking to him, but I didn't see any red flags, either."

"But then?" Will prompted her.

Kate sighed again. "But then, she started to change."

"Change, how?"

"Her clothes, first. She started dressing more conservatively. Her skirts got longer, her tops started showing less cleavage. She started wearing things that were … less quirky. Less Rose."

He could see where this was going, and it made him feel a little sick.

"Then, the piercings. She took the one out of her eyebrow first. Then the nose ring went. Then the ones from her ears. Finally, they were all gone except for a single stud in each ear."

"Which he gave her," Will guessed.

"You're catching on fast," Kate said. "Then it was the hair. Of course. He wanted her to dye it this medium brown, which she says is her natural color. Even though she didn't do it, by the time he broke up with her, all of these pieces of her had been chipped away until I don't think she felt like she had much left."

"But why?" Will wanted to know. "Why did she do all of that? Why didn't she say no? Was it … Did she love him that much?"

Kate considered that, then shook her head. "No. She thought she loved him, but I don't think she really did."

"Then what?"

Kate paused for a moment and scratched between Jane Austen's ears. The cat purred in response. Finally, she said, "The thing about Rose is, she's got this tough exterior. This *I don't give a damn what you think of me* persona. But under all that, she just wants to be accepted, like we all do."

"And acceptance is something her mother has never given her," Will added.

"Right."

They sat there quietly for a moment while Will thought about what Kate was saying.

"Aposematism," he said finally.

"Excuse me?"

"It's … animals sometimes use conspicuous coloring as a defense mechanism. Like the red milk snake. Its markings mimic the coral snake, which is highly venomous. The red milk snake is harmless, but its bright coloring warns predators away." Will straightened his glasses.

Kate pointed a finger at Will. "Now you're catching on, professor."

Professor.

"Oh, God," Will said.

"What?"

"You said her previous boyfriend was a professor. I'm not one yet, but that's where I'm headed."

Kate paused in midscratch. "Oh. Shit. I hadn't even thought of that."

"She's flashing her bright coloring at me, hoping I'll get scared and go away instead of eating her," Will concluded.

"So, what are you going to do?" Kate asked.

"I've got to find some way to convince her I'm not a predator," he said.

He just wished he knew how to do that.

The day after the barbecue at Pamela's rental house, Pamela called Rose to complain about the fact that her tasteful menu had been taken over by the common food one might find at a suburban birthday party. She complained about the impertinent way Will had spoken to her. She also complained about the amount of time Rose had spent elsewhere, first retrieving Will from the side of Highway 1, and then huddling with him outside on the patio, whispering like teenagers keeping secrets. She complained that Rose had seemed out of sorts after Will had left, a fact that Pamela had taken as a personal affront. And finally, she complained that with Rose having returned to work, Pamela was left alone and at loose ends, with nothing to do in the small beach town.

"Is there anything you're not unhappy about?" Rose demanded over the phone at De-Vine after Pamela listed her grievances.

"Well," Pamela allowed, "Jackson's steak was heavenly."

Rose didn't know if she should be pleased that Pamela had found something to be happy about, or angry because it had been someone else, rather than Rose, who had managed to accomplish that.

"Of course, you're coming over when you finish work," Pamela had concluded when she'd run out of criticism.

"I am?"

"Rosemary," Pamela said in a voice weary with impatience. "I didn't come all the way across the country to sit in a shack by myself."

"Why did you come?" Rose asked.

"Rosemary."

"No, Mom, I mean it. You don't seem to enjoy spending time with me, so, really, why did you come here?"

Pamela ignored the question. "What time should I expect you?"

"I … I can't come over. I have a date with Will," Rose said.

"Do you." She said it as a statement rather than a question.

"Yes." *As soon as I tell him about it,* she thought.

"I'm not certain about this young man," Pamela said.

"Color me surprised."

"Rosemary."

"I'm sorry, Mom," Rose said. "He's … taking me for a walk at Moonstone Beach and then for dinner at Linn's. We have reservations. I can't just back out."

"You're taking me for a walk at Moonstone Beach and then for dinner at Linn's," Rose told Will as soon as she could get him on the phone. "But it's my treat. I know you're probably broke, with the car repairs and whatnot."

Will was actually at that moment waiting for a call from his mechanic with a diagnosis and a quote for repairs. When his phone rang, that's who he'd been expecting. He'd had the car towed to the shop and had been borrowing one of the vehicles Chris kept at Cooper House until he could get his fixed.

"Well, I suppose that'll work for me." He wondered to what he owed this sudden windfall of time with Rose. "But what brought this on?"

"I told my mother I had a date with you. Now … you know. I have to go on a date with you. Otherwise, I lied to her. And people shouldn't lie to their mothers."

The corner of his mouth quirked up in a half smile. "I suppose they shouldn't. But why specifically Moonstone Beach and then Linn's?"

"Because that's what I told my mother. I had to tell her something."

❖

Will picked Rose up at De-Vine when she got off work at six thirty. He'd had to leave his car at the shop overnight, so he was driving the Ford F-150 Chris kept at Cooper House. The truck got used when Will needed to haul something or other in his capacity as caretaker, or when Chris was in town, or when one of Chris's friends was using the house and needed a way to get around. Now, Will was grateful that it was available. It would have hurt his manhood if he'd had to ask Rose to drive.

Because she'd told her mother that they'd be walking on Moonstone Beach, that was the first thing they did. Seemed like as good a place to start a date as any.

The sun was still high in the western sky when they got there, and a good number of tourists were walking on the sand with their pant legs rolled up and their shoes in their hands, or were sitting on the benches that lined the boardwalk.

The temperature in Cambria usually averaged around the midsixties in May, but it had been warmer than that, and so it was mild and comfortable as they climbed down a set of stairs off Moonstone Beach Drive and descended to the sand.

You couldn't walk very far on Moonstone Beach before you hit the bluffs or the rocks with their tide pools full of tiny crabs and sea anemones, so they walked on the sand a little bit and then climbed the stairs back up onto the boardwalk, then walked up there amid the tourists, the early evening joggers, and the squirrels that scurried along the path in front of them.

Somewhere along the way, Will reached out and took Rose's hand. He wasn't sure she would let him. They'd kissed several times, sure, but that could be explained away as impulse. If she allowed him to hold her hand, here on the beach as the sun lowered toward the water, then that would be a deliberate decision, an acknowledgment that he intended to be close to her, and she intended to let him, if only a little.

When he reached out and placed his palm in hers, then wrapped his fingers around hers, he felt her hesitate, and he waited to see which way it would go. Then she glanced at him, grinned slightly, and tightened her grip on his hand.

It felt good, holding her hand. It felt right. It felt as though his hand had found its right place in the universe, among all of the possible places it could be. It had found its home.

They continued along the boardwalk and over the bridge, and came to a stop at Leffingwell Landing, the park that stood at the northern edge of Moonstone Beach. At a picnic bench, they stopped and sat, looking out at the water and the crashing waves.

"I'm glad we're having a date," Will said. "Even if we're only doing it to get you away from your mother."

"Well," she said, "she's going to be here a month. So, we might have to move in together."

"I wouldn't mind that." He grinned. "Even though, you know. It would be fake living together."

She looked at the beach spread out before them, and her eyebrows furrowed. "I'm sorry about how she acted when we had everyone over. The way she treated you. She ... I don't know. She's not a bad person. She's just used to living a certain way, you know? I thought ..."

"You thought what?"

"Well. My father died about five years ago. I thought that without him there—without the need for her to be the perfect wife for him—she might relax a little. Stop being so status-conscious. But it didn't work out that way." A light breeze blew off of the water and tousled her hair.

"It could still. Five years isn't much when it comes to grief. Looking at it from the outside, you think, a year. That's what it's going to take for someone to get over the loss and move on. But a year is nothing. It's ... a blip."

She turned to him, concern in her eyes. "You say that like you know firsthand. Who did you lose?"

He shrugged, trying to make it seem less than it was. "My brother."

"Oh, God, Will. I'm so sorry."

"Yeah, well."

"What happened?"

He hadn't intended to talk about this, hadn't thought he would. But here it was, and part of making her trust him was in letting her know him. He sighed. "Motorcycle accident. God. My mother did not want him to buy that thing. But, he was twenty. An adult. What could she do?"

"How old were you?"

"Sixteen."

"Shit. I can't imagine." She squeezed his hand just a little tighter.

"Yeah. I thought it was going to break my parents. I thought ... I thought they were just going to shatter into little pieces and fly off with the wind. But people are strong. They find a way to survive."

Rose looked out at the birds circling the water. Eventually, in her own time, she said, "My dad was controlling. Not necessarily in a bad way, not in an abusive or intentionally harmful way. But ... he set the tone for our family, you know? He decided how things were going to be in our house. I always wondered if that kind of life was what my mother really wanted, or if she was just trying to please him. When he died … " She glanced at Will. "Heart attack. With him gone, I wondered if she'd change. If she'd find whatever it was that she really wanted, independent of him."

"What do you think she'd want?" He gazed at a couple kissing down on the sand. "If it were just up to her?"

Rose shrugged. "I don't know. I don't think she does, either."

"Do you know what you want?" he asked.

Surprised, she turned to him. "What do you mean?"

"I don't know." He gave her a look that was part question, part affection. "Seems to me like a lot of what you've done with your life has been a reaction to something. To your mother, to your father, to the life they had laid out for you and that you knew you didn't want. And that's ... well, I think that's healthy. You knew where you didn't want to go, and you got away from that. But, you're away. And here you are, free and able to live whatever kind of life you want. I'm just wondering if you know what that is."

She started to answer, then paused. "I thought I did."

"And now?"

She gazed out at the water and shrugged. "I don't know. Things are changing. What I want is changing."

"Change is good," he said, and squeezed her hand.

Chapter Nineteen

According to the agenda Rose had given her mother, they were supposed to eat dinner at Linn's. They did eat at Linn's, but it wasn't dinner. Because they were adults who didn't have to follow the rules, they opted to skip the main meal and eat olallieberry pie with ice cream instead.

"God, this is good." Rose dug into the warm pie with its mound of vanilla ice cream as they sat at a table amid the chatter of other diners. The restaurant usually wasn't full on a weeknight in May, so the noise and bustle of the place were down to a moderate level.

"Since daughters shouldn't lie to their mothers," Will said, grinning, "you'll have to fess up to the fact that you skipped dinner and had dessert instead."

"Well," Rose said, holding a spoonful of pie and ice cream, "there's lying, and then there's simply leaving out details."

"Speaking of details, how are plans for the wedding coming along?"

She threw up her hands for emphasis. Fortunately, her spoon was empty by then. Otherwise, pie might have flown in his direction. "Oh, ugh. Jeez. There are so many details. *So many* details! The florist doesn't have blush peonies, and wants to know if we can use Peruvian lilies instead. We can't get everybody's schedules coordinated for the final dress fittings. The lodge can't fit as many seats as we need in the gazebo area of the garden, and they're saying that we either need to cut the guest list or move the ceremony. We could cut the guest list—a number of people who were invited have sent regrets, and so that works out—but a lot of the people who *are* coming have been calling to ask if they can bring Cousin Bob or Aunt Sylvia. Gah. Remind me never to get married."

"Well," Will said, "we can always elope."

She nearly choked on her pie.

"What?"

"When you're ready to marry me. We can elope. Vegas is good, I've always wanted one of those Elvis ceremonies. Then afterward we can go to one of those buffets, eat ourselves into a food coma."

"Will Bachman," Rose demanded. "What the hell are you talking about?"

"You're not there yet," he said calmly. "That's fine; there's no rush."

He realized that saying such a thing this early in the game was a risk. She'd announced—many times—her decision to quit dating and eschew all things related to men. But her kisses said something different, and there was a reason she kept telling her mother that they were together. It was possible that putting it out there—letting it be known that he wanted to be with her long-term—would backfire on him and would send her scurrying under the brush like a baby rabbit hiding from a mountain lion. But it was also possible that if she knew his feelings, if she understood that he was in this, it might ease her fears and encourage her to peek her head out of her burrow and bring her furry tail into the light.

"Will, I …" She plunked her spoon down onto her plate and rubbed her eyes with both hands. "I don't think …"

He reached out and took one of her hands in his. "You're not there yet," he repeated, this time softly, intimately. "That's okay. You'll catch up, and I'll be here when you do."

She was quiet after that, and that was probably a bad sign.

She didn't pull away from him—not entirely—but she was more reserved, and as they left the restaurant, he fully expected her to tell him that she couldn't see him anymore.

So he was more than a little surprised when, the moment they were settled into the Cooper House truck, she turned to him, put a hand behind his neck, pulled him to her, and kissed him deeply, with a passion he had not expected.

His mind went blank.

The kiss had the effect of emptying out his brain, as though a drain plug had been pulled and every thought in his head had gone swirling into some dark oblivion. Without the burden of having to put coherent ideas together, he was free to just feel. His pulse started hammering in his veins, and all he could do was react—he couldn't wait anymore. This kiss could not be just a kiss, just as Rose was not just a woman.

"Come home with me," he said. "Please."

She was too busy kissing him, too busy devouring him, to answer at first. He prompted her.

"Rose. Please."

She nodded, her lips still on his, her fingers wrapped up in his hair.

"Drive," she said finally, when she drew away from him. "God. Just ... just drive."

He didn't want to crash the truck—he'd had enough automotive drama to last him a while—so he took a deep breath and tried to pull himself together before he backed out of the parking space outside Linn's and pulled out onto Main Street.

He glanced at her as he drove down Burton and got onto Highway 1. "Are you sure?"

"Don't ask me that." Her eyes were closed as she shook her head. "Just don't. Because if I think about it, I might change my mind. And I don't want to change my mind."

"If you're not sure ..."

"Will, shut up," she said.

And he did.

They arrived at the long drive leading up to Cooper House about ten minutes later. Will's hands weren't steady, so it took him two tries to punch in the right security code at the gate.

Fortunately, Will's cottage wasn't far, so he hit the accelerator and shot the truck up the winding road to the guest house door.

He slammed the truck in park, turned off the ignition, and flew out the door and around the front of the truck. He opened the passenger door for her, grabbed her hand, and pulled her out of the truck. Then he was on her, and she was on him, and he had her pressed against the side of the truck, his mouth on hers, his hands on her body.

He already had a hand sliding up the inside of her skirt when she said, "Inside. Let's ... inside."

He'd have scooped her up into his arms and carried her, but she was already running up the front porch and to the door. He chased her up there and fumbled with his keys.

"Wait a minute. Let me just ..." He dropped the keys and they jangled onto the wood floor of the porch.

It didn't help his concentration that when he bent down to pick up the keys, she ran a hand over his butt.

He snatched up the keys, fumbled around trying to find the right one, then finally got the key into the door, opened it—and then left the keys dangling from the lock as she pushed him inside, slammed the door behind them, and then launched herself at him.

She felt so many things, none of them rational and none of them manageable. Lust, passion, urgency—and fear, yes, of course there was fear. She wanted him so much, and that meant that if a day came when he decided he didn't want her—and such a day always came, in so many of her relationships—she was going to be crushed, destroyed, burned into a pile of ash that would float away on the ocean wind.

But right now, the lust and the passion and the urgency overwhelmed the fear, and she let them win. She pressed her body against him, kissing, touching, moving her fingers down the buttons of his shirt.

God, he was beautiful, with his lean physique and his tanned, taut chest and his hair, the color of the golden sand on a sunny day. He tasted warm and salty, more delicious than the sugary treat they'd had in place of dinner. And the smell of him—all fresh air and clean skin and a hint of spicy cologne.

She had her hands on him, her mouth, her body pressed against his, and he was gently nudging her toward the bedroom. When she saw the direction he was urging her to go, she grabbed the open front of his shirt and yanked him through the doorway and toward the bed.

They fell onto the mattress, in the middle of the white comforter. If she'd had her senses, she'd have teased him about keeping his bedroom so neat, so meticulously tidy. But she didn't have her senses—not the rational ones, anyway. All she had was this drive to be on him, under him, wrapped around him until she couldn't tell where she ended and he began.

His mouth was on hers, then she felt his hands on her breasts over her top, and then those same hands slid up her thighs and under her skirt. Not fast enough, not nearly fast enough. She reached up and tore her top off over her head, exposing the black, lacy bra that she could now admit—let's face it—that she'd worn in the hope that he might one day see it and take it off of her.

He lowered his mouth to the peak of her breast, tasting it through the thin, filmy lace of the bra. The heat of his breath, of his tongue penetrated the fabric and she gasped.

He lifted up onto his arms to look at her. Again, because it was proving to be so handy, she grasped his shirt and used it to haul him back down to her. She kissed his mouth, his chin, the tender hollow of his throat.

She'd imagined what it would be like to sleep with him. She'd imagined his body and the way it would feel, the way it would look. The arousal, the sensations. What she hadn't expected was the way she would feel so safe, so cherished. The way he touched her with reverence, with something like worship. No, she hadn't expected that. And that, more than anything, was what undid her.

He moved down her body, pressing tender kisses to the hollow between her breasts and to the firm flesh of her belly, tasting the indentation of her navel. When he got down to her skirt, he hooked his fingers into the waistband and pulled it down over her hips before sliding the fabric off of her legs and tossing it to the floor.

Her panties were the same black lacy fabric as the bra, and he took a moment to just look.

"I love these," he said. "Now let's take them off of you." He took her hands and pulled her up so he could unhook her bra and slip it off her shoulders, revealing breasts that were small but perfect. Then she raised her hips for him so he could slide the slight, silky fabric of the panties down, down, and off.

The shirt that had been such a convenient means of pulling him to her now had to go. She reached up and slid it off of him, leaving his firm, athletic body free for her to see, to enjoy. "Here. Let me just . . ." She reached for his belt and unbuckled it, then began unsnapping and unzipping his jeans.

She slid the zipper downward, her hand glided over him, and he leaned his head back and groaned. She pulled the fabric down and slid her hands over the firm curves of his ass.

He started to pull away from her, and she grabbed at his shoulders. "I'm not going far," he told her. "I just need to get out of these clothes."

She let go of him and sat up to watch as he removed the pants and the boxers underneath. The room was mostly dark, with only the glow of the living room light coming through the partly open bedroom door. Still, it was enough for her to see him. His body was lean but strong, like a runner, or maybe a swimmer. Everything about it was right, she thought. If he'd been too muscle-bound, she'd have found him intimidating. If he'd been too tall, they wouldn't have fit. But then, it occurred to her that maybe his body seemed perfect because it was his.

"Get back over here," she told him. Up on her knees on the bed, she moved toward where he stood.

He pushed her gently back onto the mattress and covered her with his body. And oh, his skin on hers felt glorious. It felt warm and right. He smelled like ocean air and delicious, clean man.

"Touch me, Will," she said. He made a growling noise from deep in his throat.

She didn't know what she had expected of him. If anyone had asked her—which they hadn't—she'd have predicted that he would be sweet and tentative, perhaps a little unsure, a little inexperienced. As cute as he was, there was no reason for her to think he'd had a dearth of female partners, but the brainy scientist thing didn't suggest a wealth of experience. So her eyes flew open in surprise when he slid down her body, pressed his tongue into the silky folds between her thighs, and proceeded to do things to her body that no man had ever done.

Well, yes, other men had done it. But not like this. Oh, sweet God, nobody had ever done it like this. The man had serious skills.

The way his fingers were gliding into her, the way his tongue was circling and pressing against the throbbing nub that was now becoming the center of her universe, she was quickly climbing toward sweet release. Too quickly.

"Will," she murmured, pushing at him.

"Mm," he said.

"Will." She pushed a little harder at him, but he didn't stop. And then she decided that maybe it would be all right after all if he didn't stop. And then, if he'd tried to stop she'd have had to hurt him.

"Oh, God." She was squirming, writhing, grabbing handfuls of comforter in her fists, her feet scrabbling against the bed for purchase. "Oh … oh shit. Oh, holy … Oh God oh God OH GOD!"

When the orgasm ripped through her, it was like being hit by a train. A wonderful, magical, speeding train full of unicorns and sparkle dust. She grabbed at his head, her hands gripping his hair, as waves of pleasure crashed through her body.

For the first minute or two afterward, she couldn't move or speak. When she came back to her senses, he was lying next to her, watching her face.

"How … where did you learn to do that?" she murmured. She wasn't even sure she'd managed to say it out loud.

"If something's worth doing, it's worth doing right," he said.

"Speaking of things that are worth doing …" Her hand roamed down his body and found him aroused and ready for her. She stroked him, and his eyes closed in an expression of bliss.

She hoped to God he had a condom handy, because she hadn't brought one—this had been impromptu, a sudden, overwhelming urge that she couldn't have predicted. At least, that was what she would tell people after the fact. In truth, the urge had been building for some time. And because it had been building for some time, she could, in fact, have predicted that they would end up right here, just like this.

Still. She hadn't come prepared.

"Are there any condoms?" she asked. Ridiculous that she should be embarrassed to ask, but there it was.

"Side table. Top drawer."

She rolled over, opened the drawer, and found a square foil packet. She ripped it open. Then she got onto her knees, took him into her mouth, and used her tongue on him until she could feel him trembling with arousal.

Having gotten him perfectly prepared, she rolled the condom onto him and then licked the length of him with the tip of her tongue.

He was making low, animal noises that might have included her name.

She positioned herself over his body and lowered herself onto him slowly, a little at a time, his eyes locked onto hers. He gripped her hips with his hands and began guiding her until their bodies were moving with more and more urgency.

She wouldn't have thought she could peak again after the last time—after the shattering, devastating intensity of it. But as she moved with him, her body began to hum with want, with need. She threw her head back and closed her eyes, feeling him under her, feeling his hands on the curves of her breasts.

When she was almost there, he pulled her to him, rolled her over beneath him, and thrust into her harder, faster. The change in rhythm, and in intensity, sent her up, up—and then over the edge. She cried out just as he tensed and shook with his own pleasure.

He collapsed on top of her, and she wasn't sure she could breathe. She wasn't sure she even needed to breathe. She had everything she needed, everything she wanted, oxygen be damned. When he finally did roll off of her, his absence felt like loss, like sorrow.

"Don't go," she murmured, reaching out for him.

"I'll be right back. I just have to … oh. Uh-oh."

"What? What is it?"

He got up, walked naked into the bathroom that adjoined the little bedroom, and flipped on the light. She heard him rustling around in there, and when he came back, he got onto the bed and pulled her into his arms.

"You said, 'Uh-oh,'" she reminded him.

"Um … yeah."

"What was that about?"

He pulled her close against him, and then lightly kissed her temple. "You might not want to hear this," he said.

"Will. What?"

"It's just … the condom. It broke."

She sat up. "It what?"

"It broke."

She blinked a few times, processing it. "What kind of breakage are we talking about here? Like, a little hole? Or …"

"Imagine what a water balloon looks like after you throw it at someone."

"Oh, God." She pulled out of his embrace and sat up, gathering a sheet in front of her to cover her breasts.

"Look, don't worry." His voice was maddeningly calm and rational. "Melinda was more than six months ago, and I always used condoms with her. And they didn't break."

Why was he talking about Melinda when she was in his bed, naked? How did that make any sense? Then the logic of what he was saying filtered through to her.

"You're talking about diseases."

"Well, yes. And I'm just saying, I'm pretty sure I'm healthy."

"Right, right, me too," she said, dismissing the whole idea. "Once I realized how big of an asshole Jeremy was, I got tested. I'm good. Everything's good."

"Well … okay then." He was rubbing her shoulder in a gesture that probably was supposed to be comforting.

"Yeah. Okay."

She must have looked as freaked out as she felt, because he said, "I mean … you're on the pill or something, right?"

"Sure. Or something."

The fact was, she was not on the pill. She had been when she'd been with Jeremy, but she'd meant it—or at least she'd thought she had—when she'd said she was through with men. In the wake of the Jeremy fiasco, she had ceremonially renounced all things male by throwing her pill packets in the trash.

Right now, that was starting to look like an epically bad decision.

She knew she should tell Will, but A) she didn't want to destroy what had been the best night of sex in her life, B) this didn't have to be a problem, and C) she probably wouldn't get pregnant anyway.

Probably.

Chapter Twenty

Okay, so the condom broke. What were the odds that she would get knocked up? If this were an after school special, Rose figured her odds would have been about a hundred percent. But this was real life. And in real life, it couldn't be more than, what, twenty percent? Half of that? Ten? So that meant she had a ninety percent chance of not being pregnant.

If she got odds that good at Vegas, she'd cash in her savings and book a room at the Mirage.

And there was always Plan B—the morning-after pill. Those were available over the counter now. No muss, no fuss, just buy the damned thing, and any potential problem would be solved.

Easy. Simple.

The morning following the faulty condom incident, she fully intended to go to the drugstore and buy the pills. But she didn't manage to get there, because by the time Will drove her home, it was getting close to nine a.m. and she had to get ready for work. Then, on her lunch hour, she was going to go, but Patricia had a family crisis and wasn't there to relieve her, so she had to stay in the shop.

At first she didn't tell anyone, because it was embarrassing—it was a silly problem to have, a problem you had when you lost your virginity after the prom and then realized after the fact that the guy had been carrying the same condom around in his wallet since he hit puberty.

But she told her friends everything, and the pull of that was too great to resist. So when the four of them met for lunch a couple of days after the incident, Rose brought it up like she was telling them what movie she'd watched the night before.

"So, the condom broke," Rose said casually, over pizza at a little place on Main Street.

Kate had just taken a big bite from a pepperoni slice, and she nearly choked on her food. "What?!"

Rose shrugged, picked a slice of pepperoni off of her pizza, and popped it into her mouth. "The condom," she said, then motioned with her hands to indicate an explosion.

"We're talking about Will, right?" Gen said. A lifelong adherent to healthy eating, Gen had a large green salad in front of her instead of pizza. She had paused with a forkful of lettuce halfway to her mouth.

"Of course, Will. Jeez. Who else?" Rose said.

"But you said you were done with men!" Lacy pointed out.

They were gathered around a small table in a restaurant with dark wood paneling and flyers tacked to the walls advertising the local play, a rummage sale, a live music performance at a bar just off Main Street, and other random bits of local news. A few other diners were at tables enjoying pizza slices or hot sandwiches, but they were probably out of earshot. If not, they were doing a good job of hiding any interest.

"I'm done with *relationships* with men," Rose clarified. "I'm not done with sex."

"When?! When was this?" Lacy demanded to know.

"A couple of days ago. Thursday night."

"You've been sitting on this information for two days?" Kate glared at her.

Rose shrugged. "I wasn't ready to … to dissect it yet."

"But now you are?" Gen asked.

"I guess so."

"All right," Lacy said, still pouting. "We'll dissect. But no more secrets."

"You think *that's* a secret?" Rose leaned in toward the center of the table and lowered her voice. "You should hear the secret Will's been keeping. He's a master at sex! I mean, the man is a god."

The other three stared at her, eyes wide, mouths gaping.

"Will?" Gen repeated. "The cute but geeky science nerd?"

"I know!" Rose threw up her hands to indicate the sheer scope of her surprise. "Who would have known? When he did this … thing with my … I thought my limbs and the top of my head were going to fly off."

"Wow." Gen looked thoughtful as she absorbed the information. "Now, Jackson—he's known to be a legend. But Will? I guess it's always the quiet ones."

"Jeez," Kate said. "Lucky girl."

"Yeah, well. Let's just hope that luck holds. Because, condom," Rose reminded them.

"Okay, but you're on the pill, right?" Lacy asked.

Rose grimaced. "That's exactly what Will said."

Kate gasped. "You're *not*?"

"Well." Rose began to explain, and as she did, she sounded like a kid making excuses for not doing her homework. "I was done with men! And when Jeremy and I broke up, there had to be a … a gesture! And so, as my gesture, I … I may have thrown out my pills."

"You may have," Kate said.

"Well … yeah."

"And what did Will say when you told him that the exploded condom was your only means of birth control?" Gen asked.

Rose picked a piece of cheese off of her pizza, ate it, and didn't answer.

"You didn't tell him," Kate concluded.

"Oh, Rose," Gen moaned.

"Well, we'd just had this beautiful, epic, earth-shattering sex. I didn't want to ruin the moment. I didn't want to have this big discussion! I wanted … afterglow."

"Oh, honey. You have to tell him," Kate said.

"There's nothing to tell," Rose insisted. "He knows about the exploded condom, obviously. And there's a ninety percent chance I won't get pregnant. When—if—there's something to tell, then I'll tell him."

Lacy scrunched up her nose in skepticism. "Is it really ninety percent?"

"Hell, I don't know." Rose threw her hands skyward again. "But that's what I'm going with. I'm going with ninety percent."

"But surely you took that Plan B pill, right?" Gen said.

"Well …"

"You didn't? Why not?" Kate demanded.

"Well …" Rose said again.

Lacy gasped and clapped a hand over her mouth. "Oh, my God. You didn't do it because you don't want to. You're falling in love with him and you want to have his cute, geeky, sciency baby!"

Kate laughed. "I guess you're not so through with men after all."

"That must have been some really great sex," Gen said.

"And then … oh, yeah," Rose said, not even bothering to deny their accusations about her feelings for Will. "I forgot to mention one other thing. He might have said—casually—that he wants to marry me."

For the second time in the conversation, the other three froze in surprise.

"Was this after the condom incident?" Kate asked when she recovered her voice. "An *if you're knocked up, I'll marry you* kind of thing?"

"No, he said it before the sex."

"Will proposed to you." Gen was staring at her.

"No, no. I was talking about your wedding, and I said something about how planning a wedding is hard work. And he said when we're ready, we can go to Vegas. Have Elvis do it."

"Oh, so it was a joke," Lacy said.

"The thing is, I don't think it was," Rose said, playing with the food on her plate, the fluttering of nerves and excitement in her belly robbing her of her appetite. "He kind of seemed like he meant it."

"Oh," Lacy sighed.

"Wow," Gen said.

Kate raised her eyebrows. "This is going to be interesting."

Ever since the night of pie and sex, Rose and Will's fake relationship had seemed to evolve into a real one. That had been Will's plan all along, and it was going swimmingly.

They were spending a lot of time together, most of that time ending with both of them naked. They didn't talk about what this was—whether it was a relationship, simple fun, or something else—but that was okay. Will knew what it was for him: It was love. He figured Rose would come around to that herself eventually, if she hadn't already.

And if she didn't, well, he'd help her along.

Pamela was still in town, and would be until after Gen and Ryan's wedding, and whenever he and Rose got together, she commented about how thankful she was that he was keeping her busy so she wouldn't have to spend time with her mother.

Will understood that, but on the other hand, he figured that if he was going to be a permanent fixture in Rose's life, as he was determined to be, then he might as well start getting his future mother-in-law used to the idea.

About a week and a half after the pie and the condom, Will called Rose and asked if she and her mother would like to come to his place for dinner.

"My mother?" She said it in a tone that suggested the word itself was entirely new to her.

"Yeah. I just thought, she's in town to spend time with you. Might as well do something together. Make it nice."

Rose let out a heavy sigh. "Will. Why in God's name would you want to do that, after the way she treated you the night of the barbecue? Why would you subject yourself to that?"

It was a fair question, but he was ready with the answer. "That was our first meeting. She didn't have time to prepare, mentally. Now, she's had time to get used to the idea of me. It's going to go a lot better. You'll see."

"You say that because you don't know her," Rose said dryly.

"You're right, I don't. Let's fix that. At best, she'll decide she likes me. And at worst, I'll see firsthand just what you're up against. It'll make me more empathetic when you complain about her."

Rose paused, and he could tell she was considering it. "That's not a bad point," she conceded.

Will wasn't much of a cook, but he knew how to make a roast chicken, so he did that, along with some red potatoes with butter, garlic, and dill, and a nice green salad. He fussed around some, putting fresh flowers on the table and making pretty place settings, with colorful cloth napkins and his best dishes—which were his only dishes.

At first when he was waiting for them to arrive, he didn't think he was nervous. But he was repeatedly wiping his hands on his pants, and then he realized he was doing that because his palms were sweating.

So, okay. Maybe he was nervous.

By the time they knocked on the door, the house smelled nice, like hot, juicy chicken and simmering herbs. He figured that at the very least, he wouldn't embarrass himself too badly.

He'd expected to see the same pinched, judgmental look on Pamela's face that she'd worn the last time they'd met, but it wasn't there. Instead, she was smiling politely. And he thought, *Well, of course.* He wasn't the one who had changed her attitude. It was Cooper House.

Christopher Mills's vacation estate, with its manicured gardens, its tennis courts, its swimming pool big enough to float an aircraft carrier, was just the kind of thing that would impress a wealthy, status-conscious society woman from Connecticut. It would have impressed her a lot more if Will had owned it.

"Why, the grounds are lovely, just lovely," Pamela gushed as she and Rose came into the cottage. Will took her sweater and her purse and stowed them neatly in the coat closet.

"Yes, it's a shame Chris doesn't use it more often," Will said. "Mostly, the main house sits empty. At least I get to enjoy it."

He offered them wine, and Pamela accepted. Rose asked for a glass of iced tea instead.

When they all had their drinks, they sat in the cottage's little living room while the food continued to cook.

"That smells great," Rose said. "I didn't even know you could cook."

"I didn't either," Will said. "Seems to be going okay, though."

"It was kind of you to invite us," Pamela offered. Will thought she said it grudgingly, though that might have been his imagination.

"Let me help you in the kitchen," Rose offered.

"Thanks, but I think everything's—"

"Is something burning? I smell something burning." Rose grabbed Will's hand and charged into the kitchen, pulling him along behind.

"What's burning?" He looked in the oven and at the contents of the pot on the stove. "I don't think it is. It looks okay."

Then he caught the grin on her face and realized it had been a ploy to get him in here. For a guy known for his brains, he didn't always catch on as quickly as one might expect.

"Oh," he said when he finally got it.

"*The grounds are lovely, just lovely*," Rose mimicked in a stiff-jawed Pamela voice. Then she mimed gagging herself with her finger. "Sure, *this* place is good enough for her. She hates my house and her beach rental, but this is right up her alley." Rose boosted herself up to sit on the counter, plucked a carrot stick from the cutting board, and started chomping on it.

"How's the extended visit going?" he asked, though he already knew the answer.

"I might drown myself," Rose replied cheerfully. "Drowning sounds peaceful."

He came to where she was sitting and put his hands on her hips. "Don't do that. I'd miss you."

"Aww."

He kissed her, and instead of simply kissing him back, she wrapped her arms and legs around him so that, without him even realizing it had happened, she seemed to have climbed him like a koala in a eucalyptus tree.

That's how they were standing when Pamela peeked her head into the kitchen.

"Is everything all right in here?" she wanted to know.

"So, Mrs. Watkins, how are you enjoying Cambria?" Will asked about twenty minutes later at the dinner table as he passed the serving platter to her.

"Well, the natural scenery is lovely, of course," she said, gingerly transferring chicken and potatoes to her plate. "But the house where I'm staying is no more than adequate. But at least it's better than that *cabin* where Rosemary lives. I keep telling her, there are plenty of perfectly wonderful houses in Cambria. I don't see why she persists in living like the Unabomber."

"I like Rose's house," Will said.

"I work at a wine shop," Rose reminded her mother. "It's not like I have a 401K and an expense account."

"Details," Pamela said, waving a hand dismissively.

"Um … how is that just a detail?" Will inquired.

Rose took the platter from her mother and started loading up her plate. "My mother has informed me that if I were to make a few, shall we say, lifestyle adjustments, she'd be happy to foot the bill for a bigger place."

Will's eyebrows shot up. "But you like your place."

"I do."

"And you don't want to … adjust your lifestyle."

"True. I don't."

They both looked at Pamela.

"We're talking about a hairstyle, for God's sake," Pamela spat out. "And a few items of jewelry. I fail to see why it matters so much to you."

"I know you do, Mom," Rose said. She laid a hand on her mother's arm. "Can we talk about something more pleasant? Like that nasty rash I had last month?"

"Rosemary, please." Pamela looked at Rose with scorn.

"You know, Rose is doing very well for herself, Mrs. Watkins," Will tried gamely. "She doesn't just work at the wine store, she manages it. And once she gets her degree …"

"Degree?" Pamela said.

Rose, positioned behind Pamela's back, was using one finger to make a frantic slashing gesture across her throat. But it was too late; he'd already said it.

"What degree, Rosemary?" Pamela turned in her seat to face Rose.

"Ah … I … nothing. Who wants more potatoes?"

"Rosemary." Pamela fixed Rose with a gaze honed by years of experience in applying pressure, guilt, and manipulation. Rose cracked.

"Oh, it's just … I'm thinking of going to college. At Cal Poly San Luis Obispo. They have a viticulture program, and I thought—"

"Cal Poly?" Pamela said. "Oh, Rosemary. You were supposed to go to Yale."

"She didn't want to go to Yale," Will put in. He knew this wasn't his business, wasn't his family relationship to navigate. But he couldn't just sit here and let Pamela continue to criticize and berate Rose. "She ran away with nothing but a car and the clothes on her back to avoid going to Yale. That suggests to me that she *really* didn't want to go. A high-status school isn't everything."

"Said the Stanford man," Pamela observed dryly.

"Stanford is great," he acknowledged. "But Cal Poly meets Rose's needs. They've got the program she wants in the location she wants. And, they're reasonably affordable."

Pamela scoffed. "Affordable. She's buying an education, for God's sake, not a used car."

"Well, at this point, I won't be buying either. Now, let's just enjoy this nice meal Will made for us. Can we? Please?" Rose demonstrated enjoying the meal by putting a forkful of potatoes in her mouth and saying, "Mmm. Yummy!"

"Rosemary." Rose's mother gave her the Pamela Glare. "Will says you're finally going to college, and now you say you're not. Which is it, dear?"

Rose put down her fork and plopped her hands in her lap in defeat. "I'd like to go, but I can't afford it. Okay, Mother?"

"Well, but, I'm encouraging Rose to look into financial aid opportunities," Will added.

"Financial aid!" Pamela said it as though Rose would be panhandling with a sign that read, WILL WORK FOR TUITION. "That's for inner city, blue collar, working class—"

"I *am* working class!" Rose exclaimed.

"Well, that was your own decision, dear." Pamela delicately patted her mouth with her napkin.

"Yes, it was, and I don't regret it. At all." Rose stabbed a piece of chicken with her fork as though she were defending her life against it.

"Viticulture," Pamela mused. "To do what? Become a sommelier? Because that's just a glorified—"

"No. A winemaker. I want to make wine. I'd like to eventually have my own label." Rose said this quietly, almost timidly, without her usual verve. That's what made Will understand how much it really meant to her.

"Hmm," Pamela said.

Will hadn't known Pamela long, but he could almost hear her thought process. A sommelier might be a glorified bartender, but a winemaker? That had a certain cultured, upscale cachet. That was something she could tell her Connecticut friends about.

"Pamela," Will said, attempting to change the subject. "I'm sorry you're finding your stay in Cambria to be disappointing."

"Oh, I didn't say that." Pamela lifted her wineglass and took a sip of chardonnay.

"You didn't?" Rose asked.

"No, dear. I can quite see the appeal, actually. Did I tell you that I awoke this morning to find a family of deer on the lawn? Charming. Just charming."

Rose stared at her mother, her mouth half open.

Chapter Twenty-One

On the drive back from Will's place, Pamela glanced at Rose from her place in the passenger seat.

"You know, you might have asked me if you needed money for college."

"I might have. I also might have pounded nails into my skull. But I didn't do either of those things because they're both painful and self-destructive." She said it in a bright, conversational tone, as though they were discussing movies or fashion trends.

Pamela scowled. "Rosemary, don't be dramatic."

"If I took money from you, the first thing you'd do would be to ask me to dye my hair," Rose pointed out.

"Well, naturally, I—"

"But it wouldn't end there. After you got me looking the way you wanted, then it would be my house. And my job. And my boyfriend." It was the first time she'd referred to Will that way, even mentally, and it jolted her. But then she rallied, and continued. "And *then* you'd want me to take my shiny new degree and move back to Connecticut. Don't say you wouldn't." Rose cut off her mother as she began to speak. "Because we both know you would."

"Well." Pamela straightened her cashmere cardigan. The lack of reply was likely the closest Rose would ever come to being told she was right.

"And so," Rose continued, as though she had never expected a response, "I didn't ask you, and I didn't even mention it, and now we're both going to pretend Will didn't mention it, either."

Pamela made a grumbling noise, mumbling under her breath as she rearranged her purse in her lap. "It's beyond me why you persist in making your life so much more difficult than it has to be," she said when she was speaking intelligibly again.

"I don't make my life difficult, Mom. I make it *mine*."

Pamela's eyes widened, and she blinked a few times. Somehow, Rose got the idea that finally, finally, something she had said had gotten through.

Rose dropped Pamela off at the rental house. She'd intended to leave Pamela in the driveway and get the hell out of there. It was still early, and she could scurry back to Will's place as fast as her wheels would take her, so they could have an evening of reality-altering sexual bliss.

But she parked and got out of the car after she realized she'd left her cell phone inside the house when she'd picked Pamela up at the start of the evening.

"I've just gotta grab my phone, and then I have this … this thing I have to do … I … um … I told Kate I'd—"

"When you return to Will's cottage, please tell him thank you for dinner," Pamela said, eyeing Rose sternly.

"Ha. I will." Rose would have thought that a lifetime of lying to her mother would have made her better at it. But, no.

She followed her mother into the house and grabbed her phone from the kitchen counter. Then, as she came out into the small living area on her way to the door, she found her mother in the Barcalounger with her shoes off and her eyes closed, the chair in full recline.

Rose gaped at her mother, stunned.

"You're sitting in the Barcalounger," she said when she had recovered slightly.

"And?"

"And … I just didn't think it was your style." Rose felt as though she were stating the extremely obvious, like *Water is wet,* or *The sky is up.*

"Yes, well," Pamela said without opening her eyes. "It may lack style, but it actually is quite comfortable."

Rose stared for a moment longer before letting herself out of the house and getting back into her car.

First the charming family of deer, and now this. Was Pamela going to turn warm and maternal soon? Rose doubted it. But she supposed anything was possible.

"Have you told Will yet?" Lacy demanded the next morning at Jitters when Rose went in to get her caffeine fix before work.

"Told him what?"

"You know." Lacy pantomimed an explosion with her hands and mouthed the word, *Boom.*

"Lacy, we've been over this." Rose leaned her elbows on the counter while Lacy made espresso. "There's nothing to tell. Yet."

"That was, what, almost two weeks ago? There should be something to tell by now. Unless … you know. You already know that there's nothing to tell."

"Well," Rose said, slumping slightly against the counter.

"Well what?" Lacy pulled a shot of espresso, added steamed milk, and passed it to a customer who was waiting a few steps away from Rose.

"Well …" Rose leaned over the counter toward Lacy and said in a stage whisper, "I'm late. But I have PMS, so … you know. Everything should be fine."

"You're late," Lacy repeated.

"Yeah. But, PMS."

Lacy crossed her arms over her chest and looked at Rose sternly. "What PMS symptoms are you having, exactly?"

"You know." Rose tossed her arms into the air. "The usual. My pants are too tight, my boobs are sore, and this morning I cried because I ran out of toothpaste. Classic PMS."

Lacy leaned toward her and hissed, "You idiot, those are also classic signs of early pregnancy!"

Rose blinked at her. "They are?"

"Yes!"

"Oh." Rose must have known that, somewhere in her brain, but she'd pushed the information aside in order to interpret her symptoms in the most favorable way possible.

"You need to take a test," Lacy said. "Right now. Go over to the pharmacy and pick one up, then you can come back here and pee on the stick."

"I don't want to pee on the stick," Rose pouted. "I don't need to pee on a stick."

"I think you do," Lacy said.

The customer who had just received her latte, a middle-aged woman in a sundress and flip-flops, put a hand on Rose's arm. "I really think you should. It's better to know." The woman picked up her latte and walked out onto Main Street.

"Well, there you go," Lacy said.

Buying a pregnancy test in a town as small as Cambria presented certain problems. Everybody knew Rose, and everybody knew Will. Therefore, if Rose was seen buying a pregnancy test, people were going to look at Will funny because it meant one of two things: He was about to become a father with a woman he'd only just started dating, or that woman might have become pregnant with someone else. Either way, the likely result was pity or, at the very least, curiosity.

Since Rose had no intention of telling Will about any of this—and with luck, it wouldn't be necessary anyway—she couldn't just parade into the pharmacy and pick up a First Response box.

Thinking quickly, she ducked out of the coffeehouse, saw the tourist in the sundress gazing into a shop window, and sidled up to her.

"*Psst.*" Rose hissed at the woman as though they were secret agents at a midnight rendezvous.

"Excuse me?" The woman looked at her curiously.

"Could you do me a favor?" Rose whispered the question out of the side of her mouth.

"Um ... I guess so."

When Rose explained what she needed, the woman was eagerly on board. Rose handed her a twenty dollar bill, and a few minutes later, the woman passed her a pharmacy bag containing a Clearblue digital pregnancy test.

Rose walked back into Jitters and gave Lacy a knowing look as she went toward the back of the shop and into the ladies' room.

About three minutes later, Rose was still sitting on the toilet with her pants down around her ankles as she stared at the results window of the test stick.

PREGNANT.

She felt like she was having an out of body experience. She couldn't feel her hands or feet, and she seemed to be hovering about five inches above her own head.

Gradually, she got herself together, put down the stick, fastened her clothes—and then promptly turned around and hurled her breakfast into the toilet bowl.

Well, *that* wasn't usually a PMS symptom.

❖

Lacy made an emergency round of calls, and she, Kate, and Gen all arranged to meet Rose after work for dinner. Rose had been planning to see Will that evening, but she couldn't see him until she knew what to do. And she couldn't know what to do until she'd talked things over with her friends.

One of the cruel ironies of an unintended pregnancy was that just when you needed a drink the most, you couldn't have one. In solidarity with Rose, the whole group opted for water or iced tea over dinner instead of their usual wine. Lacking the comfort of alcohol, Rose opted for junk food instead.

They were at Kate's house, gathered at her dining table around an array of Chinese takeout boxes. When they'd arrived, they'd all given Rose hugs hard enough to threaten her ability to breathe. Now, with the initial shock out of the way, they were scooping food onto plates and launching into the debriefing.

"Okay. So." Kate lifted noodle-laden chopsticks and led off the discussion. "What are we thinking here? Because, honey, you know we won't judge you if—"

"I'm keeping it," Rose said. "I might not know much about what I'm going to do yet, but, yeah. Definitely keeping it."

"Okay." Gen nodded. "So that leads us to another set of questions. Do you want to raise this baby with Will? Or alone? And if you're going to do it with him, how will that work? And if you're going to do it alone, how will *that* work?"

"Those are the questions, all right," Rose agreed.

"Well, the first thing you have to do is tell him," Lacy said. "Then, the way he responds will help you know what to do."

Rose shook her head, her hair a vibrant red this month. And, oh God, was that another thing she'd have to give up for the pregnancy? Was hair dye bad for the baby? "I can't tell him," she said.

"Of course you can!" Kate insisted. "You have to."

"No. I really don't."

The others stared at her as though she were speaking Mandarin.

"Honey," Kate said, and put a hand on Rose's arm.

Rose pulled her arm away from Kate's grasp. "Look, you're all being judgy right now, but that's because you're not seeing it from my side of things. If I tell Will, one of two things is going to happen. Either he's going to run like hell—which, let's face it, a lot of guys would do at a time like this—or he's going to feel a sense of duty and become this committed partner. But he'd only be doing that because I'm pregnant! And I would never know whether he was in it because of me, or … or because it was the right thing to do!"

Lacy looked thoughtful. "I want to argue with you, but I kind of can't. You want to see if he wants you for you, and this is going to screw with that. No way around it."

"Right!" Rose tossed her arms out toward Lacy. "You get it!"

"As much as we might understand your point," Gen said, "it's not the kind of secret you can keep forever. At some point, he's going to notice."

"Right, but by then, we'll have had more time to see where things are going. Just between the two of us. Without offspring."

"He has a right to know," Kate said.

"I know that. I know it," Rose said. "And he will know. Eventually."

"Have you told your mom yet?" Kate asked gently.

"My mom! Oh, shit. No. She already thinks I'm … Oh, God. I'll just … I'm just not going to deal with that. She's going back to Connecticut in a couple of weeks. I'll tell her after the baby's born. Or when he's in preschool."

Somehow, it was that thought—the image of her growing child being sent off to preschool, probably with a tiny backpack and a snack—that finally broke the dam of Rose's hormone-fueled emotions. First she teared up slightly, a sensation she felt as a heat behind her eyes, and then, before she even knew what was happening, she was boo-hooing into her hands as her friends watched helplessly.

Kate dashed into the bedroom to grab a box of tissues, Gen hurried to get a glass of water, and Lacy sat beside Rose, alternately patting and rubbing her back.

And that was when Jackson walked in.

He stood inside the front door, watching the crying, the tissue-bringing, the back patting, and looked like a guy who wanted to be anywhere else but here. Prison, maybe.

"What's going on?" he asked tentatively, as though he maybe didn't want to know the answer.

"Aren't you supposed to be at work?" Kate asked, her voice sounding a little harried.

"Slow night. I'm working extra hours for that private party on Tuesday, so …"

Rose sobbed and hiccuped, a wad of tissues in her hand.

"Is there anything I can do?" Jackson offered.

"No." Kate went to him, put a hand on his bicep, and said, "Rose is having … Well. It's a personal issue."

"Does this have anything to do with Will?" he wanted to know. "Do I have to go kick his ass?"

The thought that Jackson would kick Will's ass for her was unbearably sweet, and that sent Rose into another burst of tears.

"No," Gen said. "Will didn't do anything wrong. No ass-kicking required."

"Okay. Well … I have to do something to help. Can I … Rose? Do you want a glass of wine? Or something stronger? I've got whiskey."

"No!" three of them shouted at once.

Jackson stood there, helpless.

"It's a girl thing," Kate said. "We've got this." She gave him a quick kiss on the cheek. "Maybe just kind of … you know. Make yourself scarce for a bit."

He looked so relieved it was almost comical. "Okay. Then I'll just …" He hit the door not exactly at a run, but at a brisk walk.

"He's gonna figure it out," Lacy said once he was gone.

"Oh, he is not going to figure it out," Kate insisted. "He's a guy. Guys see a crying woman, they don't think pregnancy. He will not figure it out."

Chapter Twenty-Two

Of course, he figured it out.

Will was certain that Jackson knew more than he was telling as the two of them sat at a table at Ted's a half-hour later. Jackson had called Will once he'd been ordered to get out of the house, and the two had met for a beer.

"The women are at the house," Jackson said once they were settled in with mugs of beer in front of them. "There's something going on. It's ... Kate said it was girl stuff."

"What kind of girl stuff?" Will wanted to know.

"I don't know." But Jackson was avoiding his eyes.

"Baking? Crocheting? Flying kites and talking about feminine hygiene?" Will joked. But Jackson didn't even crack a smile, so he knew it had to be serious.

"Rose is upset," Jackson said.

"Wait, Rose? What about?" Will felt a surge of dread, of concern.

"I don't know," Jackson said again. "But … she was crying. And the others were trying to calm her down. And … and when I offered her a drink, they all yelled at me."

"They yelled at you?"

"Yeah. And they told me to leave. Not that it was a burden to get the hell out of there, with all that girl emotion going on."

"I've got to go find out what's happening." Will got up from his chair and grabbed his jacket.

"No, man. Don't. I think … whatever's going on, they need a little time."

Will sat back down heavily. He felt worried, and a little bit guilty, even though he couldn't think of anything he might have done wrong.

"She's not pissed at you. At least, I don't think so," Jackson offered, seeming to read his mind. "I said that I'd kick your ass if they wanted, and they said no."

"Well, that's comforting."

"I guess."

The bar was half full, about typical for a weekday night. The Rolling Stones were playing over the sound system, a smattering of customers were sitting at the bar, and a couple of guys were arguing over their pool game. It was early, so the place didn't yet smell like sweat and spilled beer.

"Do you think it has something to do with her mom?"

"No," Jackson said.

The quick, confident response confirmed to Will that Jackson knew something he wasn't telling. The guy looked worried, and that wasn't typical of Jackson, who usually had only two modes: happy and angry.

"What's going on, Jackson?" Will asked, sitting up straighter in his chair. "If you know what this is about …"

"I don't know. I've got an idea. But if she hasn't told you yet …"

"Told me what? Jackson? Come out with it." Will was getting scared now. Scared that Rose really was angry with him, for reasons unknown. Scared that she might break it off with him. Scared that something was wrong with Rose, with her life, something that was causing her pain that he wanted to fix. What if he couldn't fix it, whatever it was? What if she was in trouble, and he couldn't help her?

"You called me because you want to tell me. Didn't you?" Even as he said it, he knew it was true. "Well, I'm here. Tell me."

Jackson squirmed in his seat, looking like a kid who'd been caught cutting class. He ran a hand through his auburn hair and grimaced.

"Aw, man. I shouldn't be doing this. If she wanted you to know …"

"Just tell me. If she needs my help, I want to help her. And I can't do that if I don't know what's going on."

"Dude. I think she's pregnant."

Will had heard it said before, metaphorically, that someone felt the world dropping out from under them. That phrase had held no meaning for him until this moment. Because right now, it really did feel as though the floor had disappeared, as though he were floating in a vertiginous, spinning freefall that would end—if indeed it did end—in a crushing impact when he finally hit the ground.

"You … I …"

"Yeah. That's about how I thought you'd react," Jackson observed.

"Did they tell you that? What … How do you know that?" Will was sputtering, dizzy, unable to focus.

"Instinct, man. Rose was crying, and they were all gathered around, and they freaked out when I suggested maybe she could use a drink. Plus, Kate might have mentioned something about a bad condom a few weeks ago."

Will was stunned not only by the idea of impending fatherhood, but also by the knowledge that the news of his faulty condom had spread so far and wide.

"But … she said she was on the pill." But even as he said that, he knew that wasn't right. That wasn't what she'd said. He'd asked if she was on the pill or something, and she'd replied, *Or something.* Which had been classic avoidance of the question. He'd have realized that at the time if he hadn't been so addled by the stupendous sex.

"Yeah, well, don't go buying onesies just yet. I don't know for sure that's what's going on, I just have a hunch."

The mention of onesies made Will clutch at his beer and chug half of it in a single draft. It helped, somewhat. But he was still conscious, so it didn't help enough.

"What should I … I don't …" He scrubbed at his face with his hands.

Jackson sighed and leaned back in his chair. "Is this gonna be a deal breaker for you? Are you about to crush her heart? Because if you are …"

"What? No. Of course not. No." The very thought was appalling. In fact, the first thought that had jumped into his mind, after the blind panic, was marriage. He'd thought about Rose and marriage before, but she wasn't ready to hear it—nor would he expect her to be after just weeks of dating. But now, if a baby were to force the issue, maybe he could … No. It had been a challenge just getting her to acknowledge that they actually were dating. This would be a jump she wasn't likely to make.

"Are you sure?" Jackson said, picking up the thread of the conversation. "Better guys than you have been known to run like hell when the little line turns pink."

"I'm sure." Will took a deep breath. "Yeah, I'm sure. Jackson … I love her."

Jackson gave Will a half grin. "I was hoping you'd say that, since she's practically my sister-in-law. If you *were* going to run, I might have had to kick your ass whether the girls wanted me to or not."

"Look who's talking," Will said. "You used to have at least three clearly marked exit routes ready before the first date."

"I've changed," he said mildly. "And anyway, this isn't about me. It's about you and Rose, and your kid. If there is a kid. I'm pretty sure there is one."

The phrase *your kid* made him dizzy again, but he rallied and managed to focus.

"Okay. So, let's say it's true. What should I do? I know I want to be with her. But Rose … she's been on this 'I'm through with men' kick, and I was just barely getting her to admit that maybe she's not. And now …"

Jackson rubbed at the stubble on his chin. "Ah. So, you're not the one who's going to freak out and hit the door. She is."

"Right."

"Let me think about that a little."

They both thought about it while they drank their beer and watched the crowd at Ted's. Will reflected that there had to be a way for him to adapt to this new information, a way to work the situation so that Rose would know she was safe with him and wouldn't feel the need to shut him out. He just didn't know what it was.

"Should I go to her?" he said at last. "Tell her I'm in? Let her know I'm not going anywhere? Because I'm not." Just saying the words gave him a new sense of determination to stick, no matter what.

"I don't know." Jackson shook his head, thinking. "Maybe. Maybe not. You know what we need? We need a girl to help us think this through."

The idea was appealing. If they could get Kate to come down here to Ted's, she'd probably have a greater sense of what Rose needed—and how Will could best give it to her—than he and Jackson did. But the women were so tight, like sisters, that it seemed likely Kate would then tell everything to Rose. And that could scare her away or make her angry, neither of which Will wanted to do.

Jackson seemed to read his mind. "We could ask Kate what she thinks, but then she'd tell Rose."

"Yeah," Will agreed. "And then Rose would feel manipulated."

"And then God help you," Jackson added.

But if that wasn't going to work, then what?

"All right," Will said after a while. "Let's break it down to the basics. Do I tell her I know? Or do I wait for her to tell me? *If* it's even true."

"It is," Jackson said.

Deep in his gut, the place where the truth lived, he knew Jackson was right.

"Okay, so ..."

"Okay." Jackson sat forward, ready to work the problem. "You tell her you know, what's she most likely to do?"

"Well, she's *not* going to start calling me darling and knitting baby booties. I think that's pretty safe to say." Will pictured the image of Rose as a motherly June Cleaver, and smiled. "She's more likely to tell me that she doesn't need me. Because it's really important to her to believe that she doesn't need anyone."

"But she does need you," Jackson said.

"I know that. But it's not about what she really does need. It's about what she *wants* to need. And she doesn't want to need anybody. Because people have always let her down in the past." He thought about that for a moment, then amended it. "Well, not her friends. But men. And her mother."

"Okay. So, if you tell her you know, then she can either become a partner with you, or she can become this tough-as-nails, single pregnant woman, toughing it out on her own and taking on the world solo."

Will gave Jackson a pointed look. "Which one of those sounds like Rose?"

Jackson shook his head. "Dude, you're screwed."

"Right. Plan A isn't going to work. But Plan B ... I could just keep quiet. Wait for her to tell me. Wait for her to do what she's going to do. Meanwhile, I'll just … I'll be there for her. I'll be rock solid. I can do that. And when she sees that …"

Jackson raised his eyebrows. "Could work. Or she could break up with you without saying why, and then you'd still be screwed."

It was a possibility. Then he thought of another possibility.

"She's … oh, God. She's not going to … Is she going to have the baby? Do you … What did Kate say?" The idea that Rose might get an abortion was a sudden, horrifying possibility. If Rose wanted an abortion because she truly didn't want to have a baby, then that was one thing. But if she was considering abortion because she thought she'd be in this alone … Well. If that was an issue, he'd have to tell her he was in this to stay. And he'd have to tell her today.

"We didn't get that far," Jackson told him. "Remember, I'm not even supposed to know. But if I had to guess, I'd say she's keeping it. They yelled at me when I offered her a drink. All of them, even Rose. Would they have done that if she wasn't keeping it?"

Probably not. That thought was comforting.

Will decided that there was only one thing to do: He would keep his mouth shut and simply be there. He'd be there when Rose was scared, he'd be there when she was happy. He'd be there if she tried to push him away. He'd just be there. In the wild, when a predator approached a skittish prey animal, it had to move slowly, carefully, to avoid spooking the prey and causing it to run. This was like that, sort of. Except that Will's goal with Rose wasn't to attack her; it was simply to love her, and to make her feel safe to accept that love.

Chapter Twenty-Three

Rose threw herself into helping with Gen's wedding. That was something she could do to get her mind off of her own problems and onto something constructive. There was so much to do, it was easy to lose herself in the tasks, the details, the putting out of small fires.

She knew that she'd be keeping the baby, but she didn't know what she was going to do beyond that. She didn't know what she would do about Will, or about her mother, or how she would raise a baby on her own. But she wasn't ready to think about those things, and thinking about tulle and taffeta, flowers and place markers, seemed so much easier.

"What's the next job? I need a job," Rose told Gen at the gallery when she stopped in during her lunch break a couple of weeks before the wedding.

"Are you sure?" Gen looked skeptical. "You've got a lot on your plate right now, and I—"

"I'm sure! All of that stuff 'on my plate' "—she made air quotes with her fingers—"is the reason I need something to do! I can't think about it right now. So I need something else to think about."

"Well, okay." Gen went to the laptop on her desk, called up a file, printed it, then handed the sheet of paper to Rose. "Here's the list of the inconsiderate idiots who haven't RSVP'd yet. Could you call them and find out who's coming?"

Rose lifted an eyebrow. "Inconsiderate idiots?"

"It seems that wedding prep is making me cranky," Gen observed.

"All right. I'm on it. If you want, I can tell them that they're being idiots."

Gen smiled, a dreamy look on her face that suggested she was happily imagining just that. “Better not,” she said finally. “Some of them are Ryan’s relatives, and I’m still trying to make a good impression.”

“Okay. Only two weeks left. How are you holding up?”

“I’m good,” Gen said. “It’s good. I’m excited, and stressed out, and I can’t wait, but I also can’t wait for it to be over.”

“That sounds about right.”

“How about you? Have you told Will—”

Rose plugged her ears with her fingers and started singing. “La la la la la! I can’t hear a thing! My ears are plugged, and I’m singing! La la la!”

Gen crossed her arms over her chest and rolled her eyes as Rose walked out the door.

Rose knew she couldn’t avoid the issue forever, but she figured she could avoid it for now. So she went back to De-Vine after her lunch break and started on the phone calls. The shop was empty. She’d already done the ordering, restocked the shelves, cleaned the place, and brought the bookkeeping up to date. It seemed that hiding an unplanned pregnancy gave her stores of energy she wouldn’t have thought possible.

She was three names down the list when a text message came in from Will.

Dinner tonight?

Rose stared at the message. Though it was a simple question, not fraught with drama or emotional baggage, she felt an ache in her chest just seeing his name. She hesitated, then answered.

I can’t. Busy helping Gen with the wedding.

It was a lie. She’d be done with the phone calls this afternoon, and then she wouldn’t have anything else to do until she got another assignment from Gen. And of course, she'd have to eat dinner. It wasn't like she was going to hunger strike until the wedding was over. Still. She wasn't ready to see him.

I can help. I can make little bags of Jordan almonds. ☺

The emoticon, coming from a grown man, was unbearably cute.

A sweet, sexy man cared about her. Why did it hurt like this? Why did it make this ache, this lump of sorrow in the middle of her belly? Part of her knew that pushing him away was childish, but another part—a bigger part—felt like her very survival depended on it.

That's sweet. Thanks. But we're good on the Jordan almonds.

A moment later he responded.

Tomorrow, then? I miss you.

Oh, God. She missed him too. So much. But the knowledge of the baby growing inside her was all she could possibly handle. She couldn't handle him, too. Now—especially now—was a time when she had to protect herself. Pregnancy made her vulnerable and raw, and this was not the time to open herself up to anything as messy and unpredictable as love.

Customers in the store, she wrote back. Then she put her phone down and looked out into the empty expanse of the shop.

She sighed.

This—all of this—was why she should have been finished with men.

When Rose got off work that evening, she went to her car and found Will leaning against the hood holding a bag from Neptune.

Her heart did an annoying little flip-flop when she saw him.

"What are you doing here?"

He pushed off the car and stood up straight as she approached. "You're busy right now, but you've got to eat. So, I figured I'd bring you something." He gestured toward the bag. "There's enough here for two. We can go down to the beach and sit at a picnic table and eat it together, or if you really can't spare the time, I'll just leave it with you and go get a burger."

He grinned his disarming, sweet, good-guy grin. It almost made Rose's knees weak.

"I guess … I suppose I can spare a few minutes to eat. But then I have to get home and work on some stuff for Gen." She wondered what was in the bag, and hoped it involved Jackson's seafood bisque.

"Okay, fair enough. Your car or mine?"

The evening was mild as they set up the food on a picnic table at Leffingwell Landing, just north of Moonstone Beach. Will had planned ahead, and he'd brought a tablecloth to spread over the worn wooden table.

Gulls wheeled overhead, and a light breeze blew off the ocean. A handful of people were at the park, including a woman who'd set up an easel for watercolor painting, and a guy playing Frisbee with his kids.

Will spread the food out on the table, and it did, in fact, include Jackson's seafood bisque.

"God, I'm starving," Rose said. Though she was very early in her pregnancy, one thing about her body that had changed already was that it had an insatiable desire for food. And this hunger wasn't like any previous hunger she'd felt. This was a soul-consuming, knee-shaking, animal desire to devour anything edible that came into her path.

Will had brought the bisque, some pieces of fresh-baked baguette, a green salad, and pasta with a spicy chicken and sausage ragù. As he opened the containers, the mouthwatering smells almost made Rose swoon.

They didn't bother with plates or bowls, and instead just dug into the takeout containers with their plastic forks and spoons.

Rose wanted to be tough and protect herself and her baby from any possible dangers, and those dangers included Will, since she couldn't be sure about him and what he would do once he learned about his impending fatherhood. Her heart was at risk, and she needed to surround it with an impenetrable fortress of strength.

But it was pretty goddamned hard to be a fortress when he brought her seafood bisque.

She was too hungry, and too tired from a day spent on her feet, to worry about that now. Right now, there was the velvety texture of warm bread and the bite of the spicy sausage, and the aroma of seafood and tangy tomato sauce. Right now, there were the seagulls and the crash of the waves, and the scent of the ocean.

"I haven't seen you much lately," Will said mildly.

Rose shrugged in a way that was supposed to be casual. "Ah. Well, you know, I've been pretty busy. Work, and my mother wanting to take up all of my time, and … and Gen's wedding." It sounded false and stilted, and she knew it. It sounded like an excuse.

"Sure." He nodded. "I've been busy too. I'm finally making progress on my dissertation."

"Really? That's great, Will. I know you were worried about it."

"I was, but recently things have, let's say, clarified for me. I can't screw around anymore. I have to get this done and get my career going. I can't be a caretaker forever." The breeze was ruffling his sandy-colored hair, and he lifted a hand to brush it out of his face.

Rose wondered what, exactly, had happened to clarify things for him, and where he'd found the sudden motivation to get his metaphorical house in order. Was it possible he knew about the baby? But then she thought, no. The only people who knew were her friends. Well, and the tourist who'd bought the pregnancy test for her. Her friends would not betray her confidence, and the tourist didn't even know Will.

She shook off the thought. It was something on his end, then. With a sudden jolt of horror, she thought about his bitchy ex, the one who wouldn't let go.

"Have you heard from Melinda lately?" Rose inquired, trying to sound like she was just making conversation.

"Ah … Yes. Yes, I have."

"And?"

He gave her a kind of sideways look that she found impossibly endearing. "Are you sure you want to hear about this?"

"I'm sure. Spill it, Science Boy."

He pulled his phone out of his back pocket, fiddled with it a little bit, then passed it across the table to her. Up on the screen was the latest text exchange between the two of them, dated two days before.

Melinda: *Will, you're going to have to acknowledge me at some point.*

Will: *I don't see why. We broke up.*

Melinda: *What's done can be undone. People break up and get back together all the time.*

Will: *I'm with Rose now. Please stop, Melinda. You're with Chris. Just be with Chris.*

Melinda: *You asshole. If you think you can get away with just ignoring me, you're sadly mistaken.*

No response from Will. Then Melinda texted again ten minutes later:

If you keep treating me like this, I'll tell Chris that you kissed me. You'll lose your job. You'll be out on the street, you tiny-dicked bastard.

That last bit made Rose grin, despite how horrible it all was. She could attest to the falsity of the *tiny-dicked* comment.

He took the phone from Rose and placed it back into his pocket.

"Did you know she was this crazy when you were dating her?"

"No." He looked thoughtful. "Well, maybe a little. She did get kind of obsessive about things sometimes. But I didn't know she was at this level of crazy."

The fact that Melinda was pursuing Will made Rose feel anxious and angry. But what he'd told Melinda—*I'm with Rose now*—filled her with a kind of giddy pride. The overall result was a seesaw of emotions she didn't quite know how to handle. But, hell. Being flummoxed by her emotions was pretty much the status quo these days.

"What are you going to do about her?" Rose toyed with a piece of a baguette. She kept her voice calm and conversational—just two pals chatting about a crazy ex—but every instinct told her to track down Melinda and pull her hair out by the roots.

"I don't know." He shrugged and looked out at the water, to where the sun was slowly inching toward the horizon. "Nothing, I guess."

"What do you mean, 'nothing'? You have to do something. She's stalking you, for God's sake." To Rose's mind, taking out a restraining order would not have been out of line. Rose had read online about companies that would send boxes of dog shit to your enemies. Right about now, that seemed like a pretty useful service.

Will returned his gaze to Rose. "I figure if I ignore her, she'll go away. She's not going to tell Chris that I kissed her, because then I'll tell him the truth: that she was the one who made a move on me. No. She's not going to jeopardize her relationship with someone as high-powered as he is. I mean, he's what she always wanted in the first place: a rich guy who looks good in a suit. I really don't even get why she's doing this."

"Competition," Rose said, sipping from the tall paper cup of iced tea Will had brought for her. "All of this started when she met me, right?"

"Right."

"Well, there you go. It was fine that you two were broken up when she thought you were lonely and sad, regretting the day that you let her walk out of your life. But then she sees you with me, and I'm much hotter than she is." She grinned at him, and shot him a wink. "In her shallow, two-dimensional way, she probably saw the hair and the tats and thought that I'm way more sexually adventurous than she could ever be. Cue the insane stalking."

"You are more sexually adventurous," Will observed.

"Of course. She was probably a missionary position, only-on-Saturday-nights girl. But don't tell me about it." She put up a hand, palm out, to stop him. "I don't want to know."

Being here with him, even if they were spending the time trashing his ex, felt so good that Rose had to remind herself that she wasn't going to do this; she wasn't going to go all gooey over him and give him her heart. She needed her heart to be safe and intact for her child. But he looked so sweet with the early evening sun on his face, his hair mussed by the breeze, that when he came to her side of the picnic table and sat next to her, so close that she could feel the warmth of his thigh against hers, she didn't even think to move away.

"I don't regret the day I let her walk out of my life," he said. "Just for the record. She wasn't right for me. She wasn't who I wanted. You are."

For a moment, her rational brain kicked in. "Look, Will. We shouldn't—"

He shut down her protest with a kiss.

And damned if it didn't work. When his lips touched hers, she went all stupid, and she forgot what she'd wanted to say. What was it about a kiss that could do this to a person? That could empty your brain and make your insides go soft? Whatever it was, Rose lost herself in it. The taste of his mouth and the warmth of his tongue, the feel of his breath on her, made her want to forget everything else and live right here, forever. Somehow, against her own volition, she stopped being the girl with the heart that needed protecting, and instead rose from her seat on the bench and settled herself in his lap.

His arms went around her and gathered her in, and she felt right. She felt at peace.

Damn it.

When the two of them came up for air, he smoothed her hair back from her face with his warm hand.

"Rose. I'm not in this for a good time. I'm in this. Completely. I just wanted you to know."

And oh, God, she wanted to believe it. Wanted to believe in this, in him. She rested her forehead against his.

"Can I come to your place tonight?" She could feel his breath as he spoke just inches from her skin. "Please?"

It was the *please* that did it. She was powerless to say no.

And anyway, she could be strong again tomorrow.

Chapter Twenty-Four

"I heard you went out with Will last night." Kate sounded a little smug.

"No," Rose protested. "I mean, yes, I saw him. But we didn't 'go out.' We mostly … stayed in. And how do you know about it, anyway?" Rose was talking to Kate on her cell phone as she was getting ready for work. Rose's place was a mess, partly because she wasn't much of a housekeeper, and partly because she and Will had stayed in bed until the last possible minute, and she hadn't had time to clean up.

"Jackson cooked the meal that Will brought to you after work last night. And Jackson has been known to gossip on occasion."

"Well … okay." Rose reached down to the floor and picked up her bra from the night before, amid fond memories of how it had gotten there. "Yes, we had dinner. But it wasn't a 'date.' " She said the word with implied air quotes.

"Uh huh," Kate said. "So, he didn't stay over?"

Rose was silent.

"Just what I thought," Kate said.

"Are you being smug?" Rose demanded. "Because you sound smug."

"Maybe a little. So does this mean you two are on again?"

"No, it does not." Walking around the house, cleaning up before work, Rose saw something on top of her refrigerator, investigated, and discovered that the pink, silky lump was last night's panties. You had to admire a man whose lovemaking resulted in panties on top of the refrigerator.

"Why *not*?" Kate's voice had the whiny tone of a toddler asking why she couldn't have ice cream.

"Because. It's just ... I'll admit I had a moment of weakness last night. More than a moment. More like ... Okay, it was about twelve hours of weakness. But that doesn't mean anything's changed. It's still a really bad idea for me to get involved with him right now. With everything that's going on."

"Honey, you're already involved."

"Yes, well, considering that I'm carrying his child, it's fair to say that." Rose sighed, closed her eyes, and pressed a hand to her forehead. "But emotionally, I can't go there, Kate. I just can't." She plopped down onto her sofa, the panties still in her hand.

"Well, he's already there. Do you really think it's fair to keep sleeping with him, knowing he's got feelings for you, if you aren't planning to see it through?" Kate sounded like a stern mother. Rose expected the next words out of her mouth to be, *I'm very disappointed in you, young lady.*

"You have a point," Rose admitted.

"So, you're going to give him a chance?"

"No. I'm going to stop sleeping with him."

Giving that up was going to be about as easy as giving up breathing. But it had to be done, for her sake and for the baby's.

"You're an idiot," Kate said.

"Hey."

Kate's voice softened. "Sweetie, you know I love you. I just don't think you're seeing the big picture."

Rose felt tears come to her eyes, and she swiped them away with her fingertips.

"Okay, well, thank you for your advice. But I really have to go now. I have to get ready for work."

"Rose—"

Rose hung up on her. She wasn't mad at Kate, not really. But she didn't want Kate to chip away at her resolve. Her resolve was already crumbling as it was.

Will was feeling pretty good that morning. The night he'd spent with Rose had him singing under his breath as he went about his daily routine at Cooper House. He checked the pool filter, which seemed to be working fine since his repairs. The gardeners had been there the day before, but they hadn't trimmed the hedges surrounding the rose garden on the house's east side. He'd have to call and get them back out here.

He took a spin through the main house to make sure the cleaning crew had dusted inside Chris's action figure case. Sometimes they didn't, and Will didn't blame them. Who really wanted to remove two hundred superhero action figures and then get them back exactly in the same places? But God help them if Chris showed up on the spur of the moment—which rarely happened—and there was dust inside his action figure case. Will checked it out, and it looked good. He left the room humming, and did a little dance move in the doorway.

Okay, so he hadn't won Rose over completely yet. She hadn't told him about the baby, and he figured that was a sure sign that she didn't fully trust him. Also, she had shut down a little as he'd said goodbye. He could see it in her face, in the set of her chin. But his memories of last night were so vivid, so lovely, that he couldn't let that bother him. He'd show her that he could be who she needed him to be, and then he would be that. And then they'd be together—all three of them. A family.

In the meantime, he had to act like a guy who was ready to support that family. It was time to stop delaying and finish his dissertation. His morning rounds at the main house done, he went back to his cottage and settled in at his laptop to write.

The data was solid, and he had all he needed. As tempting as it was to spend more time out on the beach with his birds, he knew that was just a delaying tactic, a way to hold off the demands that would come with moving his career forward. And while it would be so much easier to just keep checking the dust under a set of plastic action figures, at this point in his life, more was required of him.

He sat down and got to work.

Will was making some real progress on his manuscript when his cell phone, which was sitting next to his laptop on the desk, pinged. He checked it, and he froze when he saw Chris's message:

Hey, buddy. Just wanted to let you know Melinda's coming to Cooper House early for the wedding. She'll arrive on Saturday. I'll be there the following Friday. Said she needed a little getaway. Get the place ready for her?

Will felt his limbs go cold. Melinda was going to be on the property for six days, without Chris. It would be just the two of them. And she was still acting like a crazy stalker.

What could he do? It wasn't like he could refuse to let her come. It was Chris's place, not his. He couldn't quit, or he'd have no place to live.

He considered faking a family emergency. He could say that his great aunt was ill, and he had to return to his ancestral home to be with her. But he didn't have a great aunt, nor did he have an ancestral home.

Melinda wasn't coming here for a getaway before the wedding, he was sure of it. She was coming here to mess with him. How was he supposed to handle her? He felt about as prepared for this as he was to fly a 747.

He needed advice, and he thought about who he could ask. Jackson had a lot of experience with women—far more than

Will had—but as far as Will knew, Jackson had never dealt with a ridiculously persistent one who was hooked up with his boss, but who was relentlessly pursuing him.

But then again, who had?

There was a lot to do in the run-up to the wedding, and one of the biggest jobs was getting the old barn on the Delaney Ranch ready for the reception.

The ceremony would be held at the lodge, on the lawn in front of the gazebo. But the reception was going to be in the cavernous, picturesque barn that the Delaneys had retired about eleven or twelve years ago when they'd had a new, state-of-the-art one built. Gen had been using the barn as studio space for her artist-in-residence program, but she'd found alternate accommodations for the current artist until after the proceedings.

Will was over at the ranch a day or two after the text about Melinda, helping Daniel string white lights from the roof of the barn.

One of the things about Will's flexible work schedule was that he was always being recruited by his friends to help with this or that, and he could never claim to have an important meeting or a big client in from back East. Same with Daniel. As an artist, his schedule was his own.

Not that Will minded. This kind of thing helped him to avoid his dissertation when he wanted to, which was handy. And now that he didn't want to avoid his dissertation—he just wanted to get it done—at least the task gave him the opportunity to approach Daniel about the Melinda problem.

Daniel didn't know about the baby—Will figured that was Rose's to tell, when she was ready—but he knew about the crazy ex, and Will thought he could use whatever help he could get with that particular situation.

Will was on a ladder, with Daniel on the ground feeding strings of lights up to him, when he casually brought up the issue.

"So, my ex is coming up to Cooper House on Saturday." He hammered a nail and looped the wire of the string of lights around it. "Without Chris."

"Well, that's awkward," Daniel said. The roof of the barn was high—about thirty feet up—and Will felt a brief and disturbing sense of vertigo as he peered down at him.

"It is," Will agreed. He pounded another nail, attached more lights.

"Especially after she kissed you in the wine cellar," Daniel observed.

The two of them had been at it with the ladder and the lights for a while now, and they were both dusty and sweaty. They were taking turns regarding who would get on the ladder and who would be the guy on the ground. While they did this, Ryan was busy painting the outside of the barn, something that had been overdue for years. Most of the painting was done, but there was still some trim to finish up. Will regretted the fact that Ryan was out of earshot, because Will would have appreciated his take on the Melinda situation as well.

"The thing is," Will said, during pauses in his hammering, "it wasn't just the kiss. There have been text messages."

"What kind of text messages?" Daniel fed more lights up to Will.

"Ah … *You can't ignore me. You're not going to get away with treating me like this.* That sort of thing."

"Uh oh," Daniel said.

"Yeah."

Will climbed down from the ladder, moved it a couple of feet to the left, and climbed up again.

"And she's coming here alone."

"That's right."

"Well, shit."

"Right."

Will hammered and strung lights while they both thought about that. Sweat was dripping into Will's eyes, and he wiped it away with the back of his arm.

"Well, that's going to be uncomfortable at best, and at worst, it's going to end with you losing your job," Daniel summed up.

"And my home," Will added.

"And then there's Rose," Daniel said. "How's she going to feel about you being on the property alone with a woman you used to sleep with, and who now actively wants to sleep with you?"

Will nodded, steadied himself on the ladder, and hammered another nail. "That about covers it." He looked down at Daniel. "So, what do I do?"

Daniel ran a hand through thick, dark hair that was cropped short. He propped his hands on his hips. "Well, you've just got to get through a week, and then the wedding will be over and she'll be gone."

"Right."

"You could always take the approach of being really busy that week," Daniel suggested. "Always on the run, never around at Cooper House. 'So sorry, Melinda. I can't stop to chat about your sexual needs. I've got to arrange place cards for the reception.' That kind of thing."

"I'm a man. Men don't arrange place cards," Will said.

"You're stringing fairy lights. Don't get cocky."

"Good point."

Will climbed down from the ladder. It was good to have his feet on solid ground again.

"Or." Daniel continued his train of thought about Melinda. "You could have it out with her. Tell her that breaking up with her was the sanest thing you've ever done, and you wouldn't sleep with her if she were the last woman on earth and the future of mankind depended on it."

"That's harsh," Will said. "But true."

"Or, Plan C, you could tell Chris about her behavior. Show him the crazy-ass texts. Then he dumps her, and you're done with the whole deal."

Will rubbed at the stubble on his chin. "That's got some appeal. But people have been known to blame the messenger. And I need this job, at least until I finish my dissertation."

"How's that going, by the way?"

"Good." Will nodded. "Finally, it's good. It's coming along. I just need a little more time."

They moved the ladder to the other side of the barn, and Daniel climbed up so they could drape another string of lights over the area where the guests would be sitting. Will handed the hammer and nails up to him, and then a string of lights.

"So, which plan do you like?" Daniel wanted to know.

Will considered the question. "I'm leaning toward a combination. Tell her that breaking up with her is the sanest thing I've ever done, and then make myself scarce and stay away from Cooper House until she's gone."

"Sounds reasonable." Daniel hammered a nail into place and attached a string of lights to it. "And then you can always fall back on Plan C if nothing else works."

Ryan appeared in the doorway to the barn, his T-shirt and jeans speckled with paint. "How's it going in here?"

"We're lucky we haven't killed ourselves falling off this damned ladder," Daniel said. "Whose idea was this? God-damned fairy lights thirty feet up?"

"That would be Gen," Ryan said.

"Ah, shit. I can't be irritated with a happy bride. Especially not one as beautiful as Gen," Daniel said.

"Get your mind off how beautiful my future wife is." Ryan came into the barn and looked up, appraising their work. "Though I can't argue with you."

Daniel got down off the ladder, and they flipped the switch to turn on the hundreds of little lights. The three of them stood in a line, peering upward. In the dim afternoon light filtering into the barn, the lights looked like a blanket of stars in an early evening sky.

"Gen's going to love it. Thanks, you guys." Ryan slapped them both on the back.

"How's the painting coming along?" Will asked.

Ryan grinned at him. "Since you asked, I could use a little help. Why don't you boys grab that ladder and come on outside?"

Ryan went out, and Daniel glared at Will. "You just had to ask, didn't you?"

Chapter Twenty-Five

Rose was so bloated that she'd barely gotten her pants buttoned that morning. And she was cranky. And she was simultaneously nauseated and so hungry she wanted to eat the entire contents of the Cookie Crock Market.

Pregnancy sucked, and it was only the first trimester.

She was supposed to meet her mother for breakfast before going to work, and she wasn't in the mood for it. But then again, she was rarely in the mood for Pamela.

She'd considered ways to get out of it—excuses like helping Gen with wedding prep or being called in to work early—but in the end she'd decided that avoiding her mother was childish. Maybe she was maturing, and maybe it was the maternal hormones rushing through her body, but she decided that it would be a good thing to try to bond with her mom.

After all, she was going to be a mother herself. She would need her mother's insight, if only to give her a guide for what not to do.

Rose arrived at her mother's beach house at a little after eight. She knocked and cracked the door open, and was surprised to hear her mother singing. Her mother didn't sing.

"Mom?" Rose called as she came in.

"Oh, Rose. Come in. I've just about gotten everything ready." Pamela came out of the kitchen holding a pitcher of orange juice. She placed it on the little dining table, which was arranged with pretty place settings and a vase of flowers in the center.

"Wow. This looks great." Rose could smell bacon cooking, and there was a plate of pancakes on the table, along with a bowl of fluffy scrambled eggs. When Pamela had invited her over for breakfast, Rose had pictured an array of pastries from the bakery along with a fruit salad from the market. Pamela didn't cook. At least, she never had in Rose's memory. That's what employees and caterers were for.

"Just sit right down while everything's still hot," Pamela said.

"You cooked," Rose said. "And you look … happy. What the hell's going on?"

"Oh, stop." Pamela waved Rose's comments away with her hand. "I just had a good morning, that's all. I went for a walk and I saw a family of deer crossing the road. There really are quite a lot of deer here. Charming. And then I went out onto the path that leads through … oh, I can't remember the name of it. But it was a lovely natural area overlooking the water."

"Fiscalini Ranch?" Rose provided.

"Yes, that's it. Thank you. Such beautiful wildflowers. And sea lions, down on the rocks. It was lovely. Rose, you really are quite fortunate to live here."

Rose made a show of going out the door and checking the address on the front of the house to make sure she'd arrived in the right place. She came back in, saying, "Yep, this is the address. Now what did you do with my mother?"

And then, the most unexpected thing happened. Pamela actually *laughed*.

Not only that, but Pamela had put some of the decorations that had come with the house back up on the walls. A sign reading, HEAVEN IS A LITTLE CLOSER IN A HOME BY THE WATER was back in its original spot over the fireplace. There was still no sign of the garden gnome in the front yard, however.

"Mom. Did something … happen?" Rose asked as she sat down at the table and spooned some eggs onto her plate.

"No. Why?"

"You just seem different. Kind of … well, jeez. I'll just say it. You seem happy."

Pamela poured herself a glass of orange juice from the pitcher. "Well, for goodness sake, you act like you've never seen me happy before."

"If the shoe fits …"

"Rosemary."

"I'm sorry." Rose filled her plate with pancakes and bacon. "It's just … I thought you didn't really like it here."

"Well, I'd have preferred the house I originally reserved. But I'm making the best of things."

That actually seemed to be true. Pamela had never been one to make the best of things. Pamela's instinct, when faced with a circumstance that was less than ideal, was usually to bend everyone else to her will.

"So, how is the wedding preparation coming along?" Pamela asked. Her voice sounded chirpy. It was unsettling, and maybe a little bit creepy.

"Fine. Really fine. I've just about nailed down all the non-RSVPers. Lacy's got the place cards finished. Kate's written a really nice speech for the reception. And Will says the barn looks great." Rose mentally winced as she realized her mistake of mentioning Will. Now her mother was going to ask about him, and Rose wouldn't know what to say.

"How is your young man?" Pamela inquired, right on cue.

"Oh, here we go."

"Where exactly is that, dear?" Pamela smiled placidly.

"I just know how you work, Mom. You're going to grill me about Will, and then when that's done, you're going to tell me all the reasons we're not right for each other. Well, he's not my young man, so you can just forget it." Rose gave the speech with a piece of bacon trembling on the end of her fork.

Where Pamela usually would have stiffened and pressed her lips into a tight line at this point in the conversation, instead, she smiled.

"Nonsense, dear. He seems lovely."

Rose's eyes widened. "He does?"

"Of course."

Rose reached over and pressed her hand to her mother's forehead. "Huh. No fever. I could have sworn you were delirious."

Pamela glared at her. "Rosemary."

Rose knew that she was pressing her luck by taunting her mother. But sparring with Pamela was a habit she'd never had occasion to break. And anyway, Rose had the nagging suspicion that with the good humor and cheer, Pamela was somehow setting her up. Rose would relax, reveal something she wasn't ready to reveal—like the presence of a third party at the table—and then Pamela would revert to her usual form, all fiery judgment and scorn.

Rose wasn't having it.

"So," Pamela tried again. "Why, exactly, isn't he your young man? I thought things between you were going quite swimmingly."

"I wouldn't say that."

"Why not? What happened between you?"

"Oh, nothing," Rose deadpanned. "I just wouldn't say that. The word. 'Swimmingly.' "

Pamela let out a sigh and put down her fork. "Oh, Rosemary. Can't you see that I'm trying?"

Rose could, and the least she could do was give something back. "Okay. The truth is, nothing happened between me and Will. It's fine. We're fine. I'm just not sure that I'm ready to get into a big, involved relationship."

"And that's what he wants? A big, involved, relationship?"

"Apparently."

"Well." Pamela picked up the napkin from her lap, dabbed her lips with it, and draped it carefully back over her linen slacks. "I'd always pictured you with someone high-powered. A lawyer, perhaps. Or someone high-placed in corporate business."

"Here we go," Rose said again.

"But you clearly aren't interested in going that direction," Pamela continued as though Rose hadn't spoken. "And, given the kind of lifestyle you do seem to prefer, Will seems like a good match for you."

Was there implied scorn? Had there been something withering in Pamela's voice when she referred to Rose's lifestyle? Oddly, there hadn't been. And if Pamela's comment hadn't implied scorn, had it then implied … *acceptance*?

Rose had always thought that if her mother were to one day stop criticizing her, she'd feel the peace only experienced by accomplished yogis. But instead, she felt exposed, like a tortoise without its shell.

She'd been wolfing down eggs, pancakes, and bacon, but now she felt the food sitting uncomfortably in her stomach. Maybe that was daughterly angst, and maybe it was the baby.

God, how was she going to tell her mother about the baby?

"You look a little green, dear," Pamela observed.

"I just … uh …" Rose got up from the table and wheeled around, trying to remember where the bathroom was in the unfamiliar house. When the answer didn't immediately come to her, she darted out the front door, bent over, and vomited on the spot where the garden gnome had once stood.

Pamela stood in the doorway, grimacing.

"If you had a stomach virus, you shouldn't have come." She shuddered delicately.

“I don’t have a virus,” Rose said. She straightened, went inside, and rinsed her mouth out with water from the kitchen sink. Then she went back outside to hose down the place were the gnome would one day live again, secure in the knowledge that it had escaped disaster.

Will was working furiously on his dissertation, his head fully absorbed in the minutiae of bird adaptation, when the intercom mounted in his kitchen buzzed. Someone was at the security gate.

He went to the intercom and pushed the TALK button. “May I help you?”

“Is that Will?” a voice inquired.

“Yes, this is Will. May I help you?” he asked again.

“Will, this is Pamela Watkins.” She added, unnecessarily, “Rose’s mother.”

Will felt a jolt of panic. This couldn’t be good.

“Of course, Mrs. Watkins. I’ll open the gate.” He pushed the button to roll back the big iron gate that protected the property from intruders and solicitors. If only there were a moat.

He was nervously waiting outside the guest house when Pamela came driving up in her rental car.

The other times Will had seen Pamela, she’d been wearing designer suits, the kind he imagined women of a certain age wore to meetings about charity galas. So he was surprised when she got out of the car looking much more casual in a pair of white capris and a camel-colored sweater with the cuffs and collar of a crisp white shirt peeking out from underneath. It was the kind of ensemble Martha Stewart might wear to browse for antiques. He liked her better this way.

“Mrs. Watkins. What can I do for you?” He was slouching, his hands stuffed into the pockets of faded jeans, his T-shirt on its second wearing. He was wearing flip-flops, and his hair was mussed. Only now did he realize the impression he must be making.

"May I come in?" She gestured toward the guest house. "I have something I'd like to discuss."

"Of course."

Was there ever a time when the sentence *I have something I'd like to discuss* led to something positive? Usually, such a sentence didn't precede the news that you'd gotten a promotion or won the lottery. It was more commonly associated with breakups and firings. Since Will didn't work for Pamela and he wasn't romantically involved with her, he figured he was at least safe from those.

He ushered her into the small house and panicked a little when he saw what a mess it was. His dining room table was covered in the detritus of his research, papers and notebooks surrounding his open laptop.

"Here, please sit down." He ushered her to the sofa, where he had to remove a small pile of clean laundry he hadn't yet folded and put away. "It's not usually this messy." He clutched the clothes to his chest. "It's just ... you caught me in the middle of working on my dissertation. I kind of put off doing anything else."

"I see." Pamela sat primly on the edge of the sofa. Will offered her a glass of ice water, and when she accepted, he went to get it from the kitchen.

By the time they were both settled into the small sitting area, Will had worked himself up into a substantial case of nerves. What could she want? What kind of trouble, exactly, was he in?

He took a drink from his own water glass in the hope that it would buy him time to compose himself. But while he was drinking, Pamela said, "So, I understand that you've impregnated my daughter."

Will choked, drawing a fair amount of the water into his trachea. He coughed, barely avoiding spewing water onto Pamela's crisp white capris.

When the spasms of coughing subsided, he sputtered, "What?"

"So you're saying it's not true?"

"Ah … no. I guess what I'm saying is that I'm surprised you know about it."

"Well." Pamela sat with her purse—Will supposed she'd call it a pocketbook—on her lap. "That was refreshingly honest."

"I guess I don't see the point in lying when the cat's already out of the bag, so to speak."

Somehow, the idea of the baby had been abstract up until now, but talking about it with Pamela made it real. He felt a little sick, and he felt his hands shaking.

"Why, you've gone positively white," Pamela observed.

"Look, Mrs. Watkins …" Will began.

"Call me Pamela."

"All right. Pamela. I don't know for certain that Rose is pregnant, but I suspect that she is." His voice sounded surprisingly steady to his own ears.

"You mean she hasn't told you?" Pamela seemed shocked by this development.

"No."

"Is it possible that … there's some mistake?"

Will thought that what she really wanted to ask was, *Is it possible that it's not your child?* The fact that she hadn't asked it raised her a bit in Will's estimation.

"Maybe you should have this conversation with Rose." Will squirmed a little, uncomfortable with the way this all was going.

"I would." Pamela smacked her purse down on the table beside her. "But if I asked, she wouldn't tell me."

"That makes two of us," Will muttered.

"Well." She folded her hands atop her knees. "What I'd like to know is, what do you plan to do about it?"

While the rest of the conversation so far had been hard, this part was easy. "I plan to be a father to our child and a partner to Rose in whatever way she'll have me." The words came easily, because he knew what he wanted, because every word of it was true. "I don't suppose she'll marry me—not right away, anyway—but if she ever decides she's ready for that, then that's what we'll do. In the meantime, I'm going to be there for her, for the baby, in every way I can."

Pamela's eyes widened, and she was very still. It was clear to Will that she hadn't expected that answer. What had she expected, then? That he was packing his things for an abrupt escape to another country?

"You're a student," Pamela said. "A *caretaker*." The sound in her voice when she said the word wasn't disdain so much as emphasis—as though she were trying to make him understand a fact he hadn't quite comprehended before now.

"Yes. I am. And I'm working very hard to finish my dissertation so I can get work in my field. Which will be much more financially stable than caretaking."

"I see."

Pamela sat, still and quiet, for a few moments. Then she picked up her purse, stood, and headed for the front door. When she reached it, she turned and extended her hand for Will to shake.

"Thank you for meeting with me today, Will. It's been enlightening."

Will wasn't sure where this left them. They hadn't come to any kind of understanding, though Pamela seemed somehow satisfied that she'd gotten what she came for.

"Are you going to tell Rose that you know? Or that I know?" Will asked, releasing her hand.

"Oh, I don't think so."

"You're not?" That came as a surprise.

Pamela tilted her head back slightly to create the illusion that she was looking down on him, though he was taller than she was by a good four inches. Will could imagine Rose being on the receiving end of that look throughout her childhood.

"Will," she said. "If I were to tell Rose what I suspect, she would immediately erect walls so high and thick that they would rival those at San Quentin." She raised her eyebrows. "Do you think I'm wrong?"

"Uh ..." He straightened his glasses. "No. I think you're probably right."

"And that's why you've kept quiet about it as well." It wasn't a question.

"Yeah."

"Good, then. We understand each other. And we both understand Rose." She nodded at him, a crisp *goodbye* nod that one might see in a movie about British royals, and walked out the door.

Will had been working with the assumption that Pamela didn't understand Rose at all. But now he realized he might have to reassess in light of her spot-on analysis. That was one thing to consider. The other was that she'd clearly come here to size him up, and had left without telling him her conclusions.

Well, she was going to have to accept him, one way or another. He was her grandchild's father, and that much wasn't going to change.

He was here to stay, whether Pamela Watkins liked it or not.

Chapter Twenty-Six

With only a week to go until the wedding, Gen was getting nervous. She hadn't been nervous before; at least, she didn't seem that way to Rose. But now, with the countdown nearing its end, she was losing her usual calm, forcing her friends to ply her with liberal amounts of wine just to keep her functioning.

"Ryan's cousin Richard isn't coming! Which wouldn't be a big deal, since Ryan barely even knows his cousin Richard, except for the fact that five people—five!—now want to bring additional, uninvited guests to take his spot!" Gen was pacing, her wild, red curls in a state of disarray that mirrored her mood. "Do you have any idea what kind of family politics are involved in deciding who gets Richard's spot? Do you?!"

Rose, Kate, and Lacy were sitting in the living room of Gen's new house with a seating chart spread open on the coffee table in front of them. The empty spot was at Table Five, between Ryan's aunt Molly and Gen's second cousin Jake.

"And then there's the goddamned seating chart!" Gen went on. "You'd think I could just drop whoever gets the spot into the seat I was going to give to Richard. But, no. Oh, no! Depending on who it is, I'm potentially going to have to scrap the whole thing and start over!"

"Honey." Kate got up from the sofa, went to Gen, and put a hand on her arm. "This isn't a disaster. This is just … a detail. None of this matters. Whoever sits in the open spot at Table Five, you're still going to be married to Ryan a week from now. That's what's important." She rubbed Gen's arm with gentle strokes.

"Right. It's just a detail," Gen said. "That's what you'd think. That's what they want you to think."

"Who?" Kate looked mystified.

"The people who write the bridal magazines with all those happy, glowing brides!" Gen picked up one of the magazines in question and threw it onto the coffee table with a smack. "They want you to think that it's all about love, and butterflies, and … and champagne flutes! But in fact, if I put Ryan's cousin's girlfriend in that spot, then my uncle's secretary's daughter is going to be all bent out of shape, and she's going to call my aunt Eleanor, and my aunt Eleanor is like a pit bull with a goddamned chew toy when she wants something, and she's going to call everyone I know, and *I will never hear the end of it.* Never!" Gen fell into the club chair that was positioned to one side of the sofa, her arms and legs limp.

"Sweetie, you need a drink. And a hot bath. And … I don't know. You need to watch some mindless television and forget about all this for a while," Lacy suggested.

"Ugh. I can't. Everybody who wants Richard's seat needs to know *yesterday* whether they're going to get it. Because there are flights to book, reservations to make …" Gen plunged her hands into her hair.

"I'll tell you what," Rose said. "Put me in charge of the seating chart. I'll do rock-paper-scissors and pick somebody, and then all the malcontents can blame me. When they complain, you can roll your eyes and tell them how badly I bungled everything. Then you can tell them—sorrowfully, of course—that it's just too late to fix my screwup."

Gen sat up straight and looked at Rose. "That's not bad."

"There you go," Lacy said in a soothing voice. "Rose will take the fall, and you and Ryan will live happily ever after."

"That's really good," Gen said thoughtfully. "That could work. Rose, you're a great friend."

"This is true," Rose agreed.

"Just pick whoever you want," Gen said, calmer now. She closed her eyes and leaned back in the chair. "I don't care anymore."

Rose looked over the list of potential invitees. "Well, I guess I can cross Ryan's ex-girlfriend off this list."

"No!" Gen's eyes flew open.

"No?" Rose said.

"I may or may not have this little, immature fantasy about her coming to the wedding and ruing the day she let him go." Gen sighed. "If she loses rock-paper-scissors, then so be it. But I want to have my fantasy a little while longer."

After they dealt with the seating chart crisis, the seamstress came over so they could all do the final fittings for their dresses. Doing that in the last week before the wedding had seemed to Rose to be cutting it close, but the seamstress had insisted that people gain or lose weight in the emotional turmoil of wedding planning, so it was best to do a fitting just one week out.

Rose shouldn't have been surprised when the zipper of her dress—a silky, swooping, blush-pink strapless number with a tea-length skirt—wouldn't go up. But she was. The first thing she thought was, *I'm only eight weeks pregnant. I can't be getting bigger yet.* But then she realized that the first trimester of pregnancy had brought with it a ravenous hunger that had her eating constantly and indiscriminately. So, there was that.

"Oh, my," the seamstress said as she tugged at Rose's zipper, to no avail.

"Well," Kate said, appraising Rose with her hands on her hips. "You *have* been eating like a lumberjack."

"I can't help it!" Rose wailed. "It's the hormones! I'm hungry all the time! What am I supposed to do, starve the baby?"

The seamstress raised an eyebrow at Rose. "You're pregnant? You might have mentioned that before."

"I didn't think it would matter! I'm only eight weeks!" For some reason, it was this—the bridesmaid dress being too tight to zip—that threw her into despair about the pregnancy. Up until now, she'd been holding herself together well, probably because the idea of a baby seven months from now seemed abstract and obscure. But now, the fact of her expanding waistline was impossible to ignore, and she burst into tears.

"Oh, hey," Gen said, rushing over to Rose and rubbing her back. "Don't worry. It's okay. Sheila can fix it. You can, can't you, Sheila?"

"Of course." The seamstress nodded crisply. "That's what these final fittings are for."

"See?" Gen said encouragingly.

"No, she can't!" Rose wailed. "Sheila can't fix the fact that I'm single and pregnant, and my job doesn't pay enough to support a baby, and I'm never going to be able to go to college now. And Sheila can't fix it that … that Will's probably going to forget he ever knew me as soon as he knows that I'm knocked up. Can you fix all that, Sheila? Can you?!"

"Well, no," Sheila allowed.

"Oh, Rose. If you really think Will's going to abandon you and the baby, then I don't think you're giving him enough credit," Lacy said. Lacy, looking radiant in the same bridesmaid gown that Rose couldn't zip, gazed at her with concern.

"You know, she's right," Gen said. Gen, whose own fitting was done, was the odd one out in jeans and a T-shirt. "I don't think you're being fair to him."

Rose dropped into Gen's club chair, the half-zipped dress billowing around her like a silky cloud. "I don't know," she said miserably. "I'd leave me if I were him."

"No, you wouldn't," Kate said.

Rose let out a sigh. "No. I guess I wouldn't."

"You're just scared," Lacy said. "Anyone would be. But it's going to be okay. And if you'd just tell him—"

"I can't!" Rose wailed.

"If you'd just tell him," Lacy tried again, "then you'd see that he's a better man than you're giving him credit for."

"You don't get it." Rose shook her head and wiped the tears from her face. "I don't want him to stay with me *because he's a good man.* I want him to stay with me *because he wants to be with me.* And once I tell him … once he knows …"

"Then you won't know which it is," Kate finished for her.

"Right!"

The others were all gathered around Rose as she cried. Kate was perched on the arm of the sofa, Gen was sitting on the coffee table, and Lacy was kneeling next to Rose's chair. They all formed a protective barrier around her, and she wished she could just go through life that way, with her friends shielding her from anything that might hurt her.

"You know, at some point, you're just going to have to trust him," Kate said.

"I don't know how," Rose said in a voice that was small and scared.

"You do it by just … deciding to do it," Gen said.

"Listen," Sheila said from where she was hovering in the doorway to the living room. "I hate to interrupt, but I've got another appointment at two. If I could just take Rose's measurements …"

Rose took a deep breath, wiped her eyes, and hoisted her new, heavier body out of the chair. "Let's do it," she said. "I'll have time to cry some more later."

❖

Melinda had arrived on Saturday, as scheduled. He didn't see her much the first couple of days, and Will wondered if that was because she was setting some kind of trap. He stayed away from Cooper House as much as he could, working with his laptop and his research notes at a table at Jitters during the day. In the evenings, he spent his time working on Project Rose.

They'd fallen into a pattern: He would ask her out, she would refuse, and he would show up at De-Vine when she got off work as though she'd never turned him down. She'd see him, make some noises about how she had things to do at home, and he'd persuade her to have dinner with him or just take a walk with him. Sometimes it resulted in him going back to her place and spending the night. When it didn't, that was fine, too. Just spending an hour or two with her before going back to Cooper House gave him the strength and comfort he needed to get through the following day.

He figured, if they kept this up long enough, she'd have to admit they had a relationship. And once she admitted it, well, that was something they could build on.

He was at Jitters, working on his dissertation and thinking about what he could do that evening to persuade Rose to see a movie with him, when his phone dinged with a text.

I can't figure out the remote for the TV. Please come to the main house and help me.

Melinda.

He texted back:

Sorry, I can't. I'm not on the property. Call Chris, I'm sure he can help.

Will supposed it was less than subtle of him to mention Chris—reminding Melinda that she had a boyfriend, and it wasn't Will—but he was willing to try anything.

Less than an hour later, she texted again:

The water in the pool isn't warm enough. I need you to come and adjust the heater.

Will rolled his eyes, took a deep breath, and then texted back:

Again, I'm not on the property. Call Chris. He can tell you how to do it yourself.

When an hour went by without any further texts, he figured she'd given up. With a latte and a scone in front of him, he delved into his work. He was fully absorbed in a chapter detailing his conclusions about the increase in the snowy plover's bill length when his phone dinged again.

This time, it wasn't Melinda. It was Chris.

Mel says she needs help with some things at the house, and you're refusing. What's going on???

Will considered the option of drowning his phone in his coffee, but then he remembered how expensive phones were and how many student loan payments he had ahead of him. Instead, he responded:

What's going on, as I explained to Melinda, is that I'm not on the property. I'm doing errands in town. I didn't think it was urgent.

In a moment, Chris texted back:

Got it. I'll tell her to be patient. If you could help her out when you get home, I'd appreciate it.

Telling Melinda to be patient was like telling the ocean not to be wet, so Will had little expectation that it would help. The only thing he could do was delay going home a little longer.

He finished his latte and wrote another paragraph, trying not to stress himself out about what Melinda was going to do, but failing miserably.

Lacy came over to his table and picked up his empty mug. "Get you another coffee?" she offered.

"No, thanks. I'm good."

"Really?" Lacy looked at him appraisingly. "Because you don't look like you're good. You look like you're worried about something."

"Is it that obvious?" He looked at Lacy miserably.

"Yeah, it is. So, what's up?"

Will took a moment to privately assess the situation. Lacy certainly knew about Rose's pregnancy—assuming Rose was, in fact, pregnant, which he thought was a fair bet. Lacy though that Will *didn't* know, but seeing him brooding at his table with Dostoyevskian angst, she probably wondered whether he'd figured it out. He wasn't quite ready to tip his hand yet, so it would be good to make her think he was still in the dark. Also, when Melinda made her inevitable move against him—whatever that turned out to be—the more people who knew what she was really up to, the better.

"Have a seat, and I'll give you the short version," Will said.

Lacy sat, and Will closed his laptop and gathered his papers into a neat pile.

"Did Rose tell you about what's going on with my ex?"

"You mean the stuff about the crazy stalker texting?"

"Exactly. Well, she's at Cooper House from now until the wedding, and she's still doing it." He was telling her this partly as a means to his own ends, sure. But it was also possible that Lacy might have some useful advice for him. Lacy was a woman, and Melinda was a woman. Maybe Lacy spoke Melinda's strange and unfathomable language. Will most assuredly did not.

"You mean she's there alone? Without Christopher Mills?"

"Yes."

"Oh, boy."

"Exactly. Lacy, you're a girl."

She gave him a wry grin. "Nice that you noticed."

"What is Melinda after?" He raised his hands helplessly, then let them drop. "She doesn't want me. She never did. We used to fight over all of the many, many ways she thought I wasn't good enough for her. So what is she doing? What's the point?"

Lacy leaned forward and propped her elbow on the table, her chin resting on her hand. "I don't know Melinda, but I know women like her. And I think it's more about competition than anything. Rose said she tried to kiss you."

"Yeah."

"And you blew her off."

"Well … of course I did."

"Right. Okay, here's how I see it. You two broke up, and that was fine, because she hooked up with a mega gazillionaire and that made her the winner. But then she saw you with Rose, and you seemed to be happier with her than you ever were with Melinda."

"I didn't just seem to be happier," Will put in. "I was."

"Okay. So Melinda had to kiss you, because if you kissed her back, she was still the winner. It would mean you preferred her over Rose. But you didn't kiss her back."

"And I don't prefer her over Rose," Will said. "Just to be clear."

"Sure," Lacy agreed. "So now, Melinda is a double loser. Not only did you break up with her, but you also refused her advances. Now, what does a compulsive gambler do when he's losing and he really needs to turn things around fast?"

If it were Will, he'd leave the table with his chips and call it a lesson learned. But he'd never been much of a gambler.

"He bets more?" Will guessed.

"Exactly." Lacy looked at him with satisfaction.

Will thought about that. "She's escalating because she doesn't want to walk away a loser."

"I think so," Lacy said.

"So, how do I make this stop? Tell her that Rose is dead to me and I'll only love Melinda until the day I die?"

"Well." Lacy cocked her head slightly in thought. "That would probably do it, but being a winner is no fun if no one else knows about it. So, she'd probably tell Chris, Rose, and whoever else she could get to listen that you'd declared your love for her."

"So, no, then. It's good I didn't do that."

"Probably," Lacy agreed.

Will raked his hands through his hair. "Well … I appreciate your analysis. I do. And I think it's probably right. But what I need now is advice. How do I make this stop?"

She sat back in her chair and looked at him with pity. "That, I don't know. I guess you've just got to Melinda-proof yourself and wait it out until she moves on to something else."

"Melinda-proof?"

"Sure. You know, make it so she doesn't have anything to use against you."

"Which I accomplish how, exactly?" He was growing increasingly flustered by this conversation, even though Lacy was offering him some valuable insight.

She shrugged. "I guess you do it by telling Rose everything she's done and everything she's doing, so there won't be any surprises if Melinda decides to pull something."

"I've done that already. Rose knows everything."

"Good." Lacy looked impressed. "That's good. Most men would freak out and try to keep everything a secret, hoping it'll all go away. You've got good instincts."

"Thanks, I guess." He fiddled with his glasses and thought about what she'd said. "Does that mean I should tell Chris everything, too?"

"Oh, God no. Maybe your instincts aren't as good as I thought."

"But why? You just said—"

"I said to tell *Rose* everything. Rose is inclined to believe you, because she cares about you, and because she doesn't give a rat's ass about Melinda. But Chris is sleeping with Melinda, which gives her the edge with him. A pretty considerable edge."

"Ah."

They sat there and thought about his dilemma for a while. Jitters was mostly empty this time of day, so Lacy had the time.

"Oh!" she said finally, sitting up straight in her chair.

"What?"

"I know! I know what you should do!"

He hoped fervently that she had something, some idea for how to navigate this minefield of female competitiveness. "I really want that to be true."

"You use Daniel," she said, a note of triumph in her voice.

"Okay. How?"

Lacy leaned forward, her elbows on the café table, apparently excited about her plan. "You get him to make a move on her at the wedding. It's perfect. Think about it. A hot guy—an artist, which makes him more interesting—flirts with her, dances with her, maybe makes an overt pass at her. It's going to distract her from you, and with luck, you'll get through the wedding and reception without her making a scene. At least, one that involves you." She screwed up her face in thought. "Actually, Jackson would be perfect for this. But he's off the market now, so …"

"I hate to do that to Daniel," Will fretted. "I lose a crazy stalker but he gains one?"

"Yeah, but he's not in a relationship, so she can't hurt him there. And he's also not employed by Christopher Mills. She doesn't have any ammunition against him."

What Lacy said was true. What could Melinda possibly do to Daniel if things went badly? Get him in trouble with his girl-friend? He didn't have one. Cause problems with his employer? He didn't have one of those, either. If Melinda were truly crazy, and presented some kind of physical risk, then the plan would be a no-go. But she wasn't. At least, not as far as Will knew.

"That could actually work," he said.

"Of course it could!" Lacy grinned.

"Will he do it?" Will wondered.

"Of course he will. Offer to buy him a beer or two."

Will thought that a favor of this magnitude might require more than a few beers. It might require a whole brewery.

Chapter Twenty-Seven

"So, I need you to make a pass at my ex-girlfriend."

Will and Daniel were jogging on the Marine Terrace Trail at the Fiscalini Ranch Preserve. The morning was cool and mild, and the waist-high grass, growing golden with the late spring weather, undulated in the breeze. Wildflowers in purple and yellow dotted the landscape as the two of them ran side by side at an easy pace. They were both in pretty good shape, so they were sweating but not yet out of breath. Every now and then, a squirrel darted past on the path ahead of them.

"Melinda? The nut job? What for?"

Will explained Lacy's suggestion that if Melinda were distracted by an attractive man, she might not have time to make trouble.

"So, yeah. I wondered if you could flirt with her at the wedding. Just … you know. Keep her occupied. And keep her mind off me."

Will's muscles felt pleasantly loose and warm as they ran. They passed an elderly couple with a cocker spaniel on a leash, and nodded their greetings.

"Aw, man. That doesn't sound like a very good deal for me," Daniel said. "For one thing, if I'm busy chatting up your crazy ex, then I *won't* be chatting up women I might actually like."

"That's valid," Will agreed.

"And what if she likes me, and she's as predatory as you say she is? What if I can't get rid of her afterward? I mean, with my charm, how's she gonna walk away?"

Will grinned. "Somehow I doubt that'll be an issue."

Daniel ignored that. "Plus, I'd feel like a gigolo."

Will scoffed at him. "I'm not asking you to sleep with her. I'm just asking you to lure her away from Chris and flirt with her. Make a pass. Dance with her. Offer her some champagne and cake. Women love champagne and cake."

"Everybody loves champagne and cake," Daniel observed.

"So it should be easy then."

They ran a few more yards as Daniel thought about it.

"Man, I don't know," he said finally.

"Look," Will said. "I wouldn't ask you to do this. I really wouldn't. But she's going to try … *something*. Her texts are all, 'You can't just ignore me,' and, 'You won't get away with this.' I just want you to distract her. Keep her busy, so she's not thinking about me."

"Right," Daniel said, panting a little with the exertion of the run. "Because you're so irresistible women go crazy with lust when they're around you."

"I guess so," Will said. He grinned. "It's not like I can control the magnetism."

Daniel shot him a wry look.

"The way I see it," Will continued, "the big hurdle will be, what if she's not attracted to you?"

"Impossible," Daniel said.

Will thought about that. Daniel was tall and handsome, with dark hair, a well-built physique, straight teeth, and nice hazel eyes. It seemed to him that women would like that sort of thing. But who knew what went on in women's minds?

"All the same …" Will began.

"Look," Daniel said as they crested a hill on the trail. "If my natural charisma doesn't do the job, I'll just suggest to her—subtly, of course—that you and I have a rivalry going on. That if she were to be seen playing footsie with me, it would drive you out of your mind with jealousy. That ought to do it. Of course, we both know that the kind of women I go for are way out of your league. But Melinda doesn't have to know that."

"Rose is way out of my league," Will offered. "But she likes me anyway."

"There's that."

They ran another fifty yards or so and then flopped down on a bench, breathing hard, sweat glistening on their arms and faces. Dark circles of perspiration bloomed on Will's T-shirt, under his arms and at his neckline.

"You know, that rivalry angle could work," Will said when his breathing slowed.

"Of course it could."

He glanced at Daniel. "You're kind of good at this. Which worries me."

Daniel raised an eyebrow at him. "Do you wanna malign my natural talents, or use them to your benefit?"

"Use them. I want to use them."

"Fine then." He smacked Will on the back companionably. "I'll have her eating out of my hand. Maybe literally."

The idea was comforting, but on the other hand, Will thought that he'd do well to Melinda-proof his life, just as Lacy had suggested.

And that started with Rose.

Giving Rose an update on the Melinda situation served two purposes: It made him Melinda-proof—as Lacy had said, Melinda would have nothing she could use against him if he had no secrets from Rose—and it also gave him an excellent excuse for taking Rose out after work.

Usually, when Will wanted to spend time with Rose, he had to expend a certain amount of effort talking her into it. But saying he needed to talk to her about Melinda made it hard for her to put up the usual resistance. That could have been because she thought Melinda might actually cause trouble, or it could have been the fact that relationship drama—especially when it involved an ex that wasn't yours—was notoriously hard to resist.

Either way, when Will showed up at De-Vine at seven p.m. on the Thursday night before the wedding, Rose put up her hands to ward him off, opened her mouth to make some excuse or another—and then immediately dropped her defenses when Will told her they needed to talk about his crazy ex-girlfriend over dinner.

"Why? What has she done now?" Rose wanted to know.

"Ah … well, more of the same, mostly. But now I have a plan, and I thought you should know about it."

"Huh. Well, you could just tell me now. I don't see why dinner has to be involved."

"Dinner has to be involved because I'm starving," Will countered. *And because a pregnant woman needs to have regular, nutritious meals.* He didn't say that last part, but it was on his mind all the same.

She started to argue with him, and then threw up her hands. "Oh, hell. All right."

He would have liked to have taken her out to a restaurant, somewhere nice, maybe Neptune. But he'd been doing a lot of that lately, and his meager income wouldn't support that kind of thing for any length of time. Instead, he took her back to his cottage on the Cooper House property, where he planned to make a meal for her. He'd gone to the market earlier that day in anticipation of her agreeing to come home with him. If she'd refused, he'd have had far too much food here for just himself.

He brought her inside, gave her a glass of sparkling water (he knew better than to offer wine), and went into the tiny kitchen, where he got to work boiling water for pasta and chopping vegetables on a cutting board.

"So, spill," Rose said, leaning one hip against the counter as she watched him prepare the food. "What was it you wanted to tell me about Melinda?"

He carefully sliced a zucchini into uniform rounds. "Well, she's here, for one thing."

"Right." Rose nodded. "You told me she was coming. Without her significant other." She rolled her eyes.

"Sure." He continued to cut and chop. He gave her a quick glance out of the corner of his eye. "I also told you about her crazy texts."

"'Oh, Will, why did you forsake me? One day you'll see the error of your ways.' Yadda, yadda, yadda," she recited.

"Pretty much," he said, amused.

"So, what's the new headline?" she prompted him.

"Lacy came up with a plan for how to manage her at the wedding," Will told her.

Rose's eyebrow, the one pierced with a small, silver barbell, shot up. "Lacy did?"

"Yes."

"When did you talk to Lacy about this?"

He stopped chopping and looked at her. "Do you want to know her plan, or do you want to know every detail of the conversation?"

"Both," Rose said. "Of course, both. But start with the plan."

He straightened from where he'd been bent over the cutting board. He put down the knife, leaned back against the counter, and folded his arms over his chest. "Daniel."

"Daniel," Rose repeated.

"Yep. He's going to flirt with Melinda. Distract her. Maybe even hit on her. I assume he'll stop short of actually having sex with her. But, you know. That's his call."

Rose's mouth fell open. "You're joking."

"No. Lacy suggested it, and I asked him, and he said he'd do it. He's just got to keep her busy until it's time for her to go home. Which is the day after the wedding. So … it could work."

"Huh," Rose said.

"I just hope she's attracted to him," Will said.

"Oh, she will be." The answer was immediate and definite.

"What makes you say that?" Will wanted to know.

Rose waved her arms to emphasize how obvious the answer was. "Because he's Daniel. With the body, and the eyes, and the …" She gestured vaguely.

"Oh." Will was a little stung. He doubted that women would take his own attractiveness as glaringly apparent. He pushed his glasses up on his nose to reseat them.

"Aww." Rose grinned at him and stroked his shoulder. "You're jealous."

"Well, a little."

"Don't be. I would never go for a guy like Daniel."

"Why not?" he asked.

"Because I'm done with all of that. For one thing."

"Yeah?" He could hear the defensiveness in his own voice. "What's the other thing?"

"The other thing is, if I weren't done—which I am—he's not the one I'd go for."

He looked at her, and all at once something honest and vulnerable passed across her face. A look, a blink, a sudden, subtle moment when her façade was gone and he could see her—the real her—standing there wanting to be loved.

He crossed the room to her, put his hands on her shoulders, and kissed her.

She seemed to melt beneath him as a moan escaped her throat.

"Oh, God, Will," she murmured against his cheek. "Please ... don't hurt me." She pulled back from him just a little and looked into his eyes. "Because you could. I just ... I'm trying so hard to be safe, to be smart, but I can't—"

"You don't have to try so hard," he whispered to her. "Not with me."

He kissed her again, tasting her, gathering her to him, and he thought that neither of them would ever have to try, not at this, not at being together. Because it was so, so very easy.

Rose seemed to have lost control of the situation. What little control she'd had, anyway.

Why was she kissing him—again? Why was she dissolving under his touch? Why couldn't she do this one simple thing: keep her heart safe for herself and for her unborn child?

No, this wasn't the first time she'd given in, wasn't the first time she'd agreed to see him against her better judgment and then had succumbed to his advances. Because, damn it, she just felt so *good* when she was with him, and it always seemed like her man moratorium could be continued another day.

But this was worse. This time, she'd let him know that she had feelings—tender, delicate feelings that he could use against her at his will. And that was unforgiveable, because if he knew, if he realized the power he had over her, then what might he do with it? He could destroy her if he chose. He could leave her shattered.

Somehow, though, the fear was secondary to the need. Something inside her was empty, and she didn't feel empty when she was with him. She felt full and right, and complete in a way she couldn't ever remember feeling before.

What if this was a mistake, and she ended up broken in a way that couldn't be repaired?

And what if it wasn't? What if pushing him away was the unfixable error?

She didn't know what to do, but it seemed that her body did. As all rational thought was pushed out of her brain by the feel of his hands, his mouth, the warmth of his skin, her body knew how to respond without having to consult her rational mind. She kissed him back, touched him back. She threw her head back as he ran his tongue down the delicate line of her jaw.

"Water's boiling," he murmured.

She reached over, fumbling, and turned off the burner while he continued to slowly devour the hollow of her throat.

They could always eat later.

In retrospect, bringing Rose to the Cooper House property while Melinda was in residence probably wasn't a good idea. Will wasn't sure how Melinda knew that Rose was there—whether she'd been watching out a window when they'd driven up, or if she knew by some other means—but somehow, she timed it so that she was pounding on Will's door just as he and Rose were about to take their makeout session to its logical conclusion.

They were both in various states of undress—Rose wrapped in a blanket she'd pulled off the bed, Will hastily getting into a pair of sweatpants—as they came out into the living room to see what the noise was all about.

Will looked out through the peephole in his front door while tying the drawstring on his pants. "Oh, God. It's Melinda."

Rose pulled the blanket more tightly around herself. "What the hell does she want?" Will couldn't imagine the answer to that question, so he opened the door to find out.

"Melinda," he said. He'd opened the door only a crack, but before he knew what was happening, she was pushing her way past him and into the house.

When Melinda saw Rose standing there wearing nothing but a blanket and a blush, the lack of surprise on her face told Will she'd already known Rose was here, and that she'd guessed what they were up to before she'd even knocked on the door. That answered the question: She was here to interrupt them. Mission accomplished.

"Oh. Hello," Melinda said coldly to Rose.

"Something we can do for you?" Rose asked, her tone similarly icy.

"Well, there's certainly nothing *you* can do," Melinda responded. "But I need Will."

There were several ways one could take that comment, and none of them appealed to him.

"Melinda. What is this about?" he prompted her.

When she answered, she was speaking to Will, but her eyes were fixed on Rose. "The observatory roof won't open. There's a meteor shower tonight. I need you to fix it. It can't wait."

Will wasn't wearing his glasses, so he grabbed them off the table next to the sofa and put them on. "Ah … Melinda, I usually call a guy in for that sort of thing. I don't really—"

"Then call the guy in." Her voice carried some kind of threat—of what, Will wasn't sure.

"Well, I—"

"Will. You are in charge of this property when Chris isn't here. And Chris isn't here. This is your job. I expect you to do it." She turned and left the cottage, going down the front walk and toward the main house.

When she was gone, Will closed the door and turned to Rose. "I'm sorry."

"But you're not going to go, right?" she said.

As he watched her standing there wearing nothing but a blanket, her colorful hair mussed from their lovemaking and the blush of passion still on her cheeks, leaving her was the last thing he wanted to do. But, as Melinda had said, taking care of the property *was* his job. And if he didn't do it, he might find himself without an income and without a place to live.

"I have to," he said, and added, "If I don't, she's just going to come back."

"So let her come back," Rose insisted. "That doesn't mean you have to answer the door."

"I kind of do," he said, scratching at the back of his head.

"Oh, bullshit. The goddamned thing probably isn't even broken. And is there even a meteor shower tonight?"

"I have no idea."

Will found himself caught in a dilemma. On the one hand, Rose was right: Melinda likely was inventing something to get Will away from Rose. On the other hand, Melinda was right: It really was his job to take care of anything going on at the house.

"It's my job," he told Rose.

Rose's mouth puckered in anger like its purse strings had been pulled tight. "Is it your job to go over there any hour of the day or night? Are you on call all the time?"

Actually, he was. Usually, that didn't translate into any kind of inconvenience, because the house most often stood empty. But when something did happen at odd hours, he was expected to take care of it.

Explaining that to Rose didn't do much good. And the fact that she was standing there nearly naked, the rose tattoo rising gently up her smooth, bare shoulder, didn't make it any easier for him to leave.

Gathering his self-restraint and resolve, he went into the bedroom and began getting dressed. She stood in the doorway, glaring at him.

"I'll be right back," he said. "It's probably something easy to fix. It's probably just that she doesn't know how to use the controls."

"Are you believing the pure crap that you're telling me right now?" Rose wanted to know. "Are you? Because you and I both know she's luring you over there so she can pull another kiss in the wine cellar. Except this one's going to be in the observatory."

Will sighed and turned to her, becoming frustrated. Why didn't she trust him? Why was she making this more difficult than it had to be?

"I'm not going to kiss her. And I'm not going to let her kiss me. And I'm not going back to her."

Rose had anger all over her face, but under that was something else. Her eyes were getting red, and they were beginning to pool with tears. The sight of it made Will's heart flop in his chest.

"Do what you want," she said finally. "It's not like we're a couple."

That did it. Now she wasn't the only one who was mad. "Damn it, Rose. Yes, we are. And you know it. And if you'd just admit it, it would make things a hell of a lot easier for both of us. I have to go." He pressed a kiss to her lips. "I'll be back. Don't go anywhere."

He stuffed his feet into his shoes, grabbed his cell phone and his keys, and walked out the door. He hoped she'd still be here when he came back. And he hoped she'd still be wearing just the blanket.

Chapter Twenty-Eight

Rose watched him leave, and her heart pounded. Why had she been so petulant? Why had she whined at him like a spoiled child? Tending to Cooper House was his *job*. Was he supposed to ignore his job?

That's what part of her was thinking. But another part, a louder, more insistent part, told her that this whole situation was a big, steaming pile of freshly laid shit. Melinda called with some crisis invented to manipulate him, and he came. Why hadn't he dealt with her before this? And why was he letting her pull his strings like he was some kind of goddamned marionette?

He was the father of her child, for God's sake, and he was rushing off to be with another woman. Rushing off while Rose was naked and wanting him, no less. Okay, the fact that he didn't know he was the father of her child was her fault, maybe. And the fact that he was rushing off to fix something for Melinda—not to ravish her—should have made a difference. But in Rose's hormone-addled brain, it felt like he was rejecting her because he preferred his ex. No one ever said relationships made sense.

And there was that word: relationship. Who was Will to unilaterally decide they were in one? Who the hell was he to brush aside her opinions on the matter and pronounce that they were a couple, like it was some kind of goddamned executive order?

Flustered and angry, she threw off the blanket and went into the bedroom to find her clothes. When he got back here after attending to Melinda's every whim, she'd be damned if he was going to find her here, waiting in his bed. Screw that. As she put on her underwear, fastened her bra, then pulled on her jeans and her T-shirt, she grumbled under her breath, words like *shit-head* and *idiot.* And then, turning her thoughts to Melinda, *bitch.*

When she was done dressing, she hunted for her shoes and put them on. Then she stood in the middle of Will's living room trying to decide what to do. Go home? Go up to the main house and tell him off? Find Melinda and claw her damned eyes out? Trash the place first, and then do one or all of those things? The last one had some appeal, but it wasn't very practical.

She settled on the first option: Go home.

She gathered her purse and keys, got into her car, and drove off of the Cooper House property. She got onto Highway 1 and headed south toward town. She realized she was starving, because she still hadn't eaten dinner. Will had been planning to cook for her, but they'd become ... distracted.

The idea of having to go through the work of cooking for herself before she could eat seemed unworkable. Pregnancy hunger was unlike any other hunger she'd ever known. It wasn't just hunger, but also sickness, weakness, shakiness. An urgent, desperate need to devour as many calories as possible in as little time as possible, combined with an unfortunate aversion to foods she used to enjoy. A pain in the ass, was what it was.

Instead of going straight home, she turned off the highway and onto Main Street, and headed south through town toward Neptune. The place was expensive and she couldn't really afford a pricey meal. But, who the hell cared? She needed to eat, she needed it now, and at least there were friendly faces at Neptune. Jackson would be there, and sometimes Kate dropped in at the restaurant after work to eat and to visit him.

The restaurant wasn't busy, so she got seated immediately. When her server came, Rose dispensed with the drinks-first-food-later formalities and asked her to bring whatever she could get out here quickest. Within just a few minutes, Rose had a bread basket, a green salad, and a bowl of seafood bisque in front of her.

God, this was better, she thought, digging into the soup. But she still needed someone to talk to.

"Is Kate here tonight?" Rose asked the server when the woman, a cute brunette named Marcy, came over to check on her.

"No, sorry." Marcy shook her head, and her short-bobbed hair bounced. "I haven't seen her. Were you planning to meet her here?"

"Not really," Rose said, a hot roll in her hand. "I thought if she was here, I might catch her."

"Oh. Too bad. I can tell Jackson you're here, though."

Rose almost declined—surely Jackson was busy—but then thought better of it. "Sure. Would you do that? Thanks."

She and Jackson had been friends almost as long as she and Kate had. Rose had been helping Jackson with the wine list for Neptune since he'd started his job here. He wasn't a girl—and what she really needed was another girl to talk to—but she supposed he'd do in a pinch.

She had finished her soup and salad and had left the bread basket in ruins by the time Jackson came out to her table, his white chef's coat nearly immaculate despite the fact that he'd likely been cooking all day.

"Hey," he said amiably. "I see you liked the soup."

"You could say that. If I wasn't in public I'd have licked the bowl."

"You here alone?" He looked around for any sign of Will or some other dining companion.

"Yep."

"No Will?"

"Oh, no. No Will. Absolutely no Will. At all." She raised an eyebrow at Jackson meaningfully.

"Uh-oh."

"Yeah."

Jackson looked uncomfortable. "Hey, you wanna … Should I sit down? You need to talk about it?"

"Sit," Rose agreed. "Sit, sit. Even though you're not a girl."

"That's true." Jackson pulled out a chair next to Rose and sat.

"Are you super busy?" Rose asked, thinking about how rude it was for her to come in here and dominate his time. "If you have to get back ..."

"Nah." He waved her off. "The place is pretty dead tonight. I'm mostly back there busting the sous chef's balls just for sport. I think he'd appreciate the break."

"Okay. Good. Thanks." Rose nodded.

"So, what's going on?" he prompted her.

She sighed heavily and shoved aside her empty soup bowl. "I was at Will's place tonight. Naked. And his ex came in and insisted that he had to go fix the observatory roof. So he went! And there I was, feeling stupid, because, let me tell you, Jackson, naked women do not like to be abandoned in favor of random handyman jobs. Under any circumstances. And it's even worse when that random handyman job is being done for somebody's raging bitch of an ex-girlfriend, who has stated explicitly her intention to get back together."

She paused and took a breath.

"Okay, that's a lot," he said, rubbing at his chin.

"I just ... I don't know. I might have overreacted. A little. But I don't see why he has to be at her beck and call, especially when she's been very clear that she wants him."

"But he doesn't want her," Jackson said.

"How can you be sure?" Rose could hear the pathetic whine in her own voice.

"Because girls aren't the only ones who talk to each other. Guys talk. And Will told me he's not interested in her. Basically, he thinks she's a pain in the ass but he's too much of a gentleman to tell her that."

"Well ..." Rose threw her hands into the air in exasperation. "Why does he have to be so goddamned gentlemanly? Why can't he just tell her to fuck off?"

"Because he's Will," Jackson said.

Rose sighed. "Yeah."

"Say. Speaking of people being very clear about who they are and aren't interested in, didn't you tell Will that you don't want a relationship with him? Didn't you tell him that repeatedly?" Jackson looked at her like a scolding father.

"I ... I guess I might have said that."

"Uh-huh. So, can I assume that was maybe bullshit?"

Rose avoided his eyes. "Not bullshit. Exactly."

"And yet here you are, fretting over whether he's at Cooper House right now oiling Melinda's joints. Or ... something."

Rose pouted. That was the only way to describe what she was doing: She was pouting. It didn't make sense, not any of it. She couldn't account for how she'd ended up like this, pregnant and in love with a guy who might or might not be oiling some other woman's joints. Because, yes, she was in love with him. She didn't want to be, but she was.

"I don't really think he's oiling her joints," she said. "It's not that. It's just frustrating that she's manipulating him, and he's letting it happen. I don't really believe for a second that there's anything wrong with the observatory roof, or that there's even a goddamned meteor shower tonight. She made it all up because she knew I was at the house, and she probably knew I was naked. Or that I would be soon."

Jackson sighed and leaned back in his chair. "Well, I can see why you're irritated. And I agree that he's got to sort out this thing with his ex, and soon. But as far as him being faithful to you, you've got nothing to worry about. I'm telling you, he's one hundred percent on board with whatever you two have got going on together. The guy is crazy about you."

Jackson's words made Rose feel warm all over. And she didn't want to feel warm all over—not for a man. And yet, there it was.

She opened her mouth to tell Jackson the part she'd been holding back—the part about the baby—but she was sure that if Jackson knew, he'd tell Will. And she just wasn't ready for that. Not yet.

"Well," she said.

"Listen," Jackson said, piercing her with that Jackson look that made busboys and salad chefs scurry for cover. "I think you'd better tell him—sooner rather than later—that you're in love with him. Cut the bullshit. It's not doing either one of you any good."

"But I—"

"Do *not* tell me that you're not in love with him." Jackson pointed a finger at her, making her freeze in midprotest. "Because we both know that's a load of crap."

Rose opened her mouth to argue, then let out her breath in a *whoosh,* her shoulders slumping. "Yeah. It is," she admitted.

"Fine. So tell him already. Jeez."

"It's complicated," Rose said.

Jackson gave her a stern side-eye. "You think it is, but it's not. If you could just let go of whatever fucked-up narrative you've got going on inside your head that *tells* you it's complicated, you'd see that it's simple as hell. He loves you, you love him. That's it. Simple."

He got up abruptly, kissed her cheek, and said, "I've gotta go. The guys have probably set the kitchen on fire by now." Without waiting for a response, he stalked off into the kitchen, leaving her alone with her unspoken justifications.

"Well … shit," she said.

Any doubts Will had about whether Melinda was manipulating him vanished when he got a look at the problem in the observatory. Of course the roof wasn't working. How could it, when it looked like the control panel had been hit with a hammer?

He picked up a broken piece of the panel from the floor and held it in his hand. "How did this happen, Melinda?"

She rolled her eyes. "How in the world would I know? It was probably the cleaning crew you had in here. You really should check their backgrounds more closely."

He sighed and set the broken piece on a table that held maps of the night sky. "Chris has used that same cleaning crew for as long as he's owned the place. There's never been any problem before."

"Well … I don't know. Maybe Chris broke it the last time he was here and forgot to mention it."

"He didn't," Will said.

All at once, Will felt like an idiot for being here. For leaving Rose just because Melinda wanted him to. For participating in this charade that he was just doing his job. For having dated Melinda in the first place. And finally, most importantly in the whole scheme of things, for having taken this job—this easy, overly comfortable, dead-end job—instead of vigorously pursuing his career the way he should have all along.

Will pushed past Melinda and walked out the door of the observatory, heading for the stairs.

"Where are you going?" Melinda demanded.

"I'm leaving."

"What?! You need to come back here and fix this!" She was flustered, sputtering at him.

"I don't know anything about the retractable roof, except how to use it. I'll call a repair guy in the morning." He didn't slow his pace as he descended the stairs to the second floor, and then to the first.

"Will!"

He paused at the bottom of the stairs and looked up to where she stood on the landing.

"What? What do you want, Melinda?"

She began walking down the stairs toward him, and the expression on her face changed from anger and frustration to something softer. "I don't know why we can't just talk. About you and me. About us."

"There is no us," Will told her. "There's no you and me. There's just you, and there's just me. And as for me, I'm leaving."

As he reached the front door, she said, "I'm going to tell Chris."

Will turned to face her. "Tell him what?"

"About what happened in the wine cellar."

He felt his pulse quicken as his anger rose. He could feel his face turning hot. "What happened in the wine cellar was you making a pass at me and me turning you down. Do you really want to tell him that?"

"That's not how I remember it."

Will gaped at her in disbelief. "I don't know why you're doing this," he said finally. "I don't get it. You're with Chris. I don't see the *point*."

She came the rest of the way down the stairs and stood just inches in front of him, so close he could smell her perfume and feel the warmth of her body.

"I don't want to leave Chris," she said, her voice a gentle murmur. "He and I work. We just ... we work. But you." She moved even closer so that the fabric of her blouse brushed against his shirt. "What you and I had ... We could have that again, Will. He wouldn't have to know." Her voice was a whisper against his cheek. And then she moved just a fraction and pressed her lips to his.

With her mouth on his, her breath mingling with his, her body pressed against him, he felt ...

Nothing.

He put his arms on her shoulders and pushed her back from him, gently but insistently. "You need to stop this. I'm with Rose."

And he walked out the front door and closed it behind him, hoping to God that Rose hadn't left. If she had, it would be because he'd been a fool to leave her in the first place.

Chapter Twenty-Nine

Rose and Will didn't see each other again until the following night, at the wedding rehearsal. The rehearsal itself, held at the Cambria Pines Lodge, was a straightforward affair, and both of them were kept busy, she in her capacity as a bridesmaid, and Will as a groomsman. They shot looks at each other—hers angry and seething, his pleading—from across the gazebo where the ceremony would be held, but they didn't get a chance to speak. Or, more accurately, *Will* didn't get a chance to speak, because every time he approached Rose, she had some urgent matter to attend to, about who was going to hold what bouquet, or about how the ring bearer—one of Ryan's nephews—should walk, rather than run, down the aisle.

It was possible she was avoiding him.

At the rehearsal dinner afterward, though, she couldn't put him off any longer. Ryan's family had reserved a private room at Neptune, and there were place cards specifying who would sit where. Why there would be place cards at the rehearsal dinner, Will didn't know—but he was grateful for it, because Mrs. Delaney had put him next to Rose.

"You were gone when I came back," Will said when they were seated and the bread basket was being passed around the table.

"Figured that out all by yourself, did you?"

Okay, she was mad. He already knew that, since she hadn't answered his phone calls or responded to his texts, but this attitude of hers was further proof. Will didn't think it was entirely fair.

"You know, I didn't *want* to leave you for Melinda. It's not like I went up to Cooper House so I could seduce her with candlelight and chocolates." He was whispering to keep the conversation between the two of them, rather than making their relationship issues the topic of speculation among the other guests. "You look really pretty, by the way."

She was wearing a low-cut midnight blue lace sheath dress that clung to the contours of her body all the way from her shoulders to her knees. He could barely focus on what he was trying to say.

"Don't try to distract me with compliments," she said.

"Well, you're distracting me with that dress, so I guess it's even," he murmured. He thought he saw a hint of a smile, though it was possible he imagined it.

Rose's pregnancy wasn't showing yet—of course it wouldn't, this early—but there was something going on. She seemed … rounder. Softer. She maybe even glowed a little bit. Didn't they say that pregnant women glowed? Whatever it was, it made him want her so badly that he couldn't concentrate on anything else. He tried to think of what to say next—something that would make her see his side of the story—but instead, he realized he was gazing down the top of her dress and into the sweet depths of her cleavage.

"Hey, Bachman, the eyes are up here," she snapped.

He startled slightly, then blushed. "Like I said, the dress is distracting."

"You know what's distracting?" she demanded. "Your ex-girlfriend coming over during our date. *That's* what's distracting."

His lips quirked into a half smile. "I thought you weren't even admitting it was a date."

"Shut up."

"Both of you shut up," Lacy hissed at them. "Jackson's trying to give a toast."

Will tried to put aside his issues with Rose so he could focus on the evening. Jackson's toast actually was pretty touching, starting with Jackson's memories of his friendship with Ryan, detouring to Jackson's own feelings about love, and then finally coming to a conclusion with his best wishes for the happy couple. Kate, the maid of honor, followed up with her own toast, in which she quoted a couple of poems dealing with love, passion, marriage, and partnership.

Ryan's brother Liam—a rancher who had traveled from Montana for the event—spoke next, followed by his mother, who grumbled and sat down prematurely when she broke into tears during her remarks. Ryan's father patted her several times on the shoulder.

That many toasts meant there was a lot of champagne being consumed, but Will didn't have any because he was trying to be supportive of Rose. He couldn't tell her that was why he was skipping it, of course, but it was enough that he knew.

"Why aren't you drinking champagne?" she asked him in a testy voice.

"Why aren't you?" he shot back.

If he'd thought the question would make her suddenly confess her impending motherhood, he was mistaken. She merely made a face at him—something that mixed anger and frustration, combining pursed lips with furrowed eyebrows—and turned her back on him to face Gen's mother, who was drunkenly saying something at the head of the table.

"You're going to have to talk to me at some point," Will whispered to Rose's back.

"Not necessarily," she shot over her shoulder. "You're going to give up eventually."

And that right there, Will realized, was the crux of the situation. She thought he was going to give up on her, and all of this—the *I'm done with men* routine, her insistence that she didn't care about him, her refusal to tell him about the pregnancy, and finally, her angry act over what was happening with Melinda—all of it was a test. She was trying to push him away, and if she succeeded, she would have proved that he was just like all of the men who had come before, the ones who had left, or judged, or failed to appreciate everything she offered. He was being challenged, examined for his fitness to be with her. And he was not going to fail.

"No. I won't give up, not today, not ever," he told her.

She was trying to stay mad, but holy jeez, it was getting hard. It was bad enough that they'd been seated together. But then he just had to look at her with those sweet, puppy eyes.

She'd worn this dress specifically to make him sorry for walking out on her last night while she was naked and ready to give herself to him. But the fact that it was working so well was backfiring on her. When he looked at her that way he did—with so much hunger and longing—it made her want to forget whatever it was that had made her angry in the first place, shove him down on the banquet table, and climb on top of him. But that wouldn't help her to stay strong and objective. And besides, it would upstage the bride and groom.

Whatever she was going to do about Will—if, indeed, she was going to do anything about him—would have to wait until after the wedding. Being a bridesmaid would be demanding enough without having to sort out her romantic life as well.

She shifted in her seat, faced the head of the table, where Gen's mother was standing with her champagne flute aloft, pretending to be the perfect maternal figure, and tried to forget Will was sitting beside her. That was difficult to do, because she could feel his eyes on her. But she told herself she was stronger than her carnal desires. And she almost believed it.

By the time the toasts were finished and the wait staff was placing their dinner plates in front of them, Rose had almost convinced herself that she could freeze him out. He was just a guy she'd been seated next to at a dinner function. Like the time she'd gone to her friend Annette's wedding and had sat next to Annette's cousin Julio. Since Julio was gay, he'd never looked down Rose's dress with avid intensity the way Will had. So, that was one difference.

"Would you stop?" she hissed at Will when they were halfway through the entrees.

"Stop what?"

"Stop … you know. *Looking* at me."

"I like looking at you," he said simply.

He was being sweet, and that wasn't helping.

At this point, Rose would have been happy to have her mother there, because a little family squabbling would distract her from her pressing but unwise desire to crawl into Will's lap. But Pamela wasn't part of the bridal party, so she wasn't in attendance. It figured that the one time she might prove to be useful, she wasn't there. Rose struck up a conversation with Ryan's brother Colin—a lawyer from San Diego—instead.

When the dinner was over and they'd all had their desserts and coffee, Rose got up and tried to head out of the restaurant before Will could stop her. He was too quick for her, though.

"Hey." He stopped her before she even reached the door of the private banquet room. "Don't go yet. I was hoping we could talk."

"Well, we can't." She turned away from him and started toward the door.

"Rose." He put a hand gently on her bicep.

Shit.

If this were a movie, she'd have yanked her arm away from him and demanded, dramatically, that he unhand her. But this was her life, and instead, she felt an electric warmth from his touch that made her want to whimper with desire for him.

"Will. Don't." To her horror, she felt tears coming to her eyes. "This is … Can't you see I'm trying? I'm trying my hardest to do what's right for me. To be smart. To be strong. To protect myself and my …" She stopped herself before she could say *my baby*. "My *heart,*" she said instead, recovering herself. "Why won't you let me?"

The hand that was on her arm began to slowly caress her. "When will you see that you don't need to protect yourself from me?"

"I …" Here were those damned tears again. "I have to go."

People were milling around, saying their goodbyes. She pushed her way through the crowd and left him alone to make uncomfortable small talk about the day to come.

Chapter Thirty

The day of the wedding, the weather appeared to have come straight out of a Central Coast tourism brochure. The sky was a crisp blue, the temperatures in the midseventies. A light breeze blew off the ocean, bathing everything with the scent of salt water. The deer were out, grazing on people's lawns, the hummingbirds were sipping nectar from the trees, and the flowers were in vivid, audacious bloom.

"It's like a goddamned Julia Roberts movie," Rose muttered as she wrapped her bathrobe around herself and opened her front door.

There was a lot to do today, but she didn't feel up to it. She felt too sorry for herself for having slept alone. If Will were here, he might have pointed out that it was her own fault. But if Will were here, that conversation would be moot.

Feeling grumpy and sex-deprived, she went into her kitchen and ground the beans to make a cup of coffee. She'd Googled it and found that coffee, in moderation, wouldn't hurt the baby. Maybe she'd had to give up wine, but at least she still had French roast.

She was still stirring the milk and sugar into her cup when her phone rang. The screen said it was Pamela. Could Rose tolerate Pamela on zero caffeine? She wasn't sure. But if she didn't take the call, she'd still have to talk to her eventually. She took a deep and satisfying drink of her coffee, then picked up the phone and answered it.

"Hi, Mom."

"Rosemary. What time are you leaving for the ceremony? Because I wondered if you could pick me up on your way."

Rose squeezed her eyes shut. "It's not on my way, though. You're kind of on the opposite side of town."

"Yes, but I thought—"

"What's wrong with your rental car?" Rose wanted to know.

"Nothing. I just thought we could spend some time together. There's something I want to talk to you about."

Oh, crap. Pamela probably wanted to talk to her about her hair, or her tattoo, or her job, or her place of residence. The ride to the lodge would be one long lecture. She was about to make an excuse for why she couldn't do it when she realized that giving her mother a ride would give her an excuse for why she couldn't leave the wedding with Will.

"All right," she said.

"Really?" Pamela sounded surprised.

"Sure. But I have to be there a couple of hours before the ceremony. Pictures, helping Gen get ready, and all that."

"That's fine," Pamela said, sounding far more agreeable than was usually her habit. "I'll just have a cup of coffee in the lounge."

"Super. I'll pick you up at eleven thirty." The ceremony was scheduled to begin at two, and Rose had told Gen she would be there no later than noon.

"Thank you, dear."

Had Pamela ever thanked her for anything before? Rose couldn't remember.

When Rose picked up her mother, Pamela was wearing a chocolate-colored tea-length taffeta dress with a full skirt and a neckline that was deep enough to be fashionable but modest enough to be tasteful. Rose thought she was a bit overdressed—the wedding wasn't going to be as formal as those Pamela was used to on the East Coast—but nonetheless, she looked perfect, as though she'd employed a personal stylist to prepare her for the event. Which she actually might have done.

"You look beautiful," Rose said, standing in the doorway as Pamela gathered up her purse and her shoulder wrap.

"Thank you, darling."

Pamela couldn't say the same about Rose. She and the rest of the wedding party were going to get ready at the lodge, so Rose was wearing sweatpants and a T-shirt, her hair, now a pale pink, in a ponytail at the back of her neck. Rose's dress, shoes, accessories, and makeup bag were in the car.

"Your hair …" Pamela began, after they were in the car and maneuvering their way along Ardath Drive.

Oh, here we go.

"Yes?" Rose prompted her. If they were going to have a fight, then she was ready to go at it. She'd had enough criticism, enough disapproval, to last a lifetime. If Pamela wanted to go there, Rose would shred her like a wolverine with an injured rabbit.

"I was wondering how you plan to wear it," Pamela said, her voice serene. "Will it be in an updo, or down?"

Rose was speechless for a moment. Then she recovered her voice and said, "Um … Gen has a hairstylist coming to the lodge. It's going to be up, I think. I don't really know. I'm just going to let the hair lady do whatever she wants to do."

"Ah. I see. I'm sure it's going to be lovely."

Rose tried to make sense of what was happening here, but she couldn't. In their long relationship, Pamela and Rose each had a script, and Pamela was straying from that script. Why? What did it mean? And what the hell was Rose supposed to say in response?

The best tactic was to change the subject. "Uh … you said you wanted to talk to me about something?" She prepared herself for some attempt to manipulate her into living her life more in line with the Pamela way. Would this be about her relationship with Will? Her house? Her job? Her state of residence?

"Yes. Darling, I know you might have an issue with what I'm about to say, but—"

Here it comes, Rose thought.

"—I've talked to a Realtor about moving here to Cambria."

Rose was caught so fully off guard that she almost veered off the road.

"You *what*?" Her pulse was pounding, and she had to force herself to take deep breaths so she wouldn't crash the car.

"Oh, darling," Pamela began, enthusiasm in her voice. "I always thought you were crazy for settling here, so far away from anything … *relevant.* But, my goodness! It's so lovely here, isn't it? Every morning I wake up to find deer on the lawn. And the quiet! I can actually hear myself think. I've even made a few friends. Mrs. Duffy down the road from the summer house is lovely. I've had her over for tea twice now."

As she drove, Rose pressed a hand to her forehead just to make sure it hadn't flown off. So many thoughts were running through her head. What would this mean for her? Would Rose have to move somewhere else, just so they wouldn't kill each other? And most importantly, who was this woman sitting next to her in the car?

"Mom. I—"

"Oh, I know you want your privacy," Pamela continued. "I'm aware of that. But it's not like I'll be *living* with you, darling. I'll have my own activities, my own interests."

"What … what about the house in Connecticut?" Rose stammered.

Pamela waved a hand dismissively. "I'll sell it. Or possibly not. I might want to keep it. The idea of a home on both coasts is appealing. I haven't decided."

"I suppose I could live in it if I have to flee for my life," Rose muttered under her breath.

Pamela patted Rose's arm crisply and sat back in her seat, a whisper of a smile on her face. "Oh, darling. I doubt it'll come to that."

❖

Rose whisked into the suite at the lodge they would be using as their command post, her garment bag slung over her arm, a bag containing her shoes and makeup hung over her shoulder. The others were already there.

"Am I late? I hope I'm not late. I don't know what time it is. I don't even know what goddamned day it is. Somebody give me some champagne," she said. "Wait. No. I almost forgot. No champagne. Goddamn it."

Lacy went to a table on one side of the room, where an array of snacks and beverages had been laid out. She poured Rose a tall flute of sparkling cider and took it to her. "Here, honey. You're not late, but it looks like you're having a rough day."

Rose set her things down on the bed, took the glass, and peered into it. "Cider. Bleh." But she drank it anyway.

"I think I'm going to throw up. Again," Gen said from somewhere inside the spacious bathroom.

"Oh, jeez." Rose peered into the bathroom, where Gen was on her knees in front of the toilet. "Food poisoning? Hangover?"

"Nerves," Kate said. She was kneeling next to Gen, holding her hair.

"You're kidding." Rose propped one fist on her hip, the glass of cider in her other hand. "What's there to be nervous about? Ryan is the perfect man."

"I know," Gen moaned. "I know. He's perfect. It's all … it's perfect. I just … Oh." She heaved into the bowl again.

"Ew." Rose made a face and backed out of the bathroom.

"I'll be okay," Gen said. "I can do this. It's going to be fine."

There was a crisp knock on the door of the suite, and Lacy opened it.

"Hellooo!" The stylist breezed into the room with a sing-songy greeting. "Where's the beautiful bride?"

Gen waved weakly from where she was kneeling by the commode.

"Oh, my," the stylist said. "Well. We'd better get to work."

By the time the photographer arrived in the suite to take romantic, gauzy images of Gen and her friends preparing themselves for the big day, Gen had stopped vomiting and was only slightly green. That could be worked out in the retouching stage, the woman reassured them.

With the photographer snapping away, the stylist did Gen's hair, arranging it in an artfully messy updo of copper-colored curls. Next came the makeup, which did a lot to fix the green complexion problem.

By the time they helped her into her dress, Gen seemed to be past her nausea and was pressing forward, occasionally muttering to herself, "Just get through it. Just get through it."

"That's not a very romantic sentiment for the most important day of your life," Lacy observed.

"Bite me," Gen retorted.

Gen's dress was a cream-colored, strapless tulle ball gown with a beaded bodice and a sweetheart neckline. Rose had worried that the yards and yards of fabric would swallow Gen, considering that Gen wasn't very tall. But once the dress was on, along with the beaded high-heeled sandals that would give her some extra height, all of the women in the room let out a collective sigh.

"Oh," Kate said, her eyes filling with tears. "You're gorgeous."

"God. You really are," Rose added.

"Ryan's going to swallow his tongue," Lacy said.

"You'll do," the stylist said with a grin, nodding.

"Go stand near the window," the photographer said, pointing. "That dress is going to look great with the light filtering in."

One by one, the rest of them sat still for the stylist while Gen was busy with the photographer. They had their hair and makeup done, and they got into their own dresses. The strapless, sweetheart necklines mimicked Gen's gown, though the flowing, tea-length skirts were a fraction of the volume. The blush color was somewhere between pink and peach.

"Okay, let's get this thing done," Lacy declared with hearty determination when they were all ready.

"Not so fast," the photographer said. "I need some shots of all of you celebrating before the ceremony. Everybody get a champagne flute."

"I'm not drinking," Rose said.

"Pretend," the photographer ordered.

The ceremony was held in the lodge garden, on a emerald green lawn with a white gazebo. Pine trees behind the gazebo created a curtain of lush green, and on both sides, flowers bloomed in riotous colors.

Will stood in a tuxedo before the rows of chairs filled with guests, Daniel on one side of him, Jackson on the other. He peered around Jackson at Ryan, to see how the groom was doing. The poor guy looked nervous, and he was sweating. It wasn't that hot out.

"Ry. Take a breath," Will told him.

Ryan glanced at him, then let out the chestful of air he'd been holding.

Jackson chuckled and smacked Ryan on the back. "You're gonna be okay," he said.

"I don't know why he's nervous," Daniel muttered, pulling at his shirt collar. "I'm the one who's got to flirt with the stalker from hell."

"Have I said thank you?" Will wanted to know.

"You have. But I'm thinking you're gonna have to say it again."

Will wanted to focus on what Daniel was saying, but his attention kept drifting across the aisle, where the women stood, looking like spring flowers in their silky, flowing dresses.

Rose looked like just like her name—like a blush-pink rose. He could barely keep his eyes off her.

"Dude. She's still going to be here after the ceremony," Daniel murmured.

"Yeah," Will reassured himself. "Yeah, she will."

The chatter died down when the string quartet began to play "Ode to Joy," which Gen had chosen as her processional rather than the usual "Wedding March." The guests stood, and everyone turned back toward the lodge.

Gen emerged on the arm of her father, a distinguished-looking, gray-haired accountant whom she rarely saw. Will noticed that Gen looked scared, and maybe a little sick. But then she paused at the foot of the stone pathway that led to the gazebo, lifted her eyes, and saw Ryan.

Then, the most remarkable thing happened. She transformed. The fear and tension simply drained out of her, and she smiled with a radiance that was purely magical. Will glanced over at Ryan and saw something similar on his friend's face. If there had been nerves and doubt before, now there was nothing but happiness. It seemed to Will that the guests, the groomsmen, and the bridesmaids—hell, even the lodge and everything around it—could have vanished into vapor at that moment and Gen and Ryan wouldn't have noticed. Or cared.

Will looked over at Rose and saw her dabbing at her eyes with a delicate handkerchief she'd kept tucked in her hand. She looked up and saw him, and something passed between them. Some kind of knowing—the certainty that whatever her protests might have been, whatever reservations either of them might have had, the two of them simply were.

He was counting on it.

Chapter Thirty-One

It was a good thing the photographer had waited until after the ceremony to take the group shots, because before the wedding, Gen had looked ill. Afterward, she glowed with joy.

There were shots with the whole wedding party, shots with the wedding party plus the parents of the bride and groom, shots with only the women, shots with only the men, and shots with only the bride and groom. Just when Will thought they'd exhausted every possible combination of people, the photographer started taking shots with the bride plus maid of honor, and the groom plus best man, and he was certain they would all grow old here and possibly die of natural causes waiting for the photo session to end.

"Hey," he said to Rose during a moment when neither of them was required to be on camera. "You look …" He paused because there wasn't an adequate word for how she looked.

"Like one of those meringue cookies? Because I think I look like one of those meringue cookies," she replied.

"I was going to say you look beautiful."

She started to say something—probably one of those clever Rose retorts—but then apparently thought better of it. She blushed slightly. "Oh."

"Can I give you a ride to the reception?" he asked.

"Uh … no. Thanks. I have my car."

"I can bring you back here to pick it up afterward."

"Thanks, but I also have my mom. She came with me."

"Oh."

He knew he'd seen something in her eyes during the ceremony—something soft, an acknowledgment of her feelings for him—but now he wondered whether he'd imagined it. He sensed a definite cold front coming off of her now. Was this still about Melinda?

"Rose …"

"I think Gen needs me over by the fountain." With a swish of her skirt, she walked away from him.

He watched her go and thought this was exactly where she belonged: amid a garden in bloom.

When Will arrived at the old barn at the Delaney Ranch, the place was transformed. Yards of silky fabric had been hung from the rafters along with the fairy lights he and Daniel had put up, and the golden afternoon light streamed in through the doors and windows to bathe the dining tables and the dance floor.

The tables, each covered in white linen, were laid with gleaming china and silverware, with centerpieces of blush roses and dozens of votive candles in glass holders that caught the light from the flames.

At one end of the barn, a table was set up with the wedding cake, and Will went over to marvel at it. The cake, a three-tiered affair, appeared to be wrapped in delicate layers of white silk tinged in pink. On closer inspection, he saw that the silk was made of frosting. How in the world did they do that? Pink and white roses peeked out of the silk, and Will supposed they had to be frosting, too, though he'd be hard pressed to tell that they weren't real.

The roses made him think of his Rose, his delicate confection who was just as deceptive because she wasn't really delicate at all.

He looked around to see if she'd arrived yet, but he knew she hadn't. If she had, he'd have felt her. Sensed her.

"Can I help you find your seat, sir?" A waiter in a crisp uniform appeared at his side.

"Uh … sure. Thanks." Will gave his name, and the guy walked him through the tables toward the big one at the front, closest to the dance floor.

He saw from the place cards that Rose was seated beside him, and he was relieved. He'd wondered if she would pressure Gen to put her somewhere else.

He'd visited the bar and was sitting in his spot at the table with a drink in his hand—something called a Gentini that had been invented just for the occasion—when Rose arrived and plopped down in the chair next to him.

"Okay. I'm ready to be your fake date. I said I'd do it, so I'm doing it. Is that bitch Melinda here yet?" She looked around the room for the offending party.

"I don't want you to be my fake date," Will said.

"What? I thought you did. Because otherwise, Melinda—"

"I want you to be my real date. And not just today, either. I want you to be my real date today, and tomorrow, and the day after that."

That wall she put up sometimes—the one that separated her from the rest of the world—came up again. He was sorry to see it, but then again, he was up to the challenge of bringing it down.

"I'd better make sure my mom is getting settled," she said, and then she got up and drifted across the room, away from him, leaving him to feel her absence like an ache in his chest.

❖

Everyone had arrived and the reception was fully underway by four thirty. It started with milling around, drinks being served, small talk. By five o'clock dinner was served, and by six, the plates had all been cleared, the first dance by the happy couple was complete, and the other couples had started to fill the dance floor.

Will was a little bit drunk. Not very—he thought it unseemly to get drunk at a wedding reception—but he'd had enough to take the edge off. And he'd needed to take the edge off, considering that his ex-girlfriend and his current girlfriend—whether she wanted to admit it or not—were in the same room, a situation that had probably never ended well for anyone.

"Come on. Let's dance." He stood in his place at the table and extended his hand to Rose. Everyone else at the head table was already up and dancing.

She eyed him with suspicion.

"Come on," he said again. "You agreed to be my fake date. What kind of fake date would you be if you refused to dance with me?"

She scowled at him, then finally put her hand in his and stood. They walked, hand in hand, to the dance floor, and he brought her to him and put his arms around her.

He felt better immediately.

"God, you smell good," he said. Like lilacs and vanilla.

"Well, I'm not doing it for you," she muttered.

"Oh, I know. Because we're not dating."

"That's right."

The band Gen and Ryan had chosen specialized in music from the forties. Right now they were playing "Dearly Beloved":

Tell me that it's true
Tell me you agree
I was meant for you
You were meant for me

Will closed his eyes, leaned into her, and breathed in her scent.

That was when Will felt a tap on his shoulder. He looked up, emerging from another world where only he and Rose lived, and saw Chris standing beside him, looking at home in his tuxedo.

"May I cut in?"

At that moment, Will wanted to deck him. But since that wouldn't be good behavior for a groomsman, he merely gave a weak smile and nodded.

"Of course."

Rose looked just as dismayed as he did—that had to be a good sign—but Chris smiled at her and extended his arms for her to step into. "You look lovely, Rose," he said.

The surge of jealousy that ran through him was an ugly thing, an irrational, bitter thing. And suddenly, Will understood how Rose must have felt the other night when he'd left the cottage with Melinda.

"Dance with me, Will?"

He turned, and of course it was Melinda. Where in the world was Daniel? Will looked frantically around the room and saw him near the cake table, a drink in his hand, chatting up an attractive blonde.

What kind of wingman abandoned you for a blonde?

"I can't," Will told Melinda. "I have to … help Ryan with something."

She raised her perfectly groomed eyebrows. "Really? Because Ryan doesn't look like he needs help." She indicated the head table, where Ryan had gathered Gen into his lap and was whispering something into her ear.

That left only Jackson as a possible rescuer, but he appeared to be deep in conversation with Ryan's mother.

Melinda was wearing a red dress that was so tight and low-cut it could have been an Ace bandage that was too small for some kind of whole-body injury. She gave Will a predatory grin.

He was starting to sweat.

"I have to … visit the men's room. If you'll excuse me."

Having to use the john was a lame excuse—and a predictable one—but it was the best he could come up with right now.

There were no regular men's rooms, as this was a barn, after all. So he went outside to where the portable restrooms—two trailers, one men's, one women's—had been set up.

He walked up the ramp and into the men's trailer, feeling Melinda's eyes on him as he went. Once he got inside, he hoped there was someone in there who could help him by creating some sort of diversion. A small fire, maybe. But the only person in there was one of Ryan's nephews.

The little guy—the older one, Michael—zipped up as he came out of a stall.

"Hi, Will!" he said with enthusiasm.

"Hi, Michael. You having fun?"

"Sure. My mom says I can have cake pretty soon."

"That'll be good."

"Yeah."

The kid started to head straight for the door, and Will stopped him. "I'll bet your mom would like it if you washed your hands."

"Oh." He looked embarrassed. "Yeah."

When Michael ran out of the trailer, thumping his way down the ramp, Will was left alone. Melinda was out there, if not right outside the trailer, then somewhere. What was he going to do? He could stay in here, he supposed. The portable bathrooms were nicer than he'd ever imagined such a thing could be. They were clean, brightly lit, and accessible to the disabled, and there was even a mirror over the sink and a vase of flowers in a holder attached to one wall. A person could easily wait out a crazy ex-girlfriend here.

"Don't be a wuss," he told himself. "Don't hide in the bathroom like a wuss." So he gathered himself, washed his hands—because it seemed like the thing to do—and went out of the trailer.

She was waiting for him right at the foot of the ramp.

"Now we can have that dance," she said. From the look on her face, she might as well have said, *Now I can chew your face off like a werewolf.*

Neither prospect seemed appealing.

"I'm not going to dance with you, Melinda."

She put on a show of looking hurt. "Why not?"

"Because he came here with me," Rose said. She'd emerged from nowhere, looking radiant in the glow of the sunset.

"He didn't, actually," Melinda observed. "He came here alone. You came with your mother."

"It's kind of creepy that you know that," Rose said. "Will. Come back inside." She held out her hand to him.

Will reached for it—her hand seemed like a lifeline—but Melinda stepped in between them, facing Rose.

"He's going to dance with me," Melinda said, her voice fierce.

"Like hell he is."

This is bad, Will thought, not for the first time that night.

"Look. Melinda. Can we just—"

"What the hell is your story?" Rose demanded. Her arms were crossed defiantly, her face stormy. "He's not interested. *Not. Interested.* Why can't you get that?"

"Huh. That's odd. He seemed interested when we were together at Cooper House the other night. Isn't that right, Will? The observatory roof didn't get fixed, but all things considered, it was worth it."

Will felt the blood drain out of his face. This was worse than he'd feared it would be. Would Rose believe her? Surely Rose wouldn't believe her. If she did …

"You lying bitch," Rose spat at her.

Will was vaguely aware that someone else had come out here, but he was so focused on Melinda and Rose that he didn't know who. So when Melinda reared back and slapped Rose across the face—a blow that made a resounding *thwack* and left Rose with a red handprint on her cheek—he was surprised when a ball of coffee-colored taffeta flew out of the shadows and launched itself at Melinda.

The taffeta ball hit Melinda with surprising force, and she stumbled back with a shriek.

"Mom!" Rose cried out.

"Mrs. Watkins!" Will said.

"Get your hands off my daughter or I'll tear you apart," Pamela said, squaring her stance in front of Melinda. "How dare you hit a pregnant woman!"

Chapter Thirty-Two

"You know?" Rose said, stunned from the pain of the slap and also from the sudden revelation that her secret wasn't a secret.

"Of course I do," Pamela said, as though that were obvious.

"She's pregnant?" Melinda demanded. Then she scoffed. "It's probably not even Will's."

Rose launched herself at Melinda, nearly knocking Pamela—who was standing between them—to the ground. She felt hands on her as Will held her back from ripping the bitch's arms off. Melinda, sensibly, had backed a few paces away.

"What's going on out here?" Chris emerged from the barn and walked toward them, a concerned look on his face. "I couldn't find Melinda, and then I heard yelling."

"What's going on here, Mr. Mills, is that your … *girlfriend*"—Pamela said the word as though it tasted bad—"attacked my daughter."

"Who's pregnant," Will added helpfully.

Suddenly, it hit Rose that Will hadn't been surprised to hear that particular piece of news.

"You knew too?" she said, looking at him in wonder.

"Of course I knew."

"You *hit* Rose?" Chris said to Melinda.

"She called me a bitch."

"You *are* a bitch," Rose said.

Melinda bared her teeth and reached out to swing at Rose again, but Will stepped in front of Rose to take the blow, if need be, and Pamela shoved Melinda backward mightily before she could land another slap.

At that moment, Daniel strolled out of the barn, looking happy and slightly drunk. "Hey. Where did everybody …" And then he saw them. "Oh, shit."

"Daniel. Would you take Rose inside?" Will said.

"Yes," Pamela added. "She's been hit. She's hurt."

"I'm not hurt," Rose protested. "That skank couldn't land a decent shot if she were trained by Mickey Goldmill." When they all looked at her curiously, she said, "From *Rocky*. Burgess Meredith. Don't you people know your movies?"

"Come on," Daniel told her, taking her arm. "We'll get you a drink."

"She can't drink!" Pamela scolded him. "She's pregnant!"

"You are?" Daniel looked at her with wonder. "Wow. That's … wow."

"Oh, for God's sake." She pulled her arm from Daniel's grasp. "I'm not going anywhere, so don't even try it."

"What the …" Chris was rubbing at his temples. "What the hell is going on?"

"Will came over to Cooper House on Thursday night, when I was there alone." Melinda's eyes bore into Will's with fury. "He made a pass at me."

"Oh, that's a goddamned lie," Rose said. "She's just jealous because her ex has moved on to someone else."

"Ex?" Chris said.

"Uh … yeah," Will admitted. "Melinda and I … we dated before she met you. She didn't want to tell you."

Chris turned to Melinda. "Is that true?"

"I didn't think it was important to tell you," she said. "It's all water under the bridge. Or, at least it was until Will tried to kiss me."

"*She* tried to kiss *me*," Will said. "And then got mad when I said no. I have the text messages to prove it. And the security video, which I saved."

"That doesn't prove anything." Melinda glared at Will. "You could have doctored a video. You could have—"

"Just … shut up," Chris said. Melinda gasped.

Chris turned to Will. "You didn't tell me any of this."

"I didn't want … Oh, hell. This. I didn't want any of this." He gestured to the chaos around them.

Chris rubbed at his forehead with one hand and turned away from them.

"Chris, please." Melinda put a hand on his shoulder, and he shook it off.

He turned back to face Will. "I think you'd better find a new job. And a new place to live." Chris's face had turned red, but he kept his voice calm as he straightened the cuffs of his tux. "In fact, don't come back to the property. I'll have your things packed up and delivered to you."

"I think you're doing the right thing," Melinda told him, putting her hand on his arm and following him as he walked toward his car.

He pulled his arm out of her grasp and turned to her. "When we get back to the house, I want you to pack your things. I'll arrange for your transportation home."

"But Chris, I—"

"Just get in the car." He turned to the group, couldn't find anyone he wanted to be civil to, and settled on Rose. "Please tell Gen and Ryan that I apologize for the quick departure. Good night."

When they were gone, Rose looked at Will. "Oh, Jesus, Will. Your job. Your house …"

"It doesn't matter. None of it matters," he said. "I'll figure something out."

"Of course you will." Pamela patted him companionably on the shoulder. "Did you know that Will is almost finished with his dissertation?" she asked Rose.

"I'm finished, actually," Will added.

"Good for you," Pamela said, smiling.

"What's happening here?" Rose said. The events of the previous fifteen minutes had left her dizzy with confusion. Plus, her face hurt.

"What's happening is that I'm going to defend my dissertation, get my PhD, then get a decent job, probably at Cal Poly. Then I'm going to be a father to our baby."

"You are?" Rose said. She could feel tears welling up in her eyes.

"Yes. And we *are* a couple, Rose, whether you want to admit it or not. I love you. And I want to be with you. And I want our family."

She shook her head as tears fell down her cheeks. "I don't … I can't …"

"Rosemary." Pamela's voice was stern. "Can't you see that Will is the one? That he's *your* one? My goodness, even I can see that, and I'm notoriously difficult to please."

"That's true," Rose said, laughing through her tears. "You are."

Will looked into Rose's eyes. "I am your one. And you're my one."

She waved toward the barn, where the party was still underway. "I can't get married, or anything stupid like that."

"I know," Will said simply.

"You do?"

"Of course I do. I know you."

"You do." She said it on a sigh.

He gathered her into his arms and kissed her, and the rest of the world ceased to exist.

"I was supposed to distract Melinda," Daniel told Pamela. "I'm a shitty wingman."

"It would seem so," Pamela said.

Pamela and Daniel went back into the barn, leaving Will and Rose alone to ponder all that had happened.

"Did you see what my mother did?" Rose asked him. "Did you see her? She just … *zoomed* in and attacked Melinda. Like a mother grizzly bear or something."

"I saw it," he said in wonder. "Though she was moving so fast she was pretty much just a blur."

"I didn't think she really cared about me," Rose said. A fresh tear fell down one cheek, and Will wiped it away with a gentle finger.

"Of course she does. She's your mother."

"I think I have to go talk to her."

"You should." He gave her a quick, sweet kiss on the lips. "I think that's a good idea. You do that while I go find Daniel and chew him out for falling down on the job."

Rose and Will went back into the barn, where the candle-light and the music and the dancing made everything seem like a gentle dream. She was surprised to find her mother dancing with Ryan's uncle Redmond. After the dance was over, Pamela re-turned to her table near the back of the barn, away from the band. When Rose approached her, she was holding a martini and chatting with Daniel, who was laughing about something.

"I've got an issue with you," Will told Daniel, who abruptly stopped laughing and looked contrite. "Dude. I'm sorry. I got distracted."

"So I gathered."

"You should kick my ass. You really should. But maybe we could just have a beer instead."

They wandered off toward the bar, leaving Rose and Pamela alone.

"Hey." Rose pulled out a chair and sat next to her mother.

"Rose. Does it still hurt?" Pamela gently touched Rose's cheek.

"Not really. It's okay. Thanks to you. If you hadn't come charging in like … like Bruce Willis in *Die Hard,* she'd have broken my kneecaps."

Pamela smiled. "Nonsense, darling. You were ready to pummel her, and you would have if Will and I hadn't intervened. I can't say that I approve of that sort of behavior, but you would have been justified."

"You … you rescued me," Rose said in wonder.

"Well, of course. You're my daughter. Why wouldn't I?"

"I just thought—"

"My dear," Pamela interrupted. "You'll be surprised what you'll do for your own child once she arrives. And, yes, I'm convinced it'll be a daughter."

"But … how did you know? Both you and Will. Did Kate or Gen tell you? If Lacy blabbed, I'll—"

"No one had to tell me. Or Will." She waved a hand to dismiss the thought. "The signs were obvious."

"Well, jeez. Neither one of you said anything."

"Of course not. You had to let us know in your own time. We both knew that."

"Wow." Rose pondered that for a minute, and then remembered what Pamela had told her on the way to the wedding. "Are you really moving to Cambria?"

"I'd like to. I'd like to be close to my grandchild. And you."

Rose didn't know what to say. The idea of having her mother nearby was both heartwarming and terrifying. What if they didn't get along? What if they continued to fight? What if Rose had to continue to live under her mother's harsh and unyielding scrutiny?

"I'm not sure you'd like it here," Rose said, hedging her response. "I mean, it's so far away from your life in Connecticut. And it's a small town. There's no DAR. No … big society galas. Good God, I don't know what you'd do without your social status."

Pamela waved a hand and made a noise: *pfft.* "Social status. Darling, all of that exhausts me."

"*What?*" Rose was aghast. "It *exhausts* you? I thought … jeez, Mom. When I was growing up, *everything* was about social status! How I did my hair, how I dressed, where I went to school. You wanted me to go to Yale!"

"You think I wanted you to go to Yale for *status*?" Pamela said with disgust.

"Didn't you?"

"No! I wanted you to go so you could have everything!" Pamela grasped Rose's hands in hers. This display of closeness—this physical touch—was so foreign to Rose that she almost flinched.

"When I went to Brown, it was made very clear that I was there to find a man. That was the goal my parents had for me. Look beautiful, join a sorority, and marry well. The idea that there might be something more, that *I* might be something more … Well. It simply wasn't an option that was presented to me. But *you* …" She squeezed Rose's hands. "You could have done *anything,* accomplished anything. I wanted you to have the finest education so you could soar. Darling, I wanted to give you wings."

"But you did," Rose said, tears in her eyes, emotion thickening her throat. "You did. You raised me into a person who knew that I wanted to be free. I did have wings, and I used them. I flew here. I *am* the person I wanted to be. That just didn't turn out to be who you expected."

For the first time—perhaps ever—Rose considered that her mother might have had a hand in making her someone strong enough to do what she'd done so many years ago.

"I love you, Mom." It was the first time she'd said it since she drove off that day in the Mercedes, a duffel bag of clothes in the backseat and a note to her parents on the dining room table. Saying it now, and meaning it, broke down a wall she'd built around herself, a wall she could now see had not just kept her safe, but had also kept her trapped.

"Oh, Rose. I love you too." Pamela gathered Rose into her arms and rocked her like she hadn't done since Rose was small. Had she even done it then? Rose couldn't remember.

"You have another chance, you know." Rose sniffled as she pulled back from her mother's embrace. "You have another chance with your grandchild. And with me. I hope you'll take it. I hope you'll come to Cambria."

Pamela nodded mutely, her eyes shiny with unshed tears.

Chapter Thirty-Three

Will looked anxiously toward Rose and Pamela. While he was doing that, wondering what they could be saying to each other, Jackson and Ryan came over to where he and Daniel were drinking beer from longneck bottles.

Will forced himself to smile. "Where's your lovely bride?" he asked Ryan.

Ryan pointed toward the dance floor, where Gen was dancing with Lucas, Ryan's other nephew. She had to bend over to make it work, since Lucas was only six, but somehow they were managing. Gen looked amazing, happy and glowing amid yards of tulle.

Ryan turned back toward Will. "So, what the hell was going on outside? People were leaving one by one, and then we heard some kind of commotion. I wanted to come out and see what was going on, but Gen didn't want to miss the Chicken Dance." He grinned.

"You should have seen it, man," Daniel said in awe. "Melinda hit Rose—I missed that part—and then Pamela attacked Melinda, and then Will here lost his job. And his home."

"Oh, shit." Jackson looked concerned. "That's … I don't even know where to start."

"Yeah. I know how you feel." Will nodded.

"You gonna move in with Rose?" Daniel wanted to know.

"No, no. I mean, I'd like to. But she's not ready for that."

Jackson put a hand on Will's shoulder. "You can stay in Gen's old place until you figure something out. She doesn't need it anymore." He gestured toward the room around them. "Obviously." Gen had lived in an apartment on the bottom floor of Kate and Jackson's house until she moved in with Ryan.

"Thanks, Jackson. I think I'll do that, if Kate doesn't mind."

"She won't."

They all stood there drinking for a moment, considering everything that had happened.

"So, can we all stop pretending we don't know about the baby?" Ryan asked.

"I guess. Yeah." Will grinned.

"I wasn't pretending. I really didn't know. Congratulations, man," Daniel said. "Sincerely. You're going to be a great dad."

"I'm going to be a dad," Will said. The whole thing seemed so huge and awe-inspiring that for a moment, he was overcome with happiness. The job didn't matter. The cottage didn't matter. Even the dissertation didn't matter, though he was going to get that behind him as soon as possible. He was going to be a father. And a partner to Rose. Everything else seemed to fade into insignificance.

"Let's have a toast," Ryan suggested, and they all raised their bottles and glasses. "To Will and Rose. And parenthood."

Will was happy to drink to that.

After the reception, Will was still a little buzzed and didn't think it was wise to drive, so Rose—the only sober one of the three of them—drove him and Pamela. The party had gone late into the night, and it was close to two a.m. by the time they left the Delaney Ranch property.

They dropped Pamela off at her rental house, and then Rose and Will held hands as she drove through the darkness up Ardath Drive.

"I guess this is the part where you take me home, but I don't have a home anymore," Will said. He was still pretty lightheaded, but not fully drunk. "Jackson said I could stay at Gen's old place. I guess you should take me there."

"Mm hmm," Rose said. But instead of turning on Ogden to go toward Kate and Jackson's place, she just kept winding up Ardath and away from Marine Terrace.

"We're not going to Gen's old place," Will observed.

"No," Rose agreed.

He leaned back against the headrest and grinned at her sleepily. "Does this mean I get to stay at your place tonight?"

"It does," she agreed.

"Hmm. Is there going to be sex in this for me?"

"There might be. We'll just have to see."

The thought of that made the ride home a lot more interesting.

❖

There was, in fact, sex in it for him.

When they got inside Rose's cottage, she flipped on the lights, kicked off her delicate high-heeled sandals, let her hair out of its elaborate updo, shook it out, and turned to Will with a slow, lazy smile.

"Exactly how drunk are you?" she wanted to know.

"Not too."

"Tired?"

"Nope."

"Neither am I. I wonder if we can think of something to do with all this alertness we've got going."

"Oh, I'll bet we can." He moved toward her, enfolded her in his arms, and breathed in her scent, something warm and sweet and comforting. He kissed her and pressed her back against the kitchen counter.

She started with his tuxedo jacket, slipping it off his shoulders and tossing it a few feet onto the sofa. Then she started on his tie. She managed to untie it and drop it to the floor without ever breaking the kiss.

He put his hands on her neck, caressing her, feeling the warm planes of her skin, as she began to untuck his shirt and unbutton it.

"Bedroom?" he murmured.

"Yes," she sighed.

He took her by the hand and led her into the small bedroom, then paused in surprise when he saw the bed in disarray, the clothes on the floor.

"Oh. Ha. I guess I didn't get a chance to clean up this morning." She looked up at him, blushing slightly.

"I guess my clothes can keep yours company on the floor," he said with a grin. He finished unbuttoning his tuxedo shirt, took it off, and dropped it atop a scattering of her things.

"That's good. Because my bras and undies were lonely."

"Can't have that."

He took her face in his hands and kissed her deeply, his tongue caressing hers. Then his hands moved around to the back of her dress and slowly unzipped it. "I like this dress," he murmured. "I'll like it better when it's on the floor with my shirt."

She giggled and slipped out of the dress, letting the silky fabric slip to the floor.

When he saw her in only her lacy strapless bra and panties, he just stopped and looked. She was growing softer with pregnancy, her breasts fuller. He put his hand on her abdomen, where their child was growing.

"I love you, Will," she said, a slight tremor in her voice. "I didn't say it earlier. I didn't say it back. But I do. I love you."

"I'm not going to disappoint you, Rose. And I'm not going to hurt you. I promise."

"Come on." She took his hand and drew him forward. "Get undressed. Come to bed." And he did.

❖

They made love slowly, with none of the fevered frenzy that had marked some of their earlier encounters. This time wasn't just about sex. This time was about knowing that it was real, and that it was going to last.

When they were naked under the covers of her bed, he explored her, worshipped the curves of her body, the contours of her skin. He traveled her body with his mouth, his tongue, his fingers, kissing the peaks of her breasts and entwining his hands in her hair.

She wrapped her hand around him and stroked him until he groaned, his mind lost in a world where nothing but the two of them existed. He gently touched the warm folds at her core until she threw her head back and sighed.

And then, when they couldn't wait any longer, he rolled onto his back and pulled her up onto him so that she sat astride him, his hard arousal sinking deeply into her.

God, this. Could there be anything more than this?

She moved on top of him, slowly at first, and he was mesmerized by the look on her face. The abandon. The pure, transporting pleasure. The thought that he was giving that to her, making her feel that, left him humbled and incredibly grateful. He ran his hands up her body as she moved above him.

Soon, she fell into a steady rhythm, and his pleasure rose with hers. The slow need that had started in the center of him grew more urgent, more insistent, as she rocked her body atop him. As her movements grew faster, he moved his thumb to rub the little nub of her body where they were joined.

His touch made her moan, first low, and then louder. He picked up a rhythm, touching her, stroking, until she cried out, stiffened, and then quivered with her release.

She collapsed on top of him.

Not yet sated, he took her in his arms and rolled her onto her back, never breaking their connection. Looking into her eyes, he found his own rhythm, rising on the tide of pleasure until the waves crashed and he exploded in a peak of bliss.

His body melted on top of her, and then, not wanting to crush her, he moved to her side and enveloped her in his arms.

They slept, their bodies tangled together, as the sun rose, bringing a pale pink glow to her windows.

The next day—Rose's day off—they were lying in bed, the rumpled covers in a riot of disorder as they sipped coffee and ate the Pop Tarts that were the only breakfast item Rose had in her meager kitchen.

"Don't get me wrong, I love Pop Tarts," Will said, appraising the rectangular pastry with its cheerful sprinkles. "But you probably should be eating a more balanced diet."

"Yeah, yeah," she said, nudging him with her foot. She brushed some crumbs off of the covers. "So. I hate to bring practical stuff into what has, admittedly, been the best date I've ever had. But what are you going to do about the whole thing with Chris? Your job?"

"Don't worry about it," he said.

"Why not?"

"Because I have a plan."

"Really." She sat up in bed, drawing a sheet up to cover her breasts. "Do tell."

"Well. First, I'm going to have my stuff delivered to Gen's old place. Jackson said I could stay there while I figure things out. Then, I'm going to defend my dissertation. That'll go well—my adviser has seen my work and says he's sure it'll be accepted. Then, I'm going to apply for a job at Cal Poly as a professor. One of their biology guys is retiring, so there's something opening up in the fall. In the meantime, I'm going to teach summer classes at Cuesta College. I don't need the PhD for that, I can do it with just my master's."

She looked at him with interest. "Wow. You really have been thinking."

"I have."

"And you figured this all out just since last night?"

"Oh, no. Last night I was busy."

"Yes, you were." She gave him a feline grin that nearly melted him.

"I've actually been planning all of this since I found out about the baby. A guy who's going to be a father needs to step up."

"You're stepping up," she said, pleasure in her voice.

"I'm stepping up." He sipped some coffee, feeling happy with himself, and with life. "Oh, and there's another thing."

"What?"

"Once I'm on the faculty at Cal Poly, my dependents can attend part time at a reduced cost. A greatly reduced cost. Nominal, really." He grinned at her.

"I can go to college?" The excitement in her voice gratified him.

"You can go to college." He paused. "Of course, it only works if we're married. Which we don't have to be, if you don't want that. I don't want to rush anything. We'll take things one step at a time."

He looked for signs that she might be panicking, but she looked okay.

"One step at a time," she repeated.

❖

They were still lounging around, lazy and happy, when Will's cell phone rang. He looked at the display and saw that it was Chris.

He tapped the screen to connect the call, and took a deep breath.

"Hey."

"Will. Hi. Look, about last night—"

"I'm sorry I didn't tell you about me and Melinda," Will said. "I get why you're upset. I would be, too. But I didn't make a pass at her. I swear."

"I know," he said.

"You do?"

Chris sighed heavily. "Yeah. Once I had a chance to think about things … I know you didn't, Will."

Will felt himself sag in relief. "So, what's going to happen with Melinda?"

"I sent her home this morning."

Will wasn't sure what to say. Finally, he settled on, "I'm sorry."

"Yeah, well. That was never going to be a long term thing."

"I guess not."

"So, Will. About your job. I'd like you to come back."

It felt good to hear it, to get the offer. It was validation. But Will couldn't move backward at this point. He was ready to go forward. "Thanks. But after everything, I think it's better if I don't."

"Yeah. You may be right," Chris said.

"Hey. Is it okay if I come over and get some of my stuff? All I've got is a tux and my wallet. That's going to be awkward on the job hunt."

Chris chuckled. "Of course. Whatever you don't pick up today, I can have delivered to you. Where are you staying?"

"Just a sec." He held his hand over the phone and asked Rose, "Hey, what's Kate and Jackson's address? Chris wants to know where to send my stuff."

"Give me the phone, I'll tell him," Rose said.

He handed over the cell phone.

"Chris? It's Rose. Let me give you the address where you can send Will's things. You ready?" She slid her eyes over to Will, and gave the address. But it wasn't Kate and Jackson's address. It was Rose's.

When she hung up, he stared at her.

"You told him to send my stuff here."

"I did."

"Does that mean …"

"You said it last night. We're a family. So don't overanalyze it. Just come home."

Home. Family.

He liked the sound of that.

Made in the USA
San Bernardino, CA
28 May 2018